MAGIC TIME

By Kit Reed

Novels

MOTHER ISN'T DEAD SHE'S ONLY SLEEPING
AT WAR AS CHILDREN
THE BETTER PART
ARMED CAMPS
CRY OF THE DAUGHTER
TIGER RAG
CAPTAIN GROWNUP
THE BALLAD OF T. RANTULA
MAGIC TIME

Short Stories

MR. DA V. AND OTHER STORIES
THE KILLER MICE

Juvenile

WHEN WE DREAM

MAGIC TIME

by
Kit Reed

Published by
Berkley Publishing Corporation

Distributed by
G. P. Putnam's Sons, New York

Library of Congress Cataloging in Publication Data
Reed, Kit.
    Magic time
    I. Title.
PZ4.R3245Mag 1980 [PS3568.E367] 813'.5'4 79–14129
ISBN 0–399–12423–3

Printed in the United States of America

for Sam Pottle
　　—wish you were here.

Don't call me anything. Who? I'm not sure myself yet. I thought I was but it is all either simpler or more complicated than I thought.

Think of a lightbeam with dust floating down it, not dust but cosmic microdots, waiting to be picked up and, what, developed? Played?

Someone picks at random, develops. Plays. Attends.

I have a voice.

I

Boone Castle

Now it seems to me that, given empty time with no pressing engagements, no holidays requiring trying personal appearances and nobody waiting to be disappointed; given freedom from employers, landlords and bill collectors, a person would probably be just as well off going to bed for the rest of his life.

It has crossed my mind as a possibility.

I get the idea that when we pull ourselves together in the mornings, fighting fear and gravity and the laws of logic to get out of bed and get going, we are not necessarily doing it for ourselves. Who says a person has to brush his teeth and look sharp, and who says he needs to win friends and influence people when what he really wants to do is sleep or sulk or stare, and why does somebody always say, *They are counting on you*? I have had my eye on the sparrow my whole damn life so far, either that or the sparrow has had his eye on me; I have spent the better part of my life getting on with it when I did not necessarily feel like it and I can't help thinking that without the demands, without anybody around waiting for me to cough up or look sharp or fall on my ass, I would be free to sink gracefully into the cloud of existential *yeugh* that is massing nearby and always rolling, following me at a safe distance that seems to be closing. For England, Harry and St.

George, who says; for God, country and for Yale, who needs it? Then I look into somebody's face and see what is expected . . .

As a kid I could never disappoint them; if I did somebody would say, *That isn't like you.* How did they know? By the time I hit the university everybody was convinced I was going to make a major artistic statement and my first million with the first full-length feature in holofilm, they put too much freight on me and when I crashed they expected me to be cheerful: grit your teeth, fella, *noblesse oblige.* Daniel Boone Castle, lost tycoon; I wanted to stick around and try again but a hundred others had already sprung up in my place and I was supposed to go away and not depress them. I was expected to get work and send cheery post cards back to U.S.U. to prove there were no hard feelings.

Which is how I ended up working for Fred. He is so rich he thinks you can buy talent. I am supposed to be original for him, making holopix in three dimensions to go with every random thought he utters into his microphone. No matter how boring or commonplace his tapes are I am supposed to make holopix of all his trips and business dealings and half-witted philosophical maunderings, Fred going to the bathroom. Nothing is wasted. Then I edit and he shows the results to all his friends, fans and employees so they will see what a big man he is. He already has all the money he will never need but he wants more than that. He wants to be internationally famous; he is convinced that one of these holos is going to make it big and then the eyes of the world will be on Fred Fenton, man of history; watch out moonbase, hello stars. Naturally he tells everybody he made the holos himself.

Right now, I'm supposed to be making a feature-length production out of the Fenton Family vacation, an intimate look at the recreation of the idle rich that will make a larger statement about the function of leisure and the commonality of man. Fred's words, not mine. My real function is to keep him from looking like a fool. So far he has been hung up on staging things: you stand there, Dottie, you kids clump together so Boone can get you all in; he peeks into my viewfinder and then scuttles over to stand beside them while I make the picture. He has been too busy talking into his recording bug to look at anything. The guide says: "And this is the Coliseum." Fred hunches over the bug, repeating dutifully: "This is the famous Roman Coliseum." The guide says: "Noted for extravagant displays in ancient times." Fred says: "Noted for . . . "

He never knows where he's been until he gets back and looks at the holofilm. I made a lot of footage of them in front of every monument in Rome but that was only filler, because Rome happened to be on the way. The main event was supposed to be Fred and company immortalized on the panda rides and space chutes and by the pool at the fabulously expensive Happy Habitat. I even had to write a little speech for him to record as we passed under the silver archway about how even here, in heaven on earth, a man is driven to reflect on suffering humanity. Fred doesn't only want to be rich and powerful, he wants to be a star, and if everything he does is boring and stupid I am supposed to pretend it isn't; if Fred klutzes up my best shots with his corny ideas I am supposed to be polite and get on with it and I am never, ever supposed to tell him what I really think because It's Just Not Done.

Well I am tired of not doing that which is not done.

Good timing: the rules are changing.

My holocamera is broken. So is Fred's recording bug. We came to earth all right, but not in Happy Habitat.

I don't know where we are.

One minute we were humming along in the cutter, Fred hell-bent on the cosmic significance of his vacation, me on a, what, exploration of the spirit, nothing new. His wife Dottie was asleep and the two boys were fighting in the back. The next minute we were down.

It wasn't much of a crash. I looked at a lot of old movies while I was studying early film at U.S.U., and I can tell you in the old days they did it better. They would be cruising in the biplane, high above the Andes or the Himalayas when a mountain flank would loom out of nowhere and they would crash, or else the plane would be over the jungle when the engines started to sputter or over the desert when they gave out. Everybody would be hurt in the crash which, as they say in the story conferences, throws characters into sharp relief. The good ones usually got better and braver and the bad showed their true colors early on, after which they died horribly. The survivors would battle the natives, the elements, wild animals, the beast within, reaching civilization just in time for the happy ending. Audiences loved that, back then, but they weren't as tough an audience.

Our story was somewhat different.

For one thing, we were flying in a newer number, the foolproof transistorized low-emission cutter. Granted, we were over one of the last undeveloped places anywhere but we were hundreds of miles from any of the missile silos or pollution domes, flying high above the layer. One minute we were up and the next minute we weren't. If I thought about it long enough I would have to say something grabbed us and pulled us down. Nobody was even hurt. There was a thud, the side seams of the cutter split and we rolled out onto the jungle floor.

I had never been outside before.

The first thing was, everything around me was green, not house plants or trees in boxes in the indoor parks but total green like they used to have, that you can still see in the movies. We were engulfed in green, we were lying on our backs looking up at fierce jungle trees and ropy vines with monstrous orange blooms, leafy branches holding hands into infinity: beautiful, except for the hole in the jungle ceiling where we had crashed through the branches. Even the grass felt good, maybe because our choices at home are either carpets or concrete; it was

14

prickly against my back and I liked it. I could hear Fred up and stamping around and I knew I was supposed to be on my feet too, setting up the holocorder and cranking away, but I hadn't figured any of it out: where we were and why, whether there was any danger. All I saw was greenery blurring, richer than anything I'd ever seen before, and I lay there taking it in.

Can a person from the last decade of the twentieth century find happiness in a rain forest? Maybe yes.

There was Fred the indefatigable, checking out his family and making split-second decisions: ever the executive. He had decided to handle this by recording it. If he got it down then he was pretty sure he would get home to show it to his friends. Without looking I knew he had his recording bug close to his mouth: "Unexplained crash due to undetectable causes. Nobody hurt and air security so thorough it will be only a matter of minutes before the search party reaches us and takes us out of here. In the meantime, an on-the-spot report from: *A Vacation to Remember.*"

If I turned my head sideways I could see him. He was headed for the Missus, who was sitting with her legs out in front of her, looking stunned. She shrank when she saw him, which gave me the idea she got hit a lot. Poor Dottie, she was too stupid to get work so she got married to Fred for a living.

"Dottie, stop that. It's Fred."

"I know who it is."

"Wife Dorothy is unhurt and taking it pretty well. Dorothy, what are your impressions of the accident so far?" He thrust the mike in front of her but she only hit it away.

"Fred, *please.*"

He dutifully reported, " . . . a little more upset than I thought, but you've got to understand that she's not used to surprises like this one, she was all geared up for a luxury vacation at Happy Habitat, Lord knows we all were, and now—this."

"Fred, what's going to happen to us?"

For a minute he looked lost. He hooked the mike on his belt and spread his hands, big man getting smaller by the minute, Willy Loman back from another round of one-night stands. When they came for us and we got back to the office I would be expected to write continuity plus additional dialog to cover these lapses; my job was to make Fred look good. I could see him going through a series of changes, from lost man to businessman, big man, commentator. He decided the commentator could still handle it.

"Fred?"

He switched on the mike and walked away from her. "I'm going to talk to my sons Jack and Howard now. Howard, ten, looks confused but undamaged. Are you all right, Howie?"

The boys were still flat on their backs looking up at the leaves. I saw Fred nudge Howard with his toe, trying to get him to pay attention.

"Howie?"

"I'm OK, Dad."

"Good boy. Thank you, Howard." Fred curled himself around the mike, cradling it between palm and cheek the way he always did when he was dealing with inside information. "Jack, twelve, is a chip off the old block, not a tear in his eye, not a scratch on him." He was projecting from the stomach, boy did he resonate. "Jack, give the folks your impressions of this incredible accident."

"Aw Pop."

("You can do better than that, Jack. I think I can sell this one to the networks. Now, let's try again.")

"Jack?"

"Pop, would you fuck off?"

"And now, a word about our surroundings." Fred switched off his machine and came over to me. "Get up, Castle."

"Don't you want my impressions for posterity?" I knew he didn't. His friends think he makes those holopix himself.

"You know damn well you don't show up on the tapes. Now move." He poked me with his toe. "These tapes aren't going to be much use to me if you don't start making pictures."

"Why should I?"

"You have to."

Did I? I wanted to keep on lying there in the grass, just like the kids. Nothing seems real when you are spilled out in a strange country, at least not when you've made it through unhurt. At the moment the crash wasn't real, the jungle wasn't real, my job didn't seem very real. "What's the hurry."

"Quick, this part is going to be over in another couple of minutes." He was giving me little kicks. "You have to get your pictures before the rescue party comes. Take some extra jungle footage because I want to make this part seem longer than it really is, and while you're at it give me a lot of close shots of crash damage, we can really build this up. Now will you hurry before they come and it's all over?"

I sat up then, looking at the ranks of vines and trees that gave way to other ranks of vines and trees, Disney, but with overtones. I looked up at the hole we had made in the jungle canopy, that seemed to be healing. "What makes you think they're coming?"

"Don't be ridiculous, this is the last decade."

"You Maydayed?" I knew he hadn't.

"No need. Air Security has us on their scanners."

"I hope so."

"Look at the cutter, I'm sure it's still beeping."

"I don't know, Fred." The cutter looked dead to me. The instrument panel was dark and when I put my hand to the casing it was cold. "I don't know if you can count on anything."

He wasn't listening, he was fooling with his recorder. "Got to erase back to what Jack said, add some color. Maybe we could build suspense about the rescue. Did they hear us go down? Are they coming? When? That kind of thing. If they get here before we finish taping we can always fake the rest back at the studio." He pushed several buttons and then started shaking the thing. "This can be really significant, Castle, you'll write me a little, you know, 'Even in the last decade of the twentieth century man is vulnerable,' something about the fragile bark but you'll turn it both ways so it isn't only the cutter, you know, pick up on the larger meaning. This is rotten luck but I think we can turn it into a major statement."

I was sorting through the pieces of my equipment. "Hey, Fred."

"Something that'll make them sit up and take notice."

"Fred."

"Living history." He wasn't paying any attention to me; he was shaking his machine. "Castle, would you come here for a minute?"

"Look, Fred, about the holocorder . . . "

He slapped his machine. "I can't get this damn thing to play back. I can't get it to do anything."

"It may not matter."

"What do you mean it may not matter?"

"Fred, the holocorder's broken."

I thought he was going to hit me. "The hell it is."

"Sorry, Fred." It was. I showed him the case: smashed, which was strange since none of us were even shaken by the crash. I let him watch as I opened the case and everything separated from everything else and shickled out, metal parts slithering into the grass. I had the idea somehow it served him right.

"Castle, I . . . " He was swelling up in his herringbone jumpsuit, sorting through various ways to kill me: bare hands, aviator's scarf, a quick bash to the temple with the defunct recorder, all he had to do was figure out how to make it look like an accident. He hated me because I could do something he couldn't do: make pictures. He could make money but I knew how to make things up, which meant he could not do without me because I was going to salvage his material. In the old days big men needed ghost writers to do their autobiographies, and this was more of the same, except Fred needed me in three dimensions. "What good is all this if we can't record it?"

"If you want the truth, Fred, I never did see the point."

He looked me straight in the eye for once. "A man wants to leave something behind. Something people will remember."

I thought: you poor bastard. Then I slipped the needle in. "Even when somebody else does the holopix?"

It was embarrassing. He spread his hands. "When you're older you'll understand." He drooped. "Nobody lives forever, and . . . "

"OK, when we get back I'll see what I can do." I would screen all those old jungle movies again and write him a holoplay that made him a cross between Albert Schweitzer and the great white hunter. It would take a little doing but I could recreate a limited setting so he and the folks could act out their parts and when we aired it nobody would ever know it had all been done in the tank. Fred Fenton could pop into all his colleagues' living rooms in three dimensions, fighting fire, flood, adversity, Jivaro Indians . . .

"Right. Something that will live after me." He stuffed the recorder into his zipper pocket and looked around for the first time. He didn't see any rescuers approaching, there was nobody crashing through the underbrush, there was nothing coming in on the cutter radio and no engine hum above us. "Um, ah. Maybe I'd better try and get this thing going. See what you can do with the radio."

I managed to bring the radio back to life. I could send all right, which is to say the mike was live, and I could hear messages flowing in and out of the home terminal, but it didn't take long to figure out that they weren't receiving me. Somebody else was, though, I don't know how I knew but there was somebody else listening.

"Do you read me? Cutter downed at coordinates . . . coordinates unknown. Do you read me?"

If they did they weren't letting on. I flipped the switch and got back nothing but oblivious chatter on the home frequency, which wasn't receiving, and on the rest of the band, the sound of listening air.

"Castle calling. Identify yourselves."

Nothing.

I whistled into the mike. "All right, dammit, who the hell are you?"

Nothing.

I Maydayed a couple of times on the home frequency and then listened to the rest of the band listening to me. It gave me the creeps so I shut it off. When I went around front of the cutter Fred was jabbing at the innards with a length of pipe. His neck was so red I knew he had passed beyond any attempts to find out why it wasn't working and instead was taking his revenge. I thought that was a bad idea but by that time the works were already ruined. I gave Fred a minute to finish venting his anger and then tapped him on the shoulder.

He wheeled. "How soon will they be here? Five minutes or an hour?"

"Beats me."

"Tonight? Tomorrow morning?" He still had the pipe and I thought he was going to hit me in another minute. "What did they say?"

"Fred, I couldn't bring anybody in."

"This is all your fault." He was swelling up again.

"Right, I'm the one that smashed the engine."

"You bastard."

"I'm the one that wrecked it so it will never fly again."

"Shut up before I . . . "

"Go ahead, Fred. You're nothing without me."

"Bastard." He hit me; I guess that's what I wanted because it gave me a chance to hit him. I let him have it on the jaw. It barely rocked him but it made me feel better, it

20

was partial payment for all the crap I had taken, all the hours I had spent trying to give redeeming social value to the comic strip that was his life.

He was winding up to flatten me.

"Wait, Fred, please." Before Dottie could grab him he swung and knocked me down.

I didn't care. I could see the red patch spreading where I had hit him; my knuckles hurt and I was sprawling in the grass but I was more or less content because our master-servant relationship was ended. I might be unemployed but I was free to be his enemy. I could feel the grass through the back of my shirt; it was uneven and prickly; I thought there were probably real bugs crawling around the roots, real worms. He was waiting for me to get up so we could go another round but I had what I wanted, I didn't want to be hit any more so instead I rolled over; I was going to bury my face in the grass and get a whiff of fresh dirt for a change but instead I almost put my eye out because it was plastic.

I rolled back, trying to figure it out. "Hey." Then I thought: Why should I tell that bastard anything?

"Get up." He was standing on one foot; he had the other one aimed at my head but before he could let go somebody pushed him out of the frame.

"No more, Fred Fenton. No more."

I sat up and there was Dorothy, pushing hard and yelling at him. She had spent all those years trying to be the Little Woman, and now she was trying to knock him down.

He wheeled, he was just about to hit her. "Don't."

The kids rushed him from behind so he was off balance when I got up and knocked him over.

We were ringed around him, looking down; I could see the tumblers clicking behind his eyes as he looked up at us. "All right," he said at last. "All right."

Just then the back of my neck prickled and I thought I heard something, all those plastic leaves rattling, probably, but it sounded more like a rustle of distant applause or a whole group of people drawing breath at once; it wasn't even a sound, it was more a feeling. Whatever it was, it moved across the back of my neck and right on down my spine and I told myself, No, wrong, you're only going crazy. The four of us stood back and pretended not to look while Fred pulled himself together and got up. Nobody had said it yet because nobody wanted to be the first to bring it up but by that time I think we all had a pretty good idea the rescuers weren't coming.

"All right," Fred said, pulling himself together—for us? For whoever might be watching? "Let's see if we can get this thing going."

Nothing was quite right. The ground cover was a strange mixture: real dirt, grass that seemed to be plastic, although it was so realistic I couldn't be sure until I bit into it; flakes of quartz or mica or Lucite, I had to set a match to one to find out which. The tree trunk I was leaning against seemed to be real wood but if it was real the leaves weren't, they had been woven or implanted in the branches which meant that somebody had put this all here, but why? That this was a synthetic jungle seemed to be faintly reassuring. Somebody was doing this to a purpose and I had a couple of guesses about that, if I was right our situation wasn't urgent, which meant that I could sit there watching Fred's efforts over the cutter with a certain detachment. I even thought: Boy, is he going to feel silly when he finds out the truth. If that was the truth. If the grass and the leaves weren't real then maybe there was no real danger, no wild animals, quicksand, savages. But if I was wrong, what . . .

"Look at him." Dottie slid over to whisper in my ear. "Serves him right."

"What?"

"He can't buy his way out of this one, and it's driving him crazy."

Fred was deep in a parody of efficiency. He had brought

all the loose pieces of equipment out of the cutter, plus everything that had shaken loose in the crash and he was making an inventory. He had organized the kids; one picked up each item and gave it a number, and the other wrote it down.

"Poor bastard." I settled myself more firmly against the tree trunk.

"You wouldn't say that if you knew what he is really like."

He knew we were watching and he drew himself up. "I'm taking the kids to reconnoiter."

Dottie rose to stop him but I touched her arm. "Let them go. I think it's safe."

"Meanwhile you two can . . . you can . . . "

I could see he needed help so I said, "We'll guard the site."

"Excellent." He looked relieved. "You guard the site."

He had taken his old-fashioned rifle out of the cutter, the one he had brought because they said you could shoot live tigers at Happy Habitat. He was holding it in a parody of Davy Crockett, or maybe it was Daniel Boone.

Dottie said exactly the right thing. "Be careful, Fred."

He shouldered his rifle, grinning. "We'll stay within earshot. If you hear me holler, come running. Castle, I've figured out how to handle this. When we get back we can put it together from memory. Voiceover. *Memories of a Castaway.* What do you think?"

"If you're exploring, you'd better stick to the path."

The minute they left the clearing she said, "Are you sure the kids are going to be all right?"

"I'm pretty sure. I think so."

"But the snakes."

"I don't think there are any real snakes in this place, or any real anything."

"How do you know?"

I put her hand on the grass. "Feel that."

Her face changed. "Oh Boone, where are we?"

I shrugged. "I think it's OK."

"It's still a jungle."

"Fake jungles don't go on forever." I tried out my theory. "I get the idea it's this gigantic sound stage, in another minute the director is going to holler 'Cut.' "

She was patting the ground with both hands, pulling at grassblades. "What's going to happen?"

"I don't know. I just get the idea it's going to be over soon."

"I suppose we ought to tell Fred."

I looked at her. "Do you want to?"

She wouldn't answer. "Do you?"

I said, "I won't tell if you don't."

She considered. "Let's let him stew." The next thing I knew she had her arms around my neck. "Oh Boone."

"What?"

"I've been waiting for such a long time, and I hope you . . . "

"Wait a minute."

She was more or less melting against me, talking into my cheek. "Boone, I've always felt something between us, and I hope you . . ."

I tried to set her aside but it wasn't working. I'll admit she felt good against me, her hair was smooth and she even smelled good, the trouble was I had seen this too many times before: Grace Kelly in *Mogambo,* Mrs. Macomber, Bette Davis in a dozen parts. We were cast away in this jungle and there was our leader's wife snuggling up to the young buck, who, well naturally his blood rose and parts of him responded but the other parts were telling him: Wait a minute, wait a minute, wait.

"Boone, I . . . What's the matter?"

I was shaking my head.

She licked my cheek. "Boone?"

"No, baby."

"Fred won't mind."

"It's too easy."

24

"Sometimes he even . . . "

"That's not the point."

"You think I'm ugly."

"I think you're terrific, Dottie, I think . . . " You're a little bit much in that tacky jumpsuit, with the stretch-marks creeping up your sides. "I think this is some kind of setup."

"But Boone, I always thought you cared a little. You always had those camera eyes."

"I'm sorry, Dottie, it's too pat. It's what somebody wants." How was I supposed to say the rest? *It's what they want from us.* What made me think that, and who were *they*?

She wouldn't let go. "I can get you in trouble with Fred. I could say you made advances."

I peeled her off and got up. "That would be corny, Dorothy."

"You're scared of what Fred will think. You're scared of losing your job."

"Hardly. It's because . . . " Of what? Them? Me?

"We could run away together, I could be free." She was up now, still clinging. "Oh Boone, it would serve him right."

I set her off and looked at her. "If you hate him why do you stay?"

She was looking at me, considering all the possibilities. Something behind her eyes clicked and her expression changed. I relaxed because she was writing me off. "What makes you think I hate him?"

"This, for one."

Her face went through a new series of changes. She was considering. If Mrs. Macomber wasn't going to work she would go back to being the Little Wife. "I don't hate him, Boone."

"All right, then you don't necessarily like him."

She got me back. "Why do you stay?"

"It's a living. I can quit any time."

"Well I can't." Her hands flew up and down, trying to shape an explanation. "This is what I am."

"You could leave him. You could get a job."

Her irises seemed to be spiralling. "Who would I be then? If you and I can't, if you don't . . . If there isn't anybody else I'll just have to go on being Mrs. Fred."

"Shit, lady. If that's as far as your ambition goes."

She had already turned away from me. There were sounds on the path, Fred returning, and she was going to meet him. She looked back over her shoulder. "It's better than being like you," she said. "At least I know who I am."

OK, lady, your game. Set. Match.

"Oh Fred," she was saying. "I was so worried. What did you find?"

She took the rifle from him and smoothed his brow, all praise, doing a complete Home is the Hunter routine while he explained that all he had seen was more of the same and she kept on saying he could have been killed, etc., etc., he was already impatient with her and when he gave her a push and she kept on smiling I thought: OK for you, lady, maybe we get what we deserve.

The kids came rolling into the clearing with shirts full of fruit—apples, oranges, peaches. Their faces were smeared with juice and Jack handed me a peach. I was looking at the ersatz greenery—nice, but I couldn't believe anything had ever grown from it. "Was the fruit, like, lying underneath or was it tied on?"

"I picked it." There is a lot of his father in Jack. He stuck out his chin. "Where else would you get real fruit?"

"Maybe you'd better show me the trees." I had him by the elbow and we were headed out of the clearing when Fred yanked me back. "Wait a minute."

"Fred, I'm onto something, there's something I have to figure out."

"We're going to have to stick together, Castle, that's an order." His voice was sharp, he was trying for a tone of authority: this is your Captain speaking. It wasn't coming off. "Castle, it's getting dark."

"It can't be, we had lunch just before we crashed."

"Look around."

As I did the jungle dimmed as surely as if somebody had touched a rheostat. There was an afterglow coming through the trees and that was about it. I squinted at my watch but the face was clouded.

Fred said, "Something's the matter with my watch."

"The clock in the cutter is dead." Dottie came out with flashlights. "At least these work."

"It looks like we're here for the night."

I said, "What makes you think this is night?"

"It's getting dark, isn't it?" He wanted me to give him an argument so he could punch me and prove he was right. When I didn't say anything he cleared his throat. "We'd better make a fire."

The kids took flashlights and collected logs. They turned out to be real, at least I think they were, and the question snagged and started tearing at me. If this was synthetic jungle I thought I had things figured out, but if it was, what were we doing with real firewood, real fruit? Did that mean we were in the fake part of a real jungle or something worse? At the moment it seemed better to concentrate on what was at hand: making camp, feeding the fire. As long as there were life systems to maintain, we were OK, so for the time being we played Boy Scout campout, partly for the kids. Dottie seemed to be managing better than Fred or me, keeping up a patter as she dragged cushions out of the cutter to make beds for the kids; she seemed as cool as Mrs. Macomber, or was that Mrs. Miniver? Maybe she had cast herself as the mother in *Swiss Family Robinson*. I don't know what movie Fred thought he was in. He paced the clearing, squinting into the bushes, ever vigilant, while Dottie tucked in the kids, whimpering under her breath because she was just about to run out of things to do. Now that night had fallen the place seemed larger, not so much threatening as neutral, giving back nothing: no information, no clues. In the growing silence all our unanswered questions multiplied and crowded in on us. Was Fred going to get to go on being the big man, and if he wasn't, what would happen to his little woman then? I was sick of being typecast as the existential gentleman—would I ever get another chance? Whatever we had been doing when we started out that morning didn't signify; all our importance had diminished to the size of that circle of light.

Fred said, "Castle, this can't happen to me."

I looked him in the eye. "Yeah, but it's happening."

He sat, staring into his hands. "I know."

I don't know why I was yawning. The kids had rolled on their sides like dogs, even Dottie was asleep.

There was Fred beside me, still chewing it over. "This was going to be such a damn good vacation, it's an important time for me, Castle, it was my chance—well, the people at Universal Investments have had their eye on me, that holofilm was going to clinch it, show them how creative I am . . . "

"Yeah, right." Creative. On my time and talents.

"And there was something else." He was resonating again; for a minute I thought he was recording, but our equipment was smashed and he was only broadcasting to himself. "I hoped for more from this trip, more than you dreamed. You may or may not know it, Castle, but things haven't been too good between the wife and me, we've done a good job of covering up so you probably didn't notice, right?"

I was supposed to nod: Right.

"I thought if she saw how creative I was, once she saw the holoshow . . . " His voice was jagged, "Listen, Castle, if we get out of this you have to help me make that show." He grabbed my elbow. "Where is everybody?"

"It takes a while. When we don't check in at Happy Habitat they'll start looking for us."

"Who says they keep track?"

"For what you're paying they'll keep track."

"What if they don't come? What are we going to do?"

"Whatever we have to."

He was slowing down, I don't know if it was exhaustion or something in the air. " . . . kind of answer is that . . . " His head bobbled. " . . . want results . . . " He was having a hard time talking. " . . . can't do this to me."

I was alone.

I had to stay awake. If I did, then maybe whatever it was that had brought us here would slip and reveal itself. I couldn't shake the idea that this was a gigantic sound stage and now that he had all the action he was going to get the director might jump down from wherever he had been hiding and call an end to the shooting. He would thank us for our efforts and we would get to go home, we might get free tickets to the grand premiere, Fred would be a star after all. I would be cool, give our director the elbow: right, buddy, I knew it all along.

Hey, you can come out now.

"Hey?"

I fed the fire because somebody had to limit the darkness. I wasn't sure where we were or who had cast us or what would happen next, whether it was going to be the charge by the restless tiger, encirclement by stealthy natives, or the moment the next morning when one of us would go over a hill to discover the hidden valley, the ruins of the temple, the thousand foot waterfall; I didn't know whether we were going to stumble on the entrance to the lost city or the cache of diamonds or the skull with the rolled map resting in the socket, or whether it was going to be boring, inconvenient and hard right up to the moment we died of starvation or fever or not being found. Wherever we were, this was nothing that it seemed to be; at the moment we weren't in real or pretend or even Technicolor danger, we were nowhere, in something we could neither imagine nor identify.

We might never wake up.

We could wake up and see the hole above us filled by an enormous eye.

I thought we might be in some rich man's game preserve. Would we be the hunters or were we the game?

If we could escape what would we find at the borders? I thought it might be no man's land, barbed wire and towers with armed guards.

Maybe we were new trophies for an insane collector, or specimens in an intergalactic zoo. I had a quick flash of cavemen, stuffed and grinning in a museum habitat, and I sat there in the dark, counting all the possibilities and smiling. Wait, why was I smiling? When had the fire died? I thought I ought to rouse the others but I couldn't get my arms and legs to move. Instead I sat there bubbling and grinning, thinking over all those things and humming, stoned out of my mind, on what? I should have stayed awake, somebody had to, and in some inner crevice I did, right up to the moment when the bubbles rolled over everything and I went out.

In my dream I killed a tiger. I think we were on the set of *Demetrius and the Gladiators,* the Roman Coliseum in high season, with people giggling and drinking and snorting and smashing grapes against each other's lips, and in the imperial box, an old party in silver robes. I moved forward like a deep sea diver and made my bow. The hatch opened, there was a tearing animal shriek and out it came, beautiful, with the white ruff and the blazing eyes; part of me wanted to have it stuffed and lashing its tail in the corner of my bedroom, another part wanted it reduced to housecat size, it was wild and gorgeous and wanted to kill me, I had to do something about it, dream or no dream. It roared down on me in slow motion with flaming jaws and blazing eyes, the crowd went wild and then I tried my spear and found it was a laser instead. The tiger took a long time to kill, but when I thought about it later all I could remember about the dream was the tiger blurring in a bright circle around me and the crowd roaring and some beautiful thing in a blue dress screaming for help while the wind whipped her skirts around the pole where they had her handcuffed; there was another tiger or maybe it was something else blazing down on her and I had to throw myself in its path because it was the only way I would ever save her and until I saved her or we both died there was no way out of the dream. The next part was pure nightmare, her bright hair gone and toothless mouth gaping, the end of the long-lost Méliès *She*, and then I was in a hospital dream, people in white bending over me until somebody slapped down the mask and there were no more dreams.

Evaline

Sold down the river.

They sold me down the river and I know it, them with their promises. They said, You're going to love it, Mom. I said, Don't call me Mom. They said, It's all you ever dreamed of, friends your own age, lots of dope and all-night dancing. I said, I don't want any of your old men, give me *boys*. They said, Boys, then, anything, we promise to come and visit, and I bought it. I don't know, maybe I wanted it, but it all happened so fast.

Here I am, only seventy plus-plus, with a smooth face and the sweetest, tightest ass in three counties, I look sharp and I am one terrific dancer. I never bothered them, I never even called in sick but the kids packed me off with no dope, without even a decent change of clothes.

Greetings from the Golden Acres section of Happy Habitat. Which you have never even heard of, that there was a Golden Acres section, or that they specialize. Which is another thing.

Hell yes I was railroaded. I did not work all that time and suffer all that pain and train for all those hours just to end up sitting in an old folks' hatch but here I am, who could have predicted it? After Herbert senior kicked off I like to died, we were together almost fifty years. I thought my heart was going to fall out. Half of me wanted to give up and go right after him, but the other half said: Evaline, if you've gotta stick around, you might as well do it in style. I thought: Evaline, nobody likes sad old ladies, so you'd better pull up your socks. Man, I pulled up everything: belly, chins, anything that hung down. The kids didn't like it one bit when I went back to work to earn money for the operations, but who were they to complain? We worked all our lives to put them through college and set them up in life, we put off living so we could take care of them. Herbert shucked the mortal coil without ever getting a chance to smile or put his feet up, but I. I took my nut and went into clinic and had everything lifted: face, butt, voice, the works. I got on the torture racks at the health club and I started running, I could barely make it to the corner but later on I was up to three miles a day. I trained in front of the mirror until I could dance anything, I could dance all day without ever stopping; I wasn't going to be any bother to anybody and as long as I could keep on dancing nobody and no thing was going to stop me, not old age, not ugliness, not death.

I was living it up, not troubling anyone, when it all came down on me.

See I was out dancing, shaking a leg and a hip and my (lifted) ass, without a thought in my head for what they were preparing for me, my middle-aged kids Sybil and Herb with their bourgie lifestyle, Barcalounger sit-by-the-fire. I was dancing like ten jackrabbits in my tight pants with the see-through glitter blouse that looks really good since I had them lifted, I had rhinestone birds pinned in my long black curls and I knew without checking out the mirrored walls that I looked terrific, young, but when the music stopped and I was still panting I thought I could hear a little clock ticking: soon, Evaline, you are going to be old soon. I just bumped my pretty boy Tiger and he bumped back, no telling what he saw in my face, there sure was nothing in his, just him chewing and that bald grin and the little clock in my head going: soon, soon; me dancing, thinking: No. I wasn't the only one, there are a lot of oldies but goodies like me but we never get together because that is like death; as long as we stay separate we can make like young. If you didn't know you wouldn't be able to tell which were the real young ones, like Tiger, and which was us. It's a full time job, all the exercise, makeup, the terrible operations to trim this, lift that, but it's worth it because as long as we can fool others we can fool ourselves and beat the clock—as long as we remember to take our pills.

So there I was with big sexy Tiger, dancing, when one of the little boy-girl things that run the dance hall came and told me there was somebody on the phone. I pulled the thing into the dance and said, Who is it, and it said, bop bop, your kids, and I said, bop bop, I don't have any kids, and then Tiger and I took hands and swung the little thing between us, back, forth, back, forth, OUT, head first into the tables that ring the hall. I thought that would be the end of *that* but naturally when the dance was over and we came out ten days later, they were laying for me in the parking lot. We came out high as kites and sweaty from all that dancing and there were the two of them backed up against my beautiful glitmobile like the last reel of a bad movie, what a drag. They were grey, wrinkled, the worst half of the four horsemen, dumpy Sybil and boring Herb, my middle-aged children. Tiger took one look and split but when I cut out after him they yanked me back and leaned hard, I knew the look: Mother, act your age. I should have been more careful but I was still high as a kite and I just stood there bopping in the cool air, agitating my swell body, trying to catch my own reflection in the glitmobile when I should have been making the slide for life. I should have holed up with bombs

33

and bricks and made a stand right there, when Herb and Sybil closed in I should have let them have it with a flame thrower, Lord I would have made one beautiful curtain line, hollering:

You'll never take me alive.

Who knew?

When they wouldn't leave me alone I said, "All right, what do you want?"

"Mother, we've been trying to reach you for days."

"I suppose it's about money." I could see them leaning forward, rocking on their toes. They are scared to death I am going to spend it all. "All right, how much?"

"Oh Mother, you know we wouldn't . . . "

"In a pig's eye. You'd kill me for the money if you could."

"That isn't it, Mother," Herb said.

"You're afraid I'll marry Tiger and you won't inherit."

"Oh Mother." What Sybil meant was, who would marry an old bag like you?

I remembered Tiger's body. "Maybe I should."

"Don't be foolish, Mother." Herb took my hands. "We have wonderful news."

By that time we were all stuffed in the glitmobile with Herb driving, me in the back; I was a little dizzy from all that stuff Tiger and I had been taking and my joints were seizing up, which is what happens when you stop dancing on cool nights. Sybil was fooling with my viewer, by George she had put on a cassette, it was the big sales pitch but who knew? All I saw was a bunch of beautiful people dancing, the voiceover said, YOU CAN BE ONE OF US.

Well hey wow. I was trying hard to drown out the other sound, that damn clock of mine ticking: Soon, Evaline, no matter what you do. Tick. If you don't act now it's going to happen. Tick. It's going to happen soon.

BEGIN AGAIN. The little screen bloomed with color, and the music—my knee started jerking to the beat. All

34

right, it was only an ad and another day I would have said, Out with your promos, get away, but I was getting tired; my joints hurt and this thing was promising to stop the clock for me, it was the next best thing to the Garden of Eden and all I had to do was sign. They were all young, they were bopping, they were all beautiful and when I looked closer I understood that they were all my age but they were dancing as if it didn't hurt at all, I thought: Man, I wonder what they are taking. Then I saw Ashby Braden that is ten years older than I am, looking straight into the camera, saying, It's the good life in Golden Acres, Evvy, we need you here, and I got the idea that if I could only go there I would be happy.

Well, maybe if I hadn't been stoned I would have thought it through: why the kids were pushing so hard when it was going to cost them, why they already had my suitcase in the car. I should have said stow it, I should have jumped out and run for my life but the pictures and the music and the voiceover were all lapping against my jagged nerve endings and my poor dry eyeballs, soothing me with promises; the cassette was pumping perfume into the car, or maybe it was happy gas, and I was thinking: If I go there I can stop the clock. At the back of my head I heard a warning bell but I wouldn't listen.

By that time we were at the powerport, they had me on the ramp and they were leaning on me, my stuffy son on one side and on the other my boring daughter, they were saying:

"Just think, happiness."

"But I was happy where I was."

"You're going to be really happy now."

"But I haven't . . . "

"Don't you worry about a thing."

Hey.

"You're going to love it, Mother."

Hey wait.

"Your kind of people." Sybil turned her face so I wouldn't see when she started lying. "If you don't love it you can always change your mind."

But you're making it sound like a . . .

"Do they really make you younger?"

"I don't know, I. . . . "

"Ssst. *Herb.*"

"Why yes, Mother, of course they do."

. . . sound like an . .

Both of them nudging, begging me to say yes.

"Just think, dancing parties around the clock."

. . . sound like an old people's home.

"I don't know if I want to, I . . . "

"Trust us, Mother."

(They want it so badly they will say anything.)

"You're going to love it. Please?"

(They want me to go. They are my children, have I ever been able to deny them anything? A mother's heart.)

"I don't know, I . . . " was getting tired of busting my ass just to keep even, sick of pills and exercise and starving all the time, I was sick of having my joints seize up and tired of smiling into faces that are paid to keep on smiling, some bum lover will catch you at your best, high and swinging, in the middle of the big moment you will look into those eyes and see the truth: they hate you because you are old.

"Mother?" Sybil was sounding panicky.

Herb said, "Mom?"

"Don't worry, I'm going, you can relax."

Well I looked at them for the last time right before they kissed me too quickly and shoveled me into the luxury express. I was down off my high by that time, shaky and scared, yes, beginning to wonder why I had ever let them . . . They were beaming. For once they were happy, happy. That was a new coat Herb was wearing, and Sybil had on my jade.

When I got on there were two attendants to seat each of

us, strap us in, get us something purple and fizzy to drink. They were all in tight little purple bodysuits with the HH emblem on the pocket; they were sweet, clean all-American kids like we used to have in the old-time magazines, so shiny they were sexless, and I remember wondering if that was a good thing. I cheered up when a couple of neat-looking guys got on, tightening bellies that looked like washboards; they were all codpiece and sickle thighs, my age, right, but like me they had kept it. The only dollies I saw were stitch-and-paste jobs, no threat; I saw them and I saw one of the attendants reading a body scan—mine?—that came in a printout from the arm of my seat, and that was all I saw.

I would give a nickel bag to know why we all slept most of the way, why nobody woke up until we banked over the silver arch that flashes in four languages: Welcome to Happy Habitat. I would give ten nights with the person of their choice to anybody who could explain why this part that I was going to, nobody had ever heard of. The Golden Acres part was never mentioned in the fumf they send out on Happy Habitat, they never show it in the holos, I'd never met anybody who had ever been or, oh shit, come back from it. We were flying in over the part I had heard of, that is always on holovision, the glittering park and the boomerang-shaped paramotel, the spires and wheels of the fancy rides. Even when you don't believe in escape your heart leaps up when you see the place, I was thinking: the kids used to beg me to bring them here when we couldn't afford it, now they don't care any more and here I am. I thought we would come down in the plaza and fan out and join the party but we didn't, we shooshed right on by, and when I tried to see where we were going the window had gone silver, so all I saw was my own strained face. Then we were hovering and the next thing I knew we were down.

We were all stretching and rubbing our eyes (carefully, to preserve the lifts), testing muscles without understanding why we weren't stiff, and by that time somebody had thrown a switch that unsnapped all the seatbelts and opened the hatch. Outside it was all green. The air was, all right, all the perfumes of Arabia and then some, the first thing I thought was: It's everything they promised. Maybe it's going to be all right.

We all slid down the ramp at once, crashing off into a spongy place lined with roses. People hit the ground running, singing out and stripping as they ran because they wanted to be the first to fall into the pond underneath the fountain. I had never seen anything like it; somebody said, I do believe I have died and gone to heaven, but I really didn't know. I was wondering why we had gone so far away from the silver archway, why they silvered the windows so we couldn't see; I got the idea that this part was cut off from the main park and I didn't know how we were supposed to get there from here; just then somebody jabbed a shot in my ass, "Just a little feelgood, honey," and I didn't care any more. The attendants started stripping us and washing us down and we were all laughing and posing; I knew my sutures were tight and my boobs looked as good as any, I didn't know who was looking but I felt wonderful; I was stoned out of my mind and glowing, wriggling so the transparent glitter gown would settle over my hips and the next minute I was dancing, wow.

We were surrounded, we were all being lapped by sweetness and light and bathed in milk and honey and I guess we just unfolded like those crazy jungle flowers, I have never danced like that before. It was wild, and if I heard a new sound at the back of my head, something in there alongside that old clock ticking, if I suspected I heard the ghost of a murmur of a mass intake of breath, an echoed mmmm, or aaaaaah, if I thought I heard something and I pushed it back and didn't try to tell the others, it was because I was afraid the rest would end the glowing and the dancing, and maybe I should be forgiven for my carelessness because my joints were warming from the outside in and everything was new and beautiful, including me.

I told myself the sound was only us.

Boone Castle

I woke up exhausted and sore, trying to figure out how I had been stupid enough to go to sleep and all and thinking that wasn't it, I was mad as hell because somebody had done something to me and I couldn't figure it out. It was light again, the color of early morning, but I had the feeling you get when you've jetted back from someplace, your stomach is sour and your inner clock is on the fritz, your arms float up from your sides and you can't tell whether you're starving or never want to see another thing to eat. I rubbed my eyes on my fur sleeve and looked around the clearing, which was exactly as it had been last night, if that was last night, in the last minute I was awake. I had just gone out, during which . . . There were no tracks in the dew on the plastic grass, no marks in the ashes of the dead fire, no sign of any intrusions and no changes at all, except for my . . .

. . . *fur sleeve?*

My fur sleeve was attached to a fur jacket that didn't meet in front except where it was lashed across my naked chest, which somebody had painted the color of a desert island. I had on pants made out of what I thought was deerskin but rumpled like Ultrasuede, a design touch that lifted my backhairs; my sandals were cut from rubber tires that fit so closely that they must have been measured from my footprints. I got up too fast and my blood almost didn't make it, so that I had to hang onto the cutter to keep from passing out. When my head cleared I looked around at the others, zonked out and smiling in a collection of skins and home-mades with tag-ends of clothes

39

and bits of rag tied around their heads or waists for effect,
I don't know who had done this to us or what they were
trying for but all I could think of was the Swiss Family
Robinson after a few weeks on the island, and this was
happening too fast. Somebody had doped us or gassed us
and come in here while we were out cold and.

"Fred."

He was hard to rouse. His fur hat was positioned so it
kept the light out of his eyes, he was breathing deeply
and I had to kick him a couple of times before he heard.

"Dammit. Fred."

"Huh?"

"Somebody's been here."

Dottie sat up. "Boone?"

Fred was having a hard time coming to. He pushed
back the hat without even realizing what it was.

Dottie said, "Boone, what do you have on?"

Fred said, "I didn't hear anything."

Dottie was stuffing her hands in her mouth. "Oh Fred."

"What's the matter?"

"On your head."

He threw it off and jumped away, shaking and staring
hard, almost as if he expected it to crawl away.

"It's OK, Fred. It's a hat."

"Where would I get a hat?"

The boys were rolling over, examining their clothes.

"Real fur."

"Hey, neat."

"Somebody's been here," I said.

He pulled at his fringed shirt. "Good God."

"They must have come while we were asleep."

"What do they want?"

"I don't know." I looked up, not sure what I was looking for. "I think there's something they may want us to
do."

Fred was looking at the assortment of skins Dottie was
wearing. "You'd better get rid of that stuff."

"I can't."

He had his shirt over his head. "It's not safe."

"There's nothing else to wear," she said. "Our clothes are gone."

"Go into the suitcases."

"Those are gone too."

I said, "Fred, I think we'd better get out. Now."

"The rescue party." He looked over his shoulder as if he expected to see them coming down the path.

"We don't even know if there is one."

"If we leave here we're never going to be rescued."

"You want to wait around to see who did this? We don't know what else they want." I lifted my elbow and made Fred look at my fur sleeve. "Somebody did this. I don't want to play their game."

"You're a coward, Castle. Running."

"Call it what you want."

He poked at the cutter: dead. He shook his watch. He looked at Dottie, who said, "You can put this in your memoirs, Fred. That's all you care about."

"Bitch."

I said, "Do what you want. I'm going."

Dottie looked ready to leave with me and I think he knew it. He said, "Get your stuff together, Dorothy, and round up the boys. I think it's time we were on the move."

We went into the cutter for the compass but it was clouded, like a blind eye, so we left it and picked up the rifle and a couple of hunting knives. By that time the kids had come back with more fruit and we filled everything we could find and set out. As we walked, I had to switch the bag of fruit from my left shoulder to the right because the strap was stinging where it rubbed. I felt under the jerkin and I couldn't make sense of it: where I had gotten the long scratch, when as far as I knew, that tiger had only been in the dream.

The rest of that day went along like Quix Comix, with

41

us slogging through the brush single file. I don't know what we expected, whether we thought we were going to come upon a native village or a trading post complete with biplanes or whether we only kept moving because it was better than staying still. Wherever we were going, it was bound to be better than the place we'd landed, or that's what we told ourselves. As long as we stayed with the cutter we were victims, marooned, stuck in a place where They could find us, whoever They were, and as long as They knew where we were, They could come in at night and do anything They wanted. I think Fred honestly believed we could find our way out or that we would be rescued. I was thinking we were never going to get away unless we ran for it. The going was slow because the kids kept taking off down side pathways and had to be brought back while Fred had fallen into the role of, I guess it was white hunter, which meant he had to test every flat place before he let us walk across it, although he didn't know what he was looking for: the entrance to the hidden cavern, maybe, or wires that would trip a volley of spears, or maybe he was afraid we would walk over the palm frond flooring or die on bamboo spikes in an elephant trap. I was slowing us up at the rear, but I don't think Fred and I were in the same movie. I kept looking behind us because I had the idea somebody might be following because the costumes and the scratch on my shoulder made it apparent that we were not alone in this place, that whoever brought us here was not only civilized but sophisticated, and I thought if I kept looking back over my shoulder then whoever or whatever it was might slip and reveal itself.

I didn't tell the others about my shoulder. The dream was so fuzzy that I couldn't be sure I'd really dreamed it, and as the sun got higher the last outlines began shredding and drifting away, leaving only the scratch and no clear memory of how I had gotten it. In broad daylight I decided They probably did it while costuming me. If that wasn't it, I didn't want to guess; anything I said would scare the others or else convince them I was crazy.

The day went too fast. We stopped for lunch almost before we got started, feasting on the fruit the kids had gathered, and we walked through the afternoon until the light changed and told us it was twilight, even though we were all still bright and fresh as if we had just gotten up. Dottie was still going along at a good clip and the kids were loving it; I thought if this was twilight then I was ready to walk all night, and then I noticed that I was giddy as hell, high as a kite, and my shoulder had stopped hurting, which made me wonder whether somebody had slipped speed into those apples and peaches we were eating and maybe that was why we kept giggling.

The next thing I knew Dottie was dropping back to walk next to me, bumping into me, all soft boobs and round shoulders that I didn't much like because the women I want all have an edge to them, more spring, she was bumping and I was giggling, *hmmm, mmm hmm hmm,* she was bubbling:

"Boone boone daniel castle I mean Daniel Booniel . . . "

I never really liked her and there I was, bubbling right back. "Dottie spotty dotty babe . . . "

"If you change your mind I'm still avail."

"Abul, able, able." What was I doing?

"Or nots." She giggled and covered her mouth. "After all I am a wife and mother."

"Right." What was the matter with me? With us? I heard myself saying, "Righty right right."

"But then I thought, Can this be all?" She was nudging me. "Booneyboone?"

"Dottydots." I blinked hard and tried to get it together. Why hadn't I wanted?

"If you still wantle." She was flowing all over me—costume, body, hair.

"I had a reasum, um, ah, reason." What? I was finding

43

it hard to concentrate. Had to, just to keep . . . "Fo no sanks." Did I hear a distant giggle?

"But you'll give me a little snuggle for sake's sake."

"OK."

"Nobody wants me."

" 'S all right. Nice wifey, good wifey." How stoned were we? What were they doing to us? She was sniffling and even though I didn't want her I didn't mind her, it felt good and we snuggled for a minute until I realized we weren't snuggling, we were holding each other up. Somewhere inside part of me was clanging: *wait a minute, wait-wait,* but I just said, "Oh babe, poor babe," and pulled her over to where we could sit down on a rock. I was calling, "Fred, hey Fred boy, Freds?" but he and the kids were crashing ahead, and knowing we were separated, we might even be lost forever, I couldn't get myself to care.

On the other hand, now that I didn't have to concentrate on standing up I could think a little bitter. Better. I think. I just sat there feeling giddy and light-hearted because I knew how all those movies came out: you would beat off the crocodiles and outrun the native tribesmen and make friends with fifty gorillas, so the next time the natives came at you the gorillas would help you fight them off. Either that or you would drive them off with the miracle of your cigarette lighter ("the gods make fire to show you they are angry") or you and the gorillas would bombard them with rocks, or was it peaches, clinch, fade-out, The End. Wow, right, wonderful, I loved my costume but why had Casting stuck me with a woman that I didn't even want, was I going to have to mash Fred and see it through with her or were they going to write in a neat new lady for me, Sheena in a leopardskin, or Ayesha, *She* . . .

Hey. Why was I wobbling and why was this lady sagging against me, and was it in the peaches and if not what kind of laughing gas were they piping in?

44

If this was a movie it ought to be like the movies I had seen over at the archives, tacky and dated and safe, but here I was with this funny scratch on my shoulder, that was beginning to hurt again, and there was this other thing:

If this was a movie what were we doing in it?

I was in it and the Fentons were all in it but even with those great tans and authentic-looking costumes we weren't any of us stars, we were real people, which meant that no matter what happened there was no way to give this an MGM happy ending because movies are predictable, but people aren't. We could build huts and find food and wrestle crocodiles and even fight off the pigmy hordes, we could do everything within our power to make it look good but we were still only people; we could get killed and never get up again, no matter how many times the director yelled "Cut," and if we did come to what looked like the happy ending it probably wouldn't be one after all; it would turn out we were still lonely or yearning or unaccountably depressed. I kept shaking my head, trying to clear it because I wanted to figure out whether we had options, whether we could decline to be in the movie, what would happen if we refused to perform. Maybe the director would show himself and start threatening or they would try to bribe us with whiskey and colored beads, but Lord we might just end up sitting around in the middle of this showy pretend jungle suffering real boredom and depression right up until the minute we starved to death.

"Starved to death." I think I said it. I was trying to pull myself together, Lord I was stoned.

"Hey." Fred was back.

"Huh?" Had I been asleep? How long?

"I found it."

"What?"

"Village." He was yanking at both of us, trying to get us going, he was as excited as all of the Hardy Boys so I guess he was stoned too or maybe that was just the real Fred surfacing, damn the torpedoes, damn you all, Fred Fenton is going to run the show. Thinks he's going to run the show.

"Wait a minute, Fred. Maybe that's what they want."

"What?"

"I mean, we have to be careful."

"Sick of being careful." He was jiggling on the balls of his feet. Scared? Not him. Not me either. Why? "Let's go."

"Not yet." What was I doing? Fighting plotlines, maybe. Yes I would rather do it myself. "Look, it's getting dark."

"Don't worry, it's deserted. Going now."

"Fred."

He had her on her feet, shouldering her along the path with the kids following and in another minute I was going to be alone. I got up too, fighting dizziness, fighting the giggles, fighting the whole scene but not sure enough of any of it to let them leave me there, choking on questions and blinking in the artificial, right, artificial dark.

Luce

The ad I cut out had these purple arches all the way across the top but no name, only the address. It said:

NOTHING TO LOSE? COME TO OFFICE X.

Damn right I have nothing to lose. I cut it out and put it in my desk. I didn't know I was going to have nothing to lose so soon, or so fast.

I don't even know how I got stuck in my rotten life, humdrum world, humdrum job, humdrum wifelet that would start complaining the minute I walked in after work. I work my tits off to keep him and the kids in shoes and junk cereal and all he does is stick them in Dacare and pull food out of the freezer and complain while it thaws. I was not meant for that kind of life, I don't even know when it happened. When I was little there were high winds blowing all around me, dreams flying like dayglo pinwheels, a hundred million hopes; I was going to be Lucia di Lammermoor Finley, knight errant, I was going to have it all, fame, money, a love that I had been waiting all my life for; he would come blowing in on a strong new wind and light me up from the inside like Nagasaki fireworks. A face like mine and I was going to have a love like that? Hell yes I was, thought I was, kept on thinking so right up until I ended in the desk job, the row house, with Norman that keeps his beard in curlers, and I didn't even know when or how my life turned around.

I lived my whole life for the person I was going to ride through life with, did I really ever think Norman was going to be him? All right, we did get married too young and I outgrew him, but whose fault was that? A person does a lot of things for passion, that they regret later, but there is no telling an eighteen-year-old kid. Besides it was Norman that wanted to quit school to put me through college, but when I finished, would he go back to school? Not him, he wanted the free ride, the hassle-free ticket to stay home from the office, he said he wanted kids. So he whined and begged until I made a couple of deposits down at the egg bank, but he never gave a damn about those kids. They spend half the day at his father's and the rest, they're in Dacare, at least they were. If anything came up it was me that had to run home from the office to take care of it because Norman would be out at Aikido lessons, or sitting on his fat butt on the sofa, watching the holos and combing his beard. I was always having to run home about this thing, that thing, and the good jobs in the office went to the singles, damn smart bitches, is it any wonder Maeve is a vice president and I am this penny-ante clerk. Norman has his beard up in curlers half the time now, he always has a headache, so there isn't even that.

On top of which Maeve called me in late yesterday and said it was, ah, tough rocks, but they just promoted Stevie the divorced boy, they have made him office supervisor over my head. I took it all right, gulp, I could not afford to lose my temper because I have a family to support. When you have responsibilities you can't afford to say what you think and clear out.

Which meant I was already pretty bad when I got home that night, plus Norman was right on top of me as soon as I came in the door.

"Where've you been?"

"I got depressed," I said. "I went to a bar."

"You knew I've been waiting home all day with nobody to talk to." He had the curlers in again, cold cream on his face and he was still in his old blue bathrobe, he hadn't even bothered to get dressed.

"Well I've got my problems too," I said, and tried to tell him what happened on the job.

He wasn't even listening. He said, "Luce I would like to take cello lessons, there is a guy at the Conservatory who takes the installment plan."

"The installment plan, what do you mean the installment plan?" When I tried to look him in the eye he just twisted his hair around one finger. "Didn't I just tell you I'm stuck at this salary for another year?"

Then he did look at me and he was mad at me. He, Norman, was mad at me. "You're trying to stifle me. All I am is a convenience."

"I would like to help you Norman, but I don't have the jack."

He got surly and pushed me. "You're always trying to put me down."

All I ever did was try and get him to go back to school and make something of himself, that I could talk to, but he wasn't going to, not him, he wanted the soft life in this stupid house and now . . . I was getting ready to holler so I thought I had better change the subject. "Look, that is all very well, Norman, but where are the kids?"

"The kids?" For a minute I thought he was going to say, *What kids?* "Oh them, I've put them in Permacare so I can have more time for my cello."

"You—did—what?"

"I had to forge your name but they said you could make time payments." He had this craven look in his eye. "After all, I'm a person too. Look at it this way, when we get them back they're already eighteen."

"Eighteen!"

"You can visit them on Sundays," Norman said.

"You had no right to do this." He looked scared now and I realized I had picked up the brass lamp with the figure of Richard Nixon, Norman's choice, and I was hefting it.

"Dammit, I've got just as much right to be a person as you do," he said. "If it weren't for you I'd be playing in Carnegie Hall."

Which I guess is when I swung. I can't explain what happened next—hell I can't even remember half of it, all I can remember was me swinging and him yelling, and I thought: does that face belong to anybody I ever loved, and I hated it, him, what my life was, I had started off so brave and I had been euchred: no hope, no nothing, now I didn't even have the kids. I guess I let him have it. When the red haze cleared I looked down and saw he wasn't moving and I thought: damn fool, you brought it on yourself. Then I thought: What have I done?

I was too scared to stay around and find out. I didn't know if he was knocked out or something worse, didn't want to touch him to see, swung the lamp around the room a few times to make it look like a robbery and called an ambulance, in case. I was already up the wall and halfway across the ceiling so when I heard the hooter coming

I took off. It was an accident. Was it? What had I done to him?

The office. I had to get to the office, to find the ad.

NOTHING TO LOSE? COME TO OFFICE X.

Yeah nothing to lose. Yeah, right. I had to break into the office, after I got the ad out of my desk I jimmied the door to Maeve's office and cleaned out the safe, I didn't even worry about fingerprints because I was burning all my bridges, hell, I had nothing to lose. Burning all my bridges, that had a nice ring to it so when I left I sprayed the place with solvent and set fire to it. All those years wasted in that office, with nothing to show for it, all that was left of the knight errant, crumpled up in Maeve's OUT basket, I wanted to get even, leave my mark. I thought: It serves them right. The door outside was already blistering but I stopped long enough to write on it with lipstick, I didn't know if my life was over or only beginning but if I hadn't made it one way I was damn well going to make it another and so I wrote:

LUCIA DI LAMMERMOOR FINLEY: Master Criminal.

I didn't know what they were buying at Office X or even who they were, all I knew was I was out for everything I could get. The ad said good jobs in exotic places, right, well I was going to take one and by God I would rise in it, I would skim the cream off and then I would make my mark. The firepeople were screeching in so I took off for the Darvon building, by the time the police got there I was already at the far end of the last corridor on the top floor, crashing into Office X.

It was a dump. Nobody was at the desk, only a computer terminal that took my vitals and told me to sit down. One look at the place and I had misgivings but I could hear the police heading my way and so I did, by that time they were banging at the door but I couldn't move; the plastic sofa had grabbed hold and it was hugging me.

The next thing I knew I was there. I was sitting outside in a little park and it was morning. *Outside.* If there was a pollution dome it was so high above I couldn't see it; there were trees all around me, that I have only ever seen growing in parks, and what I was sitting in was, it was real grass. At least I think it was. I saw silver walls and a flashing silver arch, damn if it wasn't Happy Habitat. I thought: babe, you're in luck, you're going to rise to the top working for the best. Then I thought: how come they didn't let you in the front door like the rest of the folks, and what do they want with you? I didn't care, I was home free, out of Melba's way and away from Norman with his wifelet whining and his messy clothes, I didn't know what was going to happen to me here, how fast I could rise in the operation, but it didn't matter because I was home free and it was cheap at the price.

There were two others, just sitting up and coming to. There was me and this guy in silver coveralls that was too pretty to come in by the back door and a kid, maybe he had run away from home. I asked the pretty boy, "What do you think?"

"So far so good."

"What's next?"

He shrugged. "They promised me everything I want, so I've got to guess they're going to deliver."

"Diamonds every payday?"

"Not exactly."

"What's your kick?"

"Necrophilia."

Well I was trying to be cool so I didn't turn a hair. "To get it or get away from it?"

"Not really." His eyes were pale and clear as ponds. "What are you into?"

"Freedom. I had to get out in a hurry."

"So did I." He was powdering his nose. "What did you . . . "

"You'll read about me in the morning papers. I'm not what I seem." I got a quick flash of the old spouseroonie laid out on my former living room rug, a trickle of blood

at the mouth but nothing serious, and I got this uncom-
fortable feeling that in another minute he was going to get
up and start to whine for me. No. I said, "I'm on the most
wanted list." *I am a desperate criminal.*

"Why, that's fab."

"Thank you." He looked so admiring that I thought it
would be all right to ask, "Listen, how come these aren't,
you know, regular channels?"

He said, "I heard they have special work for us."

"Like?"

"Like things they can't get their regular staff to do." He
leaned so close his forehead almost touched mine. "It's a
new wrinkle in the operation."

"Then we can get in on the ground floor." I was thinking: Power, right!

"Quiet. Here they are."

I don't know how they got there—up from the ground, I
guess. I don't know what I expected either, big creeps in
black hoods or little creeps in lab coats but they weren't
either; they were happy teens in blue coveralls, wearing
grins like applesauce and oatmeal, lord were they ever
American. They looked like the good-looking ticket sell-
ers and ride stuffers in all the holo promos for Happy
Habitat except maybe a little sharper, and they were all
armed.

I wanted to start off on the right foot so I got up. "Hi,
kids. I'm Luce. Luce Finley, from Bostongrad?"

"Rex Richards," said my pal the necrophiliac. "Maybe
you've heard of me."

The other kid, the runaway, unlocked his arms from
around his knees and got up. "I did my folks and now I'm
here."

Well if they heard they weren't letting on. Instead they
were sizing us up, patting a shoulder here, feeling a bicep
there, running measuring bugs over our backs and giving
notes to the one with the punch terminal. He never once
looked down at his fingers; he was staring hard at us.

Even as he squinted at my left profile, which is not my best, his fingers were flickering over the keyboard, punching information in.

"What are you guys doing?"

"Classifying. Got to see where you fit."

I said, "Wherever I want. That's where I fit."

"You'll go where you're put," he said, without bothering to ask me any of the particulars. "Charisma negative." He stamped something on my arm.

"Hey, you can't do that."

He had moved on to Rex, who widened those pale eyes and showed every tooth he had in what I guess was a smile.

"Look, you bastards."

They wouldn't even look at me. They just moved on to the kid. "Class A," the one with the punchboard said, pushing him over to stand with the two girl workers. Then he pushed Rex. "Also class A., but this one . . . "

At last, I thought. He was standing in front of me. "This one is pretty ugly. We'll put her in one of the back rooms."

"Wait a minute, do you know who you're talking to?"

"Can't let you mingle with the public. Might offend."

"You're talking to Luce Finley. *Luce Finley.*" I thought for a second and retrenched. "Listen, I thought you guys needed special talents here."

"Be that as it may, lady, we're here to please the paying guests, not frighten them."

"Wait a minute, you bastard." I swung at him.

He decked me without lifting a hand. "We project a certain image in the surface operation here, we can't afford to let anything spoil it, certainly not an ugly face."

"All right then, why in hell do you want me here?"

Damn if he didn't parrot Rex: "We have special work for you."

"But you won't let me in by the front door." I was thinking about all those little twits you saw on the holo

53

ads for the place, college graduates with faces like Ms. America. They all went through channels, while I . . .

"Look," he said, "we're entering a new phase in the operation, and frankly you . . . "

"I'm not fit to meet the public?" I grabbed him by the collar. "Who are you to say?"

One of the pretty girls whispered in his ear.

"On the other hand, if you want to opt for plastic surgery . . . "

The old red river was beginning to flash behind my eyes and I lunged.

He flicked a switch and something stopped me cold. "Back room," he said to the two boys. The girls had already started down a different path, leading Rex and Billy. "Stick her in D for shakedown and training. As far as I'm concerned she can stay there." I was still struggling but there were two of them and before I could break free they had pulled me behind a bush and we were going down a hatch.

I was pissed beyond any singing of it, thinking about Rex and the kid starting upstairs with the prime choice beauties just because the stupid bastard in the coverall liked a pretty face, there they were in the hurly and the burly while the elevator took me down. There was an underground monorail waiting and one of my guards peeled off and headed down the corridor while the other one pushed me inside. The car was crowded with people in body suits, all those beautiful bodies bulging in purple, white, with one or two tougher types in black, they were all stoned, humming and dreaming, heading back from work I guess. I was thinking: they are not so damn good looking: I was thinking: all right, what have they got that I haven't got? I was getting depressed but I couldn't let anybody see it, we were all belly to belly and back to back in the elevator but when I tried to get friendly they every one of them looked away. When the doors opened and we all surged out I tried to do it in style, head up, shoulders back, big grin that Norman learned when he took lessons at Dale Carnegie, but did my guard even notice? Hell, he just gave me a shove in the right direction and took off. I got my balance and did a quick kick and two-step and pulled up in front of the desk, all smiles and looking sharp.

The desk guard was not impressed. "No funny stuff or I'll burn you."

"I'm Luce Finley," I said. "Maybe you've already heard of me."

"In here." She let her weapon point the way.

"You can already see I'm going to go places."

"Not where you're going," she said.

Boone Castle

The village Fred led us into was as neat as a movie set. The trees thinned to bushes that ringed a grassy clearing and in the middle was a circle of Hottentot huts, all the same size except for the one on the far side, next to the pyramid of skulls.

The pyramid of skulls?

Wait a minute, everybody.

"Castle, look at this."

Wait a minute.

"Boone, this is crazy."

Wait.

"Now do you believe me, Castle? Completely deserted."

"Boone, isn't it exciting?"

"Hey Mr. Castle."

"Oh, *neat.*"

Wait.

Nobody did. They broke into the clearing and I had to follow. I was not necessarily relieved to find out that the pyramid was only faced with skulls; somebody had laid them on a wooden frame, wiring them together in graduated sizes so they all sat neatly, with what looked like an infant skull crowning the heap; the worst part was that I couldn't tell whether they were real. There were fetishes attached to the huts and for a minute I thought those were shrunken heads swinging in the doorway to the master hut, but when I checked it out I saw they were only carvings. I was moving right along, checking the place out with the rest of them, but somewhere inside I was jangling, I wanted to be wary, alert, but my feet dragged and everything was muffled and I couldn't stop yawning and giggling. I had the idea that even though it was dusk once more, here in the land of artificial sunlight, it wasn't getting any darker. It was, if anything, one degree lighter, light enough for us to see the details clearly, light enough for us to explore at will. I kept thinking there was something I ought to be doing. Something I ought to. But I just. Couldn't. Keep my mind on it.

The kids were tearing in and out of huts, whizzing by like bandits on a conveyer belt, brandishing bone necklaces, abandoned masks and rattles made out of gourds, sticking feathers in their hair and snorting and giggling because this was more exciting than all of Rome put together. I wanted to slow them down, to tell them to watch out, but nobody was listening. I don't know whether it was in the fruit or in the air but I was lightheaded, moving under water, and Fred and Dottie were whirling out of control. I don't even know what it was we were supposed to be fighting, all I know is that Dottie and Fred had given up for the time being, they had silenced their warning bells and stifled their misgivings, giving in to the place with a relief that was almost voluptuous. There was square old Fred rampaging like a runaway from Boys' Town; I don't know what conclusions he had come to in his pocket-calculator mind, whether he had even thought about it or whether he was already too stoned to think, but he was doing early Robinson Crusoe, or half-assed Stanley and Livingstone while Dottie made a place around the fire, setting out clamshell plates and little arrangements of fruit, wetting her lips and pushing back her hair as if for an unseen camera. They collected rugs and cooking tools from the huts, bringing meat from the smoke house without asking whether it had come off an animal or the haunch of some earlier traveler. Wasn't there a movie where . . .

Fred was saying, "All right, Castle, are you going to stand there and starve to death?"

I was blinking hard, trying to keep my mind on it. "We don't know what we're getting into."

"I'll tell you what I'm getting into, I'm getting into making the best of things."

Dottie said, "Try the breadfruit, Boone."

"Fred, this is some kind of jungle."

"American way," Fred said, tearing at the meat with his teeth. "Frontier thinking. Make do."

"But you don't know if it's . . . "

He was getting mad. "Don't tell me what I don't know. Little Ph.D. smartass. I don't need you." He was burping and giggling. "I know the facts of life. Try some of this skin, it's terrific."

"No thanks." It did smell good.

"The facts are, we might as well take advantage."

"What would they say about you in the board room, Fred?"

He smeared a greasy hand across my front. "They'd say I know a good thing when I see it. Sit down, Castle." He pushed me down. "Take this." He gave me a piece of meat. "And take notes while you're at it, this is one hell of a chapter in the Fred Fenton story."

"This is your life." I was maundering, I couldn't help it. I was rocking where I sat, the next thing I knew I was eating. If there was some vestigial part of me still saying, *Stupid bastard, you are giving in*, the stoned and giggling part was already saying, *Way to go, babe, eat the goodies while they're on your plate.* I still don't know if it was the costume or being stoned or just a natural hatred for always being the one who shouts WOLF when nobody is listening, but I thought what the hell and sat down in the (fake) grass along with the rest of them, enjoying the food and the fire and feeling that nobody could possibly get hurt because this could not be real; it was like landing in a featherbed, knowing you're not going to fall out no matter how much you thrash. By the time we had finished eating I was feeling as reckless as they were and I remember licking the grease off my fingers and thinking: *all right, if it's going to come down, then let it come down.*

Right. Stupid. I should have known better.

We were so sleepy we didn't even leave somebody to stand guard. You might say it served us right.

Kaa Naaji

Oh, yes! I am going into the land of heart's desiring, I am promised entry into the land of dreams. That which I have hoped for without even being able to name it is going to be mine.

What more fitting reward for the man who has lighted all the lamps of India and caused her dynamos to hum again? For it is I, who rose from the dust of Mother India, I, Kaa Naa Mahadevan, who made the great discovery. I have brought riches to India, I have given her a great new source of power and now it is India who is the giver, not the suppliant. She has power to share with a grateful world.

Before I knew the nature of my mission I knew I was a person set apart. I was squatting by our fire with my arms ringed round my knees when the earth spoke to me.

What is it, Kaa Naaji, what are you longing for?

Ah, I would say to her, *I do not know.*
But you do long for something.
Yes. As I grew older I spent more time by the fire. Every night I would sit for hours in the long twilight, watching the smoke from a million cooking fires layer itself over the city of Delhi, and I would think: It is like this everywhere at twilight. Thus it will always be. At the same time the yearning licked at me with tongues of fire and told me this was not so.

Finally I put my two hands on the earth and asked her. *Mammaji, there is something I must do. It is still not clear to me. Please help me make it clear.*

Then she spoke. *Look,* she said. *Learn. In time all will be clear.*

One stifling night in the hot months the power failed all at once all over the city, and watching Delhi go dark I understood. It was the inequity. So many cook over cowdung fires, so many starve here, and all for want of power. Even the great machines of Europe and America had slowed for lack of oil to run them and there were the Arab hordes, sitting on a cache of gold, for they alone controlled the flow of oil to the world. I touched my mother the earth and vowed that I, Kaa Naa Mahadevan, would discover a new source of power.

Long were the cold winters I spent on the banks of the River Charles in America, studying all the sciences at your famous M.I.T. While others sported with women and roistered with their friends I worked into the night, searching for the catalyst. How lonely was I, and how terrible were the winters, often did I look at those snow-laden clouds and long for the clear skies of India, the circling kites, her unremitting sun, but I could not stop or waver for there was a fire within me, I was a person set apart. When I had fulfilled my mission I could rest.

Then I made my discovery and wept.

Even the sweepers' children know me now, every wedding canopy is studded with flowers spelling my name and a grateful nation has erected a statue in my memory in the gardens of the Rashtrapati Bavan; I have come to live in Akbar's gem, the great Red Fort at Agra, and looking at me you would think: There goes a very happy man.

Yet when I had fulfilled my mission my inner fire burned the same. Ah yes, my friends, I still *wanted*, but there was nothing left for me to want. I have everything, and it is not enough.

What do I have to live for now?

Everything seems stale to me. The women and the servants all lounge and think up new ways to cheat me while I languish in the Pearl Palace, trying to think up new ways to be busy. The air inside my palace dome is sweet and filled with music, the banks of the Jumna are green where Shah Jahan could never make anything take root; I have surrounded myself with clergymen and courtiers like a modern Akbar and yet I am still a person set apart, my inner fire burns unquenched, I am so alone; I sigh, listening to the rustle of my bare feet here, there, in the audience halls, on the marble floors of the Pearl Mosque.

Think of a man who has nothing left to live for; think of a man who has run out of things to do. Imagine how I seized on the mysterious purple capsule that glowed among the sweetmeats on my tray last week when the servants brought my tea. I do not know whether someone was bribed to put it there or whether, hey presto, it simply appeared. When I picked it up it spoke:

Don't worry, I'm not a bomb.

Naturally I dropped it.

Pick me up.

I watched it for a moment or two.

It said, *Hurry.*

"Excuse me my friend. Are you speaking to me?"

Who else?

"The last one who spoke to me thus was my mother the earth."

Enough of that, it said. *Pick me up.*

I picked it up.

It cleared its throat and said, *Congratulations. You are a very special person.*

"I know that. I am a national hero."

That isn't important.

"I beg your pardon."

What is important is that you can afford what we're selling, and there's more. We have plans for you.

The word snagged my hopes. "Plans?"

Drop me in water, it said.

"I do not drink water."

Well then drop me in your tea.

"Frankly I am wary of solicitation."

Forget it then. You had more to gain than we do. It lost color and started shrinking.

"Not so fast," I said, and dropped it in my tea.

It activated.

I was in a hologram, and the things it promised! I could see but not touch in this new world where there were still prizes to gain. Scent and scenes and voice all twined: *Take lives in your own hands . . .* (she was beautiful and I saved her, there was an aura of roses.) *Snuff one, save another . . .* (I was in an ice cave, I was about to . . .) *The thrill of power is yours . . .* (Here were people I could help, we would be friends.) *Savor power and excitement in this world of worlds.* I recognized the place, the silver arch and elaborate parks of that famous pleasure place that only the wealthy can enter, but if this was that place then it was that place with a difference. (I smelled the rich smoke of a million cooking fires; if they could bring that back what else could they bring?) *New dimensions of excitement . . .* I remember crying out: "Where, what must I do," and It said, *All you have to do is sign with us.* At the same time I whirled in the vision, reaching and not touching, aware as I spun that my poor feet were planted and growing cold on the marble floor of the Pearl Mosque. I cried out, "Is this possible?"

All this and more.

And so I signed.

I prepared as for a wedding. The dhobis washed and ironed my best kurthas and laid them into the cardboard suitcase I had with me at M.I.T. because I am at heart a sentimental person. I made my offerings to the dancing Shiva and I made the long goodbye with my Drupathi, that I almost loved, and on the day appointed I barred everyone from the Pearl Palace and sat down to wait. It may take every rupee I have but they promised me true friends, a woman to love, and what is life without hope? Waiting, I dreamed a long corridor, something beautiful perpetually fleeing, me in perpetual pursuit, and when I woke up I was there.

We were all in an antechamber, belly to belly and haunch to haunch, and I think the others were all even richer than I. There were Germans, rich and impatient in fine leather garments, a Texan with a golden lasso around his waist, Japanese garlanded with cameras. On one side of me was an Arab with the sharp face of a hunting kite, one of the oil sheiks with his retinue, and on the other a lithe and glittering woman who had bought everything, had seen everything, and licked her lips in anticipation because here she was promised more. Through the high, wide window I could glimpse the silver arch that the whole world recognizes, I could see the tip of the green glass parabola that I knew from the holos and I thought: Is this only Happy Habitat after all? Have I signed everything away for this? Next to me the sheik was twisting his beard and growling: "Is this all?" I could hear a rustling and then perfumes filled the air along with the sound of voices overlapping, reassurances rushing in. " . . . you are in a new dimension . . . " "Entire worlds are yours . . . " " . . . power over life and death." "Welcome to the ultimate world . . . " There was a stir, an electric crackle; the sheik's men surrounded him, facing out, as the wall behind us opened, but they lowered their weapons as a flock of beautiful young people came to us, one on one, each comforting with a touch, drawing us along a corridor, taking us further with caresses and blandishments until we were at the consulting rooms.

"It is here that we will make your program."

As the door closed behind me I could hear the murmur of a dozen different voices in a dozen other doorways, all gentle and seductive, saying, "Yes. Now." I was drawn into my chamber and to a sofa that embraced me; there were lights pulsing, there was music, an aura of *dhoop*, and as I looked into the face of the young woman who was to plan my visit her features blurred. She was saying, "Now, if we are to fulfill all your desires we must learn what your real wants are . . . " And I could feel myself melting into her eyes, asking, "What must I do?" "Everything." "What must I give?" "All." I said, "I am empty," and the voice said, "You only think you are, my dear. Now we are going to sort your memories, the pain, your wishes and your needs . . . " I said, "I only need to be needed. Let's begin."

After that I remember only a medley of sensation and fleeting dreams, nothing, until I woke to hear my own voice, choosing. "Yes. That one. Yes please."

I am resting now.

Soon I will begin.

Boone Castle

We woke in our places around the fire, but by that time the morning grass was wet, the embers were cold and the grey light that slanted through the trees was cold. I lay where I was for a minute, too stiff to roll over. My shoulder was killing me but when I tried to raise my right hand to massage it I was jerked up short by the thong. The thong was attacked to my wrist, lashing it to a stake.

When I tried to roll on my side to undo it I found out about the other three stakes, the thongs spreadeagling me. My neck was stiff but I rolled my head to one side to find out who that was breathing on my left. There was Fred looking more or less deflated, with dirt on his face and leaves tangled in his hair. Dottie was on my other side, silent because she didn't want to scare the kids, but rolling her head from side to side with a stark, crazy grin: this didn't fit any of the parts she had written for herself. If I lifted my head slightly I could make out two other pairs of feet, the kids'; they faced me across the ruins of the fire.

"Hey Boone, are you all right?" That was Jack.

"Beats me. I think so."

"What's going on?"

"I'm tied. So are your folks."

"Me too," Howard said. "Get me loose."

"I'm sorry, I can't right now."

"Get me loose. Get me loose!"

Jack said, "Is this part of it?"

"Part of what?"

"You know. Whatever it is."

"Damn if I know."

"Well I don't like this part."

"I hate it. Get me loose."

"Howard, stop whining." Fred had come to. "Castle, you'd better get us out of this, and fast."

"I'd better . . . "

"What am I paying you for?"

Dottie said, "Fred, you know he can't . . . "

"Well somebody'd better. They can't do this to me." Fred was staked on his back, shouting at the sky. "You can't do this to me." He let his voice drop. "Castle, what do you think they have in mind?"

"Who?"

"You know."

"Fred, I don't even know who they are."

"This is no accident, you know. I pay you a good salary, Castle. Dammit, do something."

I did the only thing I could; I got to work on the knots. Somebody had wet down the rawhide in the night and it had dried again so the knots were beyond our powers. Still it gave us something to do. We lay there for the better part of what must have been the morning, watching the sun go higher over the phony jungle tracery and fooling with the knots. For the first couple of hours we kept up a minimal conversation: speculation, yes, Fred had a theory but I was only an employee so he wasn't going to tell me, and if I'd had a theory the day before I had long since stopped being sure of it; complaints, mostly the kids' because it was no fun; plans, none of which were going to work until we got the knots untied. Dottie was needling Fred: how had he let this happen, why had he brought her here, all he ever thought about was what he wanted, he used her and the kids as props for his stupid holoshows. She kept it up until the sun dried our mouths and left us parched and beginning to wonder whether we might have to die here. Even with daily pollution deaths and the war tolls and medical disasters I had always thought I was never going to die, at least not any time soon, but there we were trapped in the sun and I was beginning to wonder.

I couldn't make out where the light was coming from. If I squinted I could almost make out a fretwork of wires supporting the branches above us and sometimes I thought I saw the framework or armature of a dome, but just as I thought I was bringing it into focus the sweat would blur everything. Some time during the morning my mind turned a page, flicking us all out of the jungle format and into the World War II death camp movies, where people like us did get tortured, and even the hero died. I wanted to follow that idea, figure out where it was taking me, but I was dizzy and hung over, too preoccupied to hear Dottie and Fred stirring and trying to lift their heads, or to hear the footsteps and the person calling out as he entered the clearing. I wasn't aware of any of it until I heard Dottie talking to somebody new. I looked over and saw a pair of pale brown feet in sandals, brown hairless ankles and above them what looked like a sheet-bottom, or part of a skirt, so that I was surprised when a man spoke.

"I have come to help you."

Dottie said, "What?"

"Greetings, my name is Kaa Naa Mahadevan, and I have traveled a long way for this opportunity."

"Who are you?"

"I have come to rescue you."

Dottie said, "That's wonderful."

Fred said, "What are you doing here?"

"But you are going to be my friends, and so you must call me Kaa Naaji."

"Where did you come from?"

"All my life I have waited for such an opportunity."

Fred said, "Wait a minute."

"For which I thank you." He squatted next to Dottie and with two knifestrokes, freed her hands.

She said, "What did you say your name was?"

"I have come a very great distance from Agra, perhaps you know the place?"

Dottie sat up, rubbing her wrists. "Thank you very much, Mr."

"Who the hell are you?"

"At least you will have heard of our Taj Mahal."

I was shaking my head, trying to make some sense of it: him, in this setting. What he thought he was doing. Did he know something we didn't know, and why was he so pleased?

"You can see her from my bedroom window, the Taj Mahal."

"Untie the kids next," Dottie said.

"The hell with that." Fred was straining against his knots. "Get to me."

Instead the little guy bent over my bonds. "And you, my friend?"

"Boone Castle."

He was looking from me to Fred and back. "How did you happen to . . . " I guess he was finding it hard to match us.

"Good question."

Fred said, "Untie me, you little bastard."

He was going to take his sweet time getting to Fred. "I mean, get stuck with these people?"

"It's a living." I sat up, rubbing my wrists.

He was shaking his head. "That is no excuse, my friend."

"What do you know, you . . . "

Fred was getting redder. "Who is this guy, anyway?"

"Don't ask," Dottie said, "it doesn't matter. You can just thank your stars he's come."

Everything after that was pretty wild. He had us all untied and we were sitting up, rubbing our wrists and ankles to bring back circulation, when we became aware that we were not alone in the clearing. There was an absence of sound of any kind—no animals leaping, no jungle twitters; for once there wasn't even the fake sound of fake breezes blowing through the phony leaves. There was only a silence so complete that Kaa Naaji stashed his canteen and lifted his head, listening, and one by one the rest of us stopped muttering and making little groans of relief, then we quit breathing, staring out at the surrounding jungle and waiting for whatever was about to come.

For a minute or two there was nothing: just us straining at the silence, not sure what we were listening for, staring into the underbrush without knowing what we expected to see. Nobody spoke and there was no consultation but, moving as one, we picked up spears, sticks, anything that came handy, and moved into a defensive circle: Dottie and Fred, our rescuer and me, with the kids in the center. I could feel the Fentons jangling and I was close to the edge myself but when I looked at Kaa Naaji, on my left, he was wearing the same expression as the kids: he could hardly wait for it to happen. Still there was no sound or sign but we stayed where we were, suspended, and in the next second dark shapes began emerging from the shadowed underbrush, coming at last through the final rank of bushes in little rushes, and as we watched they swarmed into the clearing: the wildest bunch of natives I had ever seen, in or outside the movies, not head-shrinking wild or people-eating wild, but fierce and terrible because nothing about them *matched*. They weren't shaped alike or colored the same and they weren't even dressed alike; there was no way they could have belonged to the same tribe or even come from the same place. Everybody had on his own idea of native costume—beads here and there, along with bones and body paint, but never used in the same patterns or colors. The native in the grass skirt and shark-tooth necklace was howling and jumping up and down between the guy in the Eskimo suit with the whalebone snowshoes and the one in the beaded penis wrapper with the lotus painted on his belly. None of the weapons matched either; they ranged from rubber bats to thugging strings to rocks and slingshots and gravity knives, one guy was roaring and swinging a mace and chain; it was as if whoever was running that place had reached into downtown Bostongrad and grabbed a handful of whatever was available, let them pick their own costumes and dumped them here. I had time to count almost every bead because once they had cleared the bushes they all stopped, rattling and menacing us from a distance not because they were afraid of us but, all right: to string it out, because something or somebody wanted all hands to savor the moment.

There we were all backed up together, shaking spears

and beginning to feel a little foolish, and there they were, ringing us like death on skates, except after a while even they looked a little uncertain, exchanging glances and then roaring and rattling some more, apparently waiting for something that hadn't happened yet, maybe it was the signal, so that each of them had to keep checking on the others when he thought they weren't looking, and I got the idea that they were all new at this. I don't know how Kaa Naaji knew it was going to work out the way it did, or why it worked at all, but he gave us instructions in a low voice and then he lofted his canteen into the ranks of the untouchables, or whatever they were, but not until he had made a little speech that could have been the end of him, except that he was very quick and managed to dodge the spear. His face was bright and when he spoke it was a cross between a warcry and an aria:

"For my new friends and the glory of Mother India."

Then he let them have it.

I don't know what was in that canteen but it started flaming the minute he put the match to it and when it landed it leveled the front ranks as surely as any grenade. Fred was getting several shots off in the opposite direction, as per instructions, and Jack and Dottie and I charged on the stragglers with our spears. The minute the thing exploded the whole gang of attackers broke ranks with craven shrieks and there was little or nothing in the way of hand-to-hand combat because they were already beaten. It was a rout.

Kaa Naaji was springing around honing his knife and humming, he thought this was a very great victory and he wanted us to celebrate. Nobody else was in the mood. Fred and I were already itchy, anxious to get out before something worse happened. We had inspected the scene of carnage in spots where the smoke had cleared, exploding one of my theories, that hadn't quite crystallized. Some things about this jungle were fake but those were real bodies—four of them, almost unrecognizable but still

smoking, popping and making little hissing sounds. Dottie had drawn the kids to the far side of the clearing and
was sitting with her face in her hands while the kids
wheeled around her with uncertain looks, not knowing
whether to laugh and sing because we had won or to be
sick because of the bodies, because of being helpless and
still lost.

I went over to the skull pyramid and caught Kaa Naaji
on his next round.

"At last I've done it . . . "

"Hey."

"Not for myself . . . "

"Kaa Naaji."

"But for the sake of friends."

"Kaa Naaji." I grabbed his arm, and made him stop.
"Hey."

"First we will rejoice and then . . . What's the matter?"

"It's time to split."

"But we have to celebrate. We won."

"I don't know what's going on or what you think you're
doing, Kaa Naaji, but this place isn't safe."

His eyes crackled. "Ah, but that is part of it."

"Part of what?"

"You know." He spread his hands. "We are in this
thing together."

"Well I think we'd better get out of it together."

He looked around with regret. "But I have waited for
this for so long, and come so far."

"You've what?"

He didn't answer. At last he said, "All right, if it will
make you happy. I want my friends to be happy."

"It would make me feel a little safer."

"Very well."

Which is how we happened to be heading down the
trail toward the sound of rushing water when we were
charged by the water buffalo. It lunged out of nowhere
with blood in its eyes and fire in its mouth and before

Fred could raise his rifle little Kaa Naaji had thrown himself on its horns with a warcry that sounded more like strangled laughter, and after a certain amount of thrashing and wrestling, sank his knife in at the base of its skull.

After the thing fell we pulled him out from under it and moved his arms and legs to be sure he wasn't broken. He wasn't even bent; he was on his feet in a blaze of excitement, hugging us all at once and laughing and dancing all at the same time, and when we finally got him quieted down he pulled a camera out from under that thing he wears instead of pants and damn if he didn't ask me to take his picture.

Which I did. Fred and Dottie were heading down the path to what was probably a river; the sound of rushing water was loud by that time, and as I raised the camera I could hear them laughing and splashing.

Kaa Naaji stood first on one side of the water buffalo and then the other, and when nothing else worked he went to its head and stood with his knife raised and one foot on its skull, and if it didn't seem quite real, who was I to . . .

If it didn't seem quite real.

I snapped the picture and after he thanked me and took back his camera I went over to the thing he'd killed and kicked it, half expecting to see bolts fly and hear the pinging of an uncoiling spring. Instead my foot sank in, thudding against the skull, and there was even a convincing amount of blood. It should have been enough but the sound track in my head was slipping out of sync now, I had the idea my own personal projector was running down, so that the last three takes were in stop motion: one of the dead water buffalo, one of Kaa Naaji, stashing his camera, and then a close shot of his face.

"All right," I said. "What's going on?"

He seemed upset by what he saw in my face. "My friend?"

"Wait a minute."

"Yes, Castle."

"Look, who the hell are you, and what are you doing to us?"

"Castle, I am your friend."

He looked so innocent that I wanted to hit him. "What do you know about friends?"

"Why what is the matter?"

"There's something the matter, is what's the matter." I was numbering all the things: the mismatched natives, the canteen, his cheerful, expectant expression right before we met the water buffalo. "There's something the matter with all of it."

"My friend, did I not help you fight off the natives, and was I not brave?"

"You were terrific."

"And did I not kill the water buffalo?"

"Right, you killed the water buffalo."

"And does that not make us all friends?"

I was losing track of the conversation. His eyes were large and liquid, his face filling up with hurt feelings. "What difference does it make?"

"I thought we were in this together. Indeed it is the whole point." He was looking more and more distraught. "If we are not in this together then there is nothing. Nothing . . . "

"What in hell are you talking about?"

"At least it is better to know the truth." He had started toward the river. "Not everything is easily bought. It is all over, this segment."

"What?"

But he wasn't talking to me. He was walking along talking to his wristwatch; what was it tuned to? "This segment over and out."

"Are you going to tell me what you're doing?"

"I thought we were in this together. Over and out." He was more surprised than I was when the wristwatch didn't answer.

"You little bastard."

If a brown person can get red in the face, he was red. He

sidled closer so nobody else could have heard what he was saying. "Promise you will say nothing of this to the others." We were at the end of the path now, just about to start down the slanting bank. Dottie and Fred and the kids were wading around in the shallows trying to assemble enough drifting logs to make a raft. I was going to join them when he stopped me, tightening his fingers on my elbow. "Look up there, where the river bends. There is the boat I am going to find."

"Explain, dammit." I grabbed him by the neck and shook hard.

"At least you are honest in your feelings."

"What are you doing to us?"

"It is not I, it . . . "

The boat was in full view now, drifting our way as surely as if it ran on an underwater track. How did he know it was coming? Where did it come from, and was it safe? Kaa Naaji was squirming under my hands, working hard to breathe. I let go so he could talk.

"I only wished you well." He shook his head, saying, "I thought we were in this together, and now . . . Listen. When you board this boat it will take you out to meet your rescuers. I was to have come with you, to accept your thanks and share in the joyful moment of your recovery, but now . . . " He was shaking his head sadly, rubbing the place where my fingers had damaged his neck. The boat had drifted close to the bank; the Fentons were wading out to pull it in. Kaa Naaji started toward them, drawing me along. "What was not to be was not to be, but when you think of me again perhaps it is the boat you will remember and that I led you to it, and not your bitterness, and perhaps when you speak of me to your grandchildren . . . "

It was getting hard to hear him because of the sound of the motor. "I'm not going to have any . . . "

"You will tell them that I fought off the natives and saved you from the water buffalo, that I helped you in danger and that I was brave."

The motor? But the thing Dottie and Fred had snaffled and were climbing into looked more like a rowboat; there weren't even any oars, there were only a couple of poles. "Dammit, Kaa Naaji."

"Ssst. My friend. Into the boat, with the others."

Now there was no doubt where the noise was coming from. There was a speedboat coming around the bend and heading in fast; the driver and his crew were crouched low because of the spray. "Wait a minute."

"As for me, I must go on to new adventures." He saw I was in the boat and pushed it off with his foot. As we parted company he said, "You may think ill of me, but at least you will be safe."

"Wait a minute." I wanted to stop the Fentons, or slow them down at least.

Kaa Naaji was saying, "At least, I think you will."

"Hold on, Fred, you don't know who those . . . "

"It's all right, Castle." Both Dottie and Fred were poling hard, going out to meet the speedboat. It was so close I could almost make out the faces.

" . . . people are." They were wearing purple uniforms. I shook my head because I just couldn't . . .

"Didn't I tell you?" Fred was wigwagging with both arms. "It's all right."

I wasn't so . . .

"Look at those uniforms. Look at the flag." The boat shooshed down on us, dashing spray. There was no holding Fred now; he pounded my arm and laughed. "Of all the damn good luck, Castle. We've come out in Happy Habitat."

Evaline

I thought it was better than advertised, there was a lot of laughing and wallowing in perfumed water, with purple stuff to drink or snort and we were stoned out of our minds, clumped and rubbing underneath the colored spray until they came for us with blow driers and makeup and fluorescent dancing clothes. We were all slinking and swanking along the mirrored runway, spilling into the great soft place where the music is pure energy and you can dance your brains out without ever once having to stop to catch your breath. You could have bounced a dime off my slick belly or rested a ruler across my tits; I would like to have a kiss for every head I turned while I was dancing, I would like a minute taken off my age. At dawn it was over and I fell in love with a wonderful guy who threw me over his shoulder and took me to his room. I looked him all over for traces, but there were no leftover stretch marks and no tiny scars where things had been removed or lifted, so I guess he was one of the help, which is probably why I don't remember anything after he kissed me on the eyelids, picking off my false eyelashes with his teeth. It probably explains why I woke up in a cold bed in a tacky room; whoever put me there had hung up my glitter suit and tucked me in between the yellow satin sheets. I hoped it wasn't my room but it was all right, there was the suitcase Sybil had thrust at me, with a hastily scrawled gummed label and underwear hanging out because she had been in such a hurry to snap it shut. All the junk I had been taking had worn off in the night and I was stiff as a board and lonely as a cloud.

I got up to look for pills. I started slow, head first, then shoulders, then sitting; by the time I had my feet on the floor I knew the place was a gyp. The rug was white Astroturf, the upholstery on the love seat was waterproof, underneath the yellow satin bedding was a rubber sheet. In case of medical disaster the whole place could be hosed down. There were grip bars in the shower and night nurse buzzers everywhere, the place seemed to be fitted to deal with incontinence and feebleness, poor old bodies letting go, it could all be hosed away. The designer may have been thinking orgy, but he was also thinking old age.

Worse yet, there weren't any pills. My last hope was the suitcase. Not a prayer. Sybil had packed the sum total of 40-plus years of sheer malice: a flannel nightgown, baggy cotton underwear, fuzzy bedroom slippers and a hideous bed jacket, Milk of Magnesia; there wasn't a red or a benny or a popper in the whole dismal kit. There wasn't an item of clothing fit to scrub a floor with. She had gone to Ugly Unlimited and picked out a lot of old-lady clothes.

That's the way our daughters like to think of us.

The message was so clear: Give up. Does she think I am using up all her chances, or filling up her space? Maybe she and Herb look at me and read their own futures. Tick. Or else they're afraid of catching it. Tick. Terminal old age. Well fuck them both.

In the cold light of day I didn't know why I had signed the paper, whether I had faced up to all those things I was holding tight inside and decided to let go or whether I did it for the children: a mother's heart.

Maybe it would be a good idea to split. I would go to the office and ask about ways out. I kicked Sybil's suitcase under the bed and made a bikini out of the satin pillow-case. I took two turns in front of the mirror wall, thinking: all *right*. I could feel those joints pinging and I was tempted to lie down until the feeling passed but I knew if I did it would be hard to get up. By that time there were needles beginning in my head and the fuzz was creeping up my throat. I had to hurry so I tied a yellow satin ribbon on my hair and went out.

"Ma'am." There was an attendant with a tray.

I said, "Uppers."

"Yes Ma'am. And a couple of other things to make you feel better." He was in a purple stretchy thing that outlined all those bulges and ridges. I ran my hand along the line from his throat to the bend in his arm, thinking this might not be so bad.

"I feel better already," I said, and popped the pills. "What's that?"

"Tiger's milk."

I drank it.

"There's a petting party in the sauna, or if you'd prefer, there is skinny-dipping in the mineral waters, or mixed doubles in the passion pit. We have a shuffleboard tournament planned later in the day with a barbecue tonight." He was punching information into a tiny computer box on his belt: which pills I had popped? "Or if you have any special requests . . . "

"I was going to . . . " What was I going to do? All those pills had met the tiger's milk and they were coursing through me. I felt so good I didn't remember what I was going to do, at least not all of it. Oh yes. Leave. Well, not right away, maybe; I felt better than I ever had.

"The Early Risers are in the solarium."

"I think I'd rather . . . "

"Or you can sign on for one of our Special Adventures."

The sun was warm on my swell body. I was feeling great, I was thinking: Man, this is cheap at the price. I said, "Is it all right if I look around?"

"Whatever turns you on."

So I bopped along in my bikini, taking in the pueblo-style building that bordered the square. Each room had its little terrace with the waterbed and the flowering tree, and from each terrace you could see the square with the dance floor and the bandstand and a lot of pairs of bare feet sticking out from under the bushes, people making it or sleeping in the grass. From the corners of the square, archways opened onto the paths to the solarium, the disco, the shuffleboard courts, the warm springs pool. It was laid out like a pleasure seeker's dream. On the pool path I saw oldies but goodies like me sunning, lounging on little hills, whooping it up in the velvet grass, and if I happened to meet somebody they would wave with a stoned grin and I couldn't help grinning back. I was thinking: all right, if I have to get old this is as good a place as any, happy to the last, *all right*. I was feeling good, and if I saw a squad in purple suits rushing somebody somewhere, I thought maybe it was a medical disaster and it was their job to take care of it, and if I saw others moving clothes and bedding out of one of the cabanas I thought: Yeah, well, these things happen, and if I wondered where were the paths that led to the rest of Happy Habitat, that we had paid so much and come so far to visit, I thought maybe they did things gradually around here, they wouldn't mind if you mingled, but before you did they wanted you looking good.

When I came back to my place there was Ashby Braden on the terrace, Ashby that was ten years ahead of me in school. Her legs were tanned and her hair was blonde this time around, she looked wonderful and for once I was glad to see her: almost eighty and still swinging.

"Ashby, babe."

"They told me you were here."

"Well Ashby, you look wonderful." I was taking in the contrast between her tan and my spotty-looking legs, I was thinking if that's what this place does for you, lead me to it, I was about to ask where she went for her clothes when she said:

"They don't want you to be afraid."

"This is the cat's ass, Ashby, why should I be afraid?"

"You shouldn't, really. Have some pills."

"I've already had pills."

"Extras," she said. "Just in case."

I popped them. "What are they for?"

"They keep you looking good and feeling good." She gave a little laugh, the last remaining sign of her age; she had even had a voicectomy, so except for the laugh she sounded like a mere slip of a thing in her tweens. "They want you to keep looking good and feeling good . . . "

"Well you certainly look wonderful."

"Oh, I am wonderful, it's just . . . " She dropped her

voice, you would have thought we were in a spy movie, "I can't help being afraid."

"Afraid it's going to stop?"

"Oh, it never stops, the parties are the greatest, the men are . . . well we don't any of us have to have old men, Ev. And they don't have to have old ladies." Her eyebrows went up and down; when we were kids about a hundred years ago she would have said *woo woo*. "We have a real swinging life here, everybody is so nice, but every once in a while . . . " She was whispering so low I had to lean close to hear, "somebody goes away and they don't come back."

"Face it, Ashby, we're no chickens."

"That isn't it."

"I mean, sooner or later everybody has to . . . "

"It isn't the oldest, it's the prettiest."

"Well heart and cancer don't always . . . "

"Ev, they weren't even sick."

That stopped me. Part of me was about to say: how do you know, and the other part of me wanted to drag her inside and make her tell me everything she knew. "Are you sure?"

"Things happen in the night sometimes, things you hear, but you never know what and then the next morning . . . " There was a shadow on the terrace, somebody coming, and she leaned closer and hissed: "People disappear."

"My dearest." We both jumped. He was on the terrace and he slipped his arm around her; he was tall and gorgeous. "I thought you would be alone."

"Oh, Armand." Ashby's face was a mixture: scared and lascivious. "Was it today?"

"Our assignation was today." He had her by the arm and he was tugging. "Come my dear, let us fly."

She was holding back. "Where are we going?"

"Someplace wonderful." He gave her another tug. "It's the apotheosis, honey. Gangbusters."

She said, "Gangbusters, you promise?"

"Gangbusters."

He wasn't very convincing and I don't think she was convinced but she said, "Oh Evaline, it's going to be gangbusters, don't wait up for me, OK?" She wanted to be happy and if her voice spiraled up at the end, well, it was something she couldn't control.

I said, "I won't, babe." He was drawing her away with him; I didn't know if I ought to let her go, didn't know how to stop them. "Oh, Ashby."

She turned. "Ev?"

"Ashby, if you'd rather stay with me."

He stroked her bare arm. "My dear, our friends are waiting."

The look she gave me was one I recognized. "Ev, I'm so tired."

"But you don't know what's going to . . . "

She looked fierce. "Don't."

I understood what she wanted. No matter what happened, she wanted it to look good—her departure, our farewells, wherever it was she was going, whatever was going to happen to her.

He was saying, "Gangbusters."

She reached out her fingers and I touched them as he drew her away, knowing as she slipped out of my reach just what she was thinking. If you can make it look good, maybe it will be good. Her voice wavered. "Wish me luck."

"Bye, Ashby honey. Have a ball."

Luce

And I thought I was going to rise in the business. I put on the uniform she gave me: grey everything, while hers was red. I hated the color but the fit wasn't bad; I wished the boots had wider tops, but the belt was neat. I let my hair down and when I brushed it out it was almost auburn. For a skinny lady, I looked damn good. I thought: Take that, 0547B. Kind of ugly, he had said. I would kind of ugly him. When I came out I gave the uniformer my best profile.

"Not bad, huh?" When she didn't say anything I said, "I mean, I'm going to knock 'em dead."

"You're, uh, not going to meet a lot of people where you're going."

"What do you mean?"

"Well, uh. Where they're putting you. Your looks aren't quite up to standard so they're going to, uh, have you working behind the scenes."

"What do you mean not up to standard." All right, I was yelling.

"Now don't get huffy. I'm not up to standard either, that's why I work down here. It's, uh, not up to standard for their purposes, you know, the All-American norm." She was backing away from me. "It's part of the image we project at Happy Habitat, everything the public sees has got to be perfect, healthy and handsome and wholesome, and you . . . "

"What's the matter with me?"

She just squinted and shook her head. "Let's face it, ugly people are a turnoff."

"Ugly people. I'll ugly people you." I was halfway across the counter, I could have smashed her in another second but she touched something on her belt and I fell back screaming because my eardrums were about to implode. She kept her hand on the button until I stood up and backed off and marched where she told me to.

I thought I would run into other recruits in the corridor. I had seen enough about HH on the holos to know how new employees were supposed to be treated. There had to be an orientation show. I got the idea that Billy Freeman and Rex the necrophiliac were off somewhere getting the full treatment in the big auditorium, feelos, smellos, the works, while I was stashed down here with no supervisor to impress, not even a friendly guide. They would all be sitting shoulder to shoulder with a lot of other beautiful but dumbs, they would be filled in on the operation. Maybe somebody would even get up there and explain the new wrinkle in the operation, what they had recruited us for. I thought I knew all about Happy Habitat and I could not for the life of me figure out why, after all those years of hiring Misses and Messers America with the pretty teeth, they had gone digging for people with nothing to lose, people that would do anything. For all I knew they were making the assignments right now, everybody else got the pretty suit and the glad hand and I got stuck down here with grey underwear and a rotten cassette. It flipped out of the dispenser as I went through the door and it directed me through the corridors to the shop. I thought when I got there I might find the welcoming committee after all, I could snow them, that was for sure. I could really impress people, if I could only find somebody to impress.

The corridor spilled me out into the shop. It was a little like coming into a jungle. There was a barrel roof hung with racks of capes and coats and fur things, suits and dresses and styles that nobody had worn outside the movies, there were togas and suits of armor and Daniel Boone outfits. I could see people in grey uniforms sorting through racks of clothes or working with sewing guns but they were all in Plexi cubicles and there was no way to get to them. A couple of them were staring: a hunchback working in furs and leathers, a fat woman in evening gowns, a dwarf in charge of World War II uniforms, and as I went by I put my hands to my face because I saw recognition in their faces: some blind bastard had stamped my UGLY and now I was stashed down here so naturally they thought I was one of them. If I was a weaker person I would have cried. Instead I followed the tunnel to the right place and damn if I didn't end in negligees.

Negligees. Me. "Manager," I yelled. "I would like to speak to the manager."

Nothing. No manager, no shop steward, no foreman; nobody came running and nothing came over the speakers. There was nobody but me, so far as I knew nobody cared what I did. How was I going to rise in the business stuck down here where nobody could see? I stuck the cassette in the monitor and it told me which was the equipment and how to use it, which was the hatch where food trays would be delivered, where the toilet was. There was a vacuum tube delivering capsules full of tired negligees, and my job was to take care of the claw holes and the knife damage, the cassette told me which kinds of stains to look for: dirt, powder burns, arterial blood, and I was supposed to decide when it was time to throw out the damaged item and punch out an order for a new one. I would take requisition orders from the terminal on my workbench. I would fill them by putting the required pieces in the capsule provided and shoosh them away through the vacuum tube.

"Listen," I said. "Where is everybody? When do I get to see the manager?"

I shook the cassette but it was finished. It was so quiet I could hardly stand it. I was alone and getting scared. I had been through all that with Norman back in Boston-grad, I had burned my bridges and come all this way and here I was in the middle of a jungle of pink and aqua negligees that I already hated and I was getting scared.

"Listen, gang, whatever you may think, Luce Finley doesn't scare."

Another capsule popped out of the vacuum tube.

"All right, who's in charge?" I tore negligees off the racks until I reached the back wall of the shop, baring the Plexi partition. All I could see on the other side was a thicket of dressing gowns. I took a scissors and went to work on the Plexi. It turned out not to be Plexi after all. I kicked it a couple of times. "Hey, why are these negligees filthy? What happened to the people who were wearing them?"

Whatever the stuff was, I could have kicked it all night without making any noise.

"WHY WON'T ANYBODY ANSWER ME?"

I thought I saw a face peering through the dressing gowns but it could have been one of those fox fur pieces, the ones with the ears, that bit each other's tails. I gave up and went to work on the negligees. Maybe this was a test, and if I did all right I would be promoted. I kept sneaking looks at my reflection; I didn't look so bad, it wasn't fair. The hatch opened and my food tray came. Goofy juice in the coffee, probably, or a burger laced with ha-ha pills, one bite and I would be happy as a dead bug in the sunshine, one sip of coffee and I would never get away.

After I didn't eat the box on my work table bleeped and a new capsule came out of the vacuum tube.

There was a hand in with the negligees. I dropped it into the scrap basket and started sorting through them, staying cool. Then my teeth started scraping and my hands were flying and the next thing I knew I was sitting on the floor crying like a fool girl. Then part of me backed off and took a look at the other part, what they had made of me and I thought: OK, lady, you have got to pull yourself together and get the hell out of here.

I quit crying and got very cool.

When I couldn't find any cracks in the wall anywhere I sat back on my heels and thought. I don't know why the dwarf hadn't tumbled. If you were skinny enough, you could probably make it out via vacuum tube. I made a scarf out of one of the negligees and wrapped my head, face and all. Then I pushed over the work table and trashed the sewing gun so nobody else would ever have to work there and I climbed up on the wreckage and shoved myself into the tube. At first I thought I was going to be stuck forever. I could feel the top of my head stretching, the damn thing took my breath and my brains were going to be next, my head was going to come off in another second if my shoulders didn't come loose. Then they did and the rest of me started moving after which there was nothing but black roaring, blood exploding in my ears.

I came to in a dressing room. It took a long time to get the scarves unwound because I could see and then I couldn't see because it was so bright.

"Armand." It was an old lady's voice. "Who is this, Armand?"

"It is nothing, my darling."

"What the hell do you mean nothing?" I popped out of the clothes basket and got a good look at them. This old lady was holding a robe up to her boobs so I wouldn't see they had been lifted; the skin on her face was tight but her hands were wrinkled, I said, "Who the hell are you?"

"She's one of the Oldies but Goodies, who are you?" There was this guy in a purple uniform holding a Scarlett O'Hara dress for her to step into. He was looking imperious. "I said, who are you?"

"I am Lucia di Lammermoor Finley, all right?"

"Oh Armand, is this part of the adventure?"

He said, "Not that I know of, darling. Now let's slip into this lovely dress."

"Oh Armand, I'm so frightened."

"Don't be frightened, Ashby dear." He was having a hard time getting her to put her arms up so he could get them into the sleeves. I saw him give her a vicious jerk. "We're going to have a lovely time."

"Hey, what are you doing to that old lady?"

He was mad at her arms for not going in right, he was getting mad at me. "What are you doing here anyway?"

"I am fucking escaping, you want to make something of it?"

"What?"

The old lady was saying, "But Armand, this dress makes me look just like a cheap . . . "

85

"Shut up." He was listening to me. "You're what?"

"Going out and up. I'm going out and up."

"Oh Armand, I'm frightened." The old lady got her head up through the ruffles. She looked like a Southern wedding cake.

"I'll protect you." He put her behind him, like they used to in the old days, when women were protected. He was looking at me. "Nobody gets out, the management won't like it."

"Keep your hand off the buzzer or I'll trash you. I'm going out and up, out and up."

I guess he knew I would hit him, maybe there was more to it than that, like, he wished he had the nerve. "OK," he said, "get away while you still can, but you never saw me, right?"

"Right." I shoved him aside and went out in the hall. There were people poking their heads through curtains, some in costumes, some in uniforms. I wanted to stop and ask what they were doing but everybody was looking past me, there was the wardrobe supervisor coming down the corridor at a dead run. He was about to let me have it when I took a curtain pole and ran right at him, I had the rod broadside but as I closed in I swung it around and smashed him on the neck and he hit the floor, whether dead or alive I couldn't tell. All along the corridor people gasped and shrank behind the curtains waiting for what, me to get mine, all hell to break loose. All right, I had made my mark and now I was waiting for them to notice. I sat right there and waited for the guards to come. It didn't take long. A whole platoon came, weapons raised.

"It's OK," I said, and put my hands up. "I'll go quietly. All I ever wanted was a chance."

They marched me out to their scooter and cuffed me to the seat. We went down a tunnel that was intersected by other tunnels; I saw food trucks moving in one direction, garbage in another, trucks full of supplies going past us in the main tunnel. I didn't know whether it looked more like the tunnels at NASA or the sub-basement of a big department store. There were crews carrying props and pieces of scenery; a gang went by carrying what looked like the Statue of Liberty in sections and another gang was going somewhere with a big red-and-gold dragon head. Somebody was coming in the other direction with a smashed Greek column and a bunch were on the floor underneath this old Rolls-Royce, like they used to have, trying to get it working. We went by an enormous chemical disposal unit with chutes running into it, and when I followed them up I saw they were part of some master vacuum disposal system. There was a conveyer belt carrying what looked like corpse cases, and that fed into the disposal unit too. On the walls at every corner were giant TV monitors, all showing parts of the surface operation: happy crowds in the bar at the green glass paramotel, people swarming under the silver arch, with a new flashing sign: LOVE AND DEATH RIDE, a mob scene in what looked like an old Greek temple, pretty boys in leather skirts mixing it up with stones and short swords. I didn't get to see how it came out because we scooted around another corner. I didn't know exactly how this underground complex fit into the larger operation at Happy Habitat but I could see there was a lot of stuff that the public didn't even know about, and I was pretty sure that in terms of the power nexus, this was where it was at. Everything that was busted or used up or didn't fit the surface picture was whooshed off down the waste removers or garbage chutes and taken care of here, and things were sent up from here, all those old bags in the funny costumes, maybe even people like me and bad Rex, but the difference was that we would be on business, we were not your enfeebled Oldies but Goodies, we had work to do. I didn't mind going along in the scooter, I didn't care where they took me because I was getting an inside look, they could not stick me in the back room again, not after what I did, after what I saw. I was going to get in on the ground floor, which is all I ever wanted.

I marched into the supervisor's office as smart as any up-and-comer. All I said was, "I did not burn all my bridges and come all this way just to work in negligees."

I guess he knew all about me, he said, "I admire a girl with your spirit."

"I am not a girl."

"Have it your way. We have a special assignment for you."

"Something with possibilities?"

"Cleanup and removal."

I leaned on the desk. "What does that mean exactly?"

"Even in an operation as smooth as ours, there is the occasional sorehead, or recalcitrant. We have our problems."

I hit my left hand with my right fist. "And we?"

"Your job is to see that there aren't any."

"Let me at it."

The super said, "You'll have to wear this hood."

"Don't start that again."

He ignored me. "You have to work fast and get out before the public notices."

"If nobody sees me, how am I going to get ahead?"

"Look at it this way. If you don't do it our way, you don't do anything. Ever again."

Yeah, it was a threat. "Have it your way."

"Look at it this way, it's a step up."

I took the hood. I was already ahead on points, I could afford to wait my time but when it comes I am going to make my play. "Where do I go?"

"The office is the next door up. They'll costume you and dorm you until the night shift goes on."

I went up the hall to Cleanup and Removals.

It seemed like as good a place as any to begin.

Kaa Naaji

I expected more. I wanted to go live in my new adventure with my friends, but Boone thought I had betrayed him and so it all went sour. There was nothing I could do to set it right because the programmer was lurking behind a tree, waiting to take me back.

"Wait, there is unfinished business."

He said, "That's all for today."

"We are not friends. I ordered friends, that was part of my arrangement."

He tapped a message into his belt. "This is a new phase in the operation, there are a few bugs in it, but if you'll just bear with us."

"Of course," I said bitterly. "It is only illusion, like all the rest. I see no reason to continue here, I . . . "

"It's real enough." He inserted my credit card in his belt and tapped another message. "We have a couple of things to work out, that's all. Tomorrow we can fix you up with something more dramatic."

"More dramatic than saving lives?" I think I wanted him to tell me that I had really killed the water buffalo.

"Kid stuff," he said. "Perhaps you would like to take one."

I was steeped in disappointment and so I gave way to sarcasm. "Perhaps I would like to take several."

Even that was lost on my Virgil, who only said, "That can be arranged."

Imagine me, a pacifist and a vegetarian, driven to such heights of rage that I said, "Beginning with you."

"That is not in the contract." He put the mask on me.

I woke in time for the cocktail hour. I took my fruit juice and joined the others in the magnificent chinchilla pit underneath the sky dome, where we sat comparing notes in the midnight and starlight, not even looking up as fireworks streaked and exploded over our heads. As I told the others I realized it was a better story than I thought, and when I showed them the hairs I had taken from the crest of the water buffalo the others applauded me. Even as they did so I was shaken by terrible doubts. I tried to tell them, I said, "My friends, I do not know what has become of them."

"What's the diff?" said Marva, who is slender and shimmers like a serpent. "It's all in fun." Then she told us of her day in the London of Jack the Ripper, where she watched several poor jades die horribly before herself succumbing to the charms of the ripper. There was still a bloody thumbprint on her temple and I said, "But those poor women . . ."

"They got what they deserved." She wet her finger and put it to the spot on her temple. "That's what put the edge on it."

"But Marva. Are they really dead?"

Simpson cut me off. "You should have seen my boys." There was no stopping him then, as he described the biceps of this one, the triceps of that one, the cries of the one who was brought to him, for he had spent his first day in the birth of ancient Greece.

I was too distracted to listen. I asked, "Where do they all come from, your boys?"

He laughed and twirled his fingers. "Who cares?"

Sheik Ahmed was rumbling next to me, fierce and restless in his white robes. He set aside his staff with the oil derrick picked out in diamonds at the tip and he said, "There are indeed a few questions remaining, for this place is either everything the advertisements promised or else it is not." Then he told us how he leaped off the riverboat to grapple with the killer alligator in the muddy riverbed in the Deep South Setting, and he described the circumstances under which he had triumphed to rescue the Memphis belle; once he had rescued and ravished her with gusto they did not walk away into the light of burning Atlanta as he had expected, but instead she was ripped from his arms, crying out for love. He turned a face like a forest fire. "What kind of place is this if it gives and then takes away?"

"One boy is as good as another," Simpson said. "What difference does it make?"

"No," said Marva. "There is only one Ripper, and I . . . "

I pursued my own thoughts. "If these others I rescued were guests, as I thought, then they would be here too."

Ahmed said, "Guests take what they want, while those poor others . . . " He shrugged.

I was thinking back: Had I betrayed Castle and the others? Were they something less than guests, were they something other? "Then those we meet in the adventures are . . . "

Neither he nor I wanted to say it and so we fell silent there in the chinchilla pit, brooding and looking at the fiery blooms that spread in the night sky above the dome. Simpson and Marva had fallen into their own reveries, honing their desires, while Ahmed and I lapsed into more complicated studies, perhaps trying to penetrate the mystery that surrounded the fulfillment of our desires. Granted, they delivered what we ordered, but at what cost? If what we suspected was true, then what should Ahmed and I do next? Were there maidens to be rescued, captives to be set free? My blood quickened at the idea. As we pondered a waiter came and refilled our glasses, this time with purple champagne for the others, sparkling purple juice for me, and as we drank, our senses dulled and everything seemed possible. Perhaps this day was only the beginning and our real adventures were yet to come. We were dreaming, looking up at the multicolored stains in the night sky, when the attendant came.

"All set now?"

We turned blurred faces to him. "Yes," I said, or think I did.

Next to me, Ahmed was rumbling. "My gold and white woman," he said. "Memphis. My beautiful Ashby."

The attendant only said, "All things pass."

Dazed, Ahmed tried to say, "No. I want . . . "

"There will be better tomorrow," the attendant said, "but now . . . "

"I have questions."

"No time for questions now," the attendant said, and brought me to my feet. "You're late for the parade. The outdoor gala is starting, there are seats available in the Golden Circle in the plaza."

"No thanks," Marva said. "I want to punch out a change in plans. Can you send me a program counsellor?"

"But you'll miss the parade." The attendant looked truly disappointed. "You're scheduled for the avalanche at the Zugspitz tomorrow. Love in the glacier? The one-legged ski instructor?"

Marva only shook her head. "I want to go back to Jack."

"I'm afraid that can't be arranged."

She took out her platinum credit card and scored the back of his hand. "That will teach you to be fresh."

"Yes Ma'am." He flushed but did not flinch; he was blond, square-jawed, wholesome; at M.I.T. they called his kind a jock. He tapped the punch-buttons on his belt. "What shall I tell the programmer?"

"Tell him I want London back, let's kill more whores."

"It's going to cost."

"I'll pay."

"Wait." What was I trying to say?

"I wish," Simpson said, and one could almost see the joyous Greek youths leaping behind his eyes, passing as if on a conveyer belt.

The attendant said, "We'll look into it, Mr. Simpson. As for you two, this way to the parade."

Ahmed was whirling in his white robes, I was full of unspoken questions, but two other attendants came from nowhere and hurried us out of the chinchilla pit and toward the plaza.

I said, "Ahmed, perhaps we should try and find out."

He put a hand on my arm and silenced me. "My friend, we must bide our time."

As we crossed the lobby we went by the Carnival Lounge; there was a neon placard flashing and I did not know whether to be reassured or troubled by what I read. The sign flashed on and off, off and on:

TONIGHT'S SPECIAL FEATURE:
MINGLE WITH THE FENTON FAMILY
IN THE FABULOUS CARNIVAL LOUNGE

I thought I saw a familiar form in the center of the band of admiring guests and I may have seen the Fenton children sitting on the bar, but if that was Castle he looked all right, he was dressed in a clean suit and lifting a glass of purple champagne, so perhaps he was also a guest here, as I had originally thought, and all my worries were for nothing. I wanted to go in to ask, to be positive, but the attendant was hurrying me along and there was no turning.

He put Ahmed and me into lounge chairs in a bank of chairs overlooking the plaza, and I sank in, wavering between uncertainties and feeling drunk in spite of the fact that I had been assured I would not be served spirits. Next to me Ahmed seethed in his velvet seat, thinking of Ashby, his lost Southern belle, and the handsome parade passing in front of us might just as well have been so many dusty desert camels for all he saw. I knew that even as a paying guest he had little recourse because it had been set out in the regulations that we could take our pleasure in the settings, we might clip the ears of animals we killed or pluck pretty flowers, but we could not bring back anybody we met there because this would violate the premise, whether because the others were also paying guests with rights and desires or something else I could not be clear. So it was that I watched the parade with diminished pleasure because Ahmed was suffering beside me and I could not be sure that was Castle back there, in the Carnival Lounge, and if so how he had gotten there, and if not, what had become of him.

Even so the parade was beautiful, the hawkers came among us with sweetmeats and balloons, fireworks bled across the sky in ferocious colors and the attendants moved among us, trying to ensure our happiness. To satisfy them and perhaps deceive ourselves we clapped and laughed and gobbled like children because there were no real children there to remind us that we were older. There were dancing girls and tigers and elephants and acrobats costumed as date palms and Balinese goddesses and gigantic chapathis, all the glories of Luxor and Agra and Angkor Vat recreated and passing in front of us; there were women of prodigious beauty and startling bits of Americana such as the eighteen-foot Hershey bar and the monstrous submarine sandwich and after that came the previews of things to come, elaborate floats tricked out to resemble the many lands of adventure offered here at Happy Habitat.

So it was that I lost Ahmed, for in the Deep South Setting there were several young ladies on the float and among them Ahmed saw or thought he saw the belle for whom he had been grieving. Before I could stop him he leaped to his feet, shouting: "There she is."

Attendants were heading our way and I said, "Ahmed, wait."

"By Allah, I must have her." He tore out of my grasp and vaulted the row in front of us. "Ashby, my magnolia."

"Ahmed, you mustn't."

He eluded the attendants, leaping over astounded patrons in their seats and crying out, "I shall rescue you."

From the float came a cry, "Oh, Ahmed," but I alone heard. By that time Ahmed was in no position to hear for an extraordinary thing had happened.

It happened and my life changed.

There was a new surge of music, an infusion of perfume, an effusion of color in the sky, and as the rest of the crowd looked upward a hatchway opened in the cobbled surface of the plaza and a small squad of attendants came springing out, silent and sinister in their black suits and hoods. They were swift as daggers, and before his beloved Ashby could cry out or Ahmed could hear her, they had seized him and removed him, they just covered his head and took him down the hatch. They closed it after them so quickly that I had to stare hard to convince myself that it had even happened. Ah, but they left one behind, or one stayed behind, and I could not shake the idea that this one had stayed behind because of me. I had the idea that the black-hooded face was turned toward me, the eyes were on me, and in the next second the figure had ripped off its hood, shouting out over the music and shaking her fists at the sky. With her head bared her hair flew, it was brilliant and flaming in the firelight, her face was contorted and knotting with rage and when she turned this rage from the sky to the oblivious crowd it grew even greater because they did not notice her at all but instead strained upward, for sparks. Except for me, Kaa Naa Mahadevan, overturned in that extraordinary second, for she looked back in my direction and our eyes locked.

Then she cried out, "Damn your eyes."

And I cried, "My darling."

"You and all your kind, damn you, look at me."

Did she see me? "I cannot stop looking."

Did she hear me? Did I hear her correctly? " . . . out," she was crying.

I shouted, "Who are you?"

I still do not know whether she was raging at the inattentive crowd or whether she was speaking directly to me, but it seemed like an answer: "Luce Finley, and you'd better look out for me."

I was ready to leap the last row of seats by that time and

join her in the plaza, but I felt hands on my arms, pulling me back to my seat. As I strained against them the hatch in the plaza opened, a hand closed on the woman's ankle and she was gone, might never have been there, except that her image was burned beyond my retinas, into my cortex, seared in my soul. The crowd never saw. I would never forget. I let them draw me back to my seat and press a perfumed handkerchief to my nose but I did so with a sense of biding my time, for I was beginning to plan. I knew now that there were parts of this place that guests would never dream of, and that my plans would run counter to the desires of the management, but I also knew that none of my real desires could be answered by made-up adventures in the settings they had devised, for all of that was artificial. I had the idea that true satisfaction would come with upsetting all their arrangements, moving outside their entertainment scheme, and so I would pretend to go along for as long as I had to but when the time came I would go deeper. I was going to uncover all the secrets of Happy Habitat, and at the same time fulfill my heart's desire.

The hope was new and even as I formed it I had to wonder: was this, too, part of their plan?

I remembered her face and thought: No.

I must find her.

Yes, it happened in that instant, as her hair flew and she raged at the fiery pinwheels exploding in the sky.

Indeed, I was in love.

Boone Castle

Rescued, just like that. It was spooky. We were safe and comfortable before we had a chance to ask questions: how they knew where to find us, where the Indian had come from, how we had fetched up so neatly here at Happy

Habitat. They brought us to the suite and installed us without even waiting for us to sob out our stories.

Wait.

The last one out the door said something about cocktails after dinner, a midnight press conference. Fred asked if it would be aired worldwide and they said that depended, which he chose not to hear. He was already telling me to get working on his speech.

Wait a minute.

He told them he was going to need new holocording equipment so we could get on with the Fred Fenton story, but the last one was already out the door. He said they could bill him but I don't think they heard. When he saw that the door was closed he held onto his temper, and even though I was standing there doing nothing he said, "Don't be upset, Castle, this is nothing that can't be fixed."

"What?" Wait.

"We'll have equipment first thing in the morning. Right now I want you to write the press conference. Make it good."

Hey, wait. "Don't you think . . . "

"Castle, enjoy the ice cream while it's on your plate."

I couldn't shut off the warning tickle, but the others were already diving into the buffet as if this kind of thing happened every day. Here we were safe in Happy Habitat, right where we had been heading before the crash. There were the intertwined double Hs on the towels and inlaid in gold in the floor, there was the double H in the moulding above the door, we had been stashed at the top of the great green glass paramotel that every kid knew from the holos, we could see the silver arch from here. While he ate Fred struck poses in front of the inner, mirror wall, working out gestures to use for the world networks and satellite relay plus syndicates. Shouldn't he be, maybe, a little worried? Shouldn't he be in touch with his companies?

For one thing, the phone was a house phone only, and for another, the HH people had promised to take care of details, but wasn't this all a little strange?

I said, "Don't you think this is a little strange?"

"What a story," Fred said. "All that doubt and hardship, and we ended up just where we wanted to go in the first place."

I said, "Maybe you should be in touch with the office."

"They can see me on the holos," Fred said. "Complacent bastards, this will set them on their ears."

"Are you sure?"

He turned on me and snarled. "Castle, this is supposed to be a vacation. Now shut up and go work on the script."

"I would like to, Fred, but I don't know what it's about."

I thought he was going to hit me. "Then make something up."

I could see Dottie was no help. She took all this as her natural right, she was busy passing food and if she thought twice about any of it, she didn't let it bother her. She was at her usual stand, handing out food and running the household, giving an extra flick of the ass because I was there and she was always better with an audience. When she thought I wasn't looking she turned to the mirror wall and patted her hair. The kids were alternately stuffing themselves and running up and down the corridors. Everybody but me was eating heavily without a thought for who had left the food or what might be in it. I don't know why it gave me the creeps but it did and I decided not to eat right then because somebody out there wanted me to. I popped a few peanuts to ward off starvation and left the rest for the Fenton family.

By that time Dottie and the kids had discovered the wardrobes hung in each closet, Lurex leisure suits and silver boots, snappy leather numbers and iridescent kaftans, too much stuff, from a lot of movies I had never even heard of. It was not comforting to see that everything fit perfectly. I said, "Wait a minute, Fred," but he was bright as cock robin in the red velvet smoking jacket with the monogram, and when I tried to ask didn't he think it was strange, those being his initials on such short notice, he said, "Don't be hysterical, Castle, they've had our reservations on file since September."

So there we were, stashed at the top of Happy Habitat. We had been rescued from the jungle in the nick of time, we were safe at last from getting lost or eaten and for the first time since we crashed we knew exactly where we were. I didn't like it. Partly it was the way we got here. The nice folks had brought us out of the wilderness by boat, and after the pickup, the baby Matto Grosso or wherever it was we had been stranded turned too quickly into a neat-looking canal with mosaic sides and grass growing down the banks. We were going too fast for me to see much but we passed from jungle vegetation to topiary shrubs with nothing in between, one minute we were in darkest Oz and the next it was hello Emerald City, we were streaming along past playgrounds and plazas and buildings that would make Brasilia look like a piece of junk. The transition was too quick.

"Fred, the transition was too quick."

"Have you written my thank-you?"

"I don't see how you can . . . "

"Forget it, Castle, I'll play this one by ear." He gave me a shove. "Get dressed. The least you can do is look presentable."

I spent a long time in the shower, letting the water run on my head and drawing in the steam that collected on the mirror wall. When I came out I still didn't have any answers. I could hear our escorts talking in the next room so I dressed quickly and went out.

They had sent a pair: a guy and a girl in white body suits. She was beautifully built and I thought hey maybe, but her manner went with the uniform: featureless. She was looking magazine pretty, like all the other help.

There was something so All-American about all of them that you had to admire it but you wouldn't want to touch it, which is what I suppose the management had in mind. There was no hanky-panky in Happy Habitat, at least not according to the ads. You paid a lot to get it perfect, pretty, clean. I tried to get closer to the girl anyway, but I might as well have been a piece of furniture. The guy was giving Fred's jacket a once-over with a magnetic whisk while she did the kids' hair and ran a beeper over Dottie's curls, smoothing the style. When they were satisfied with our looks they took us along the inner balcony to the grand escalator, it cuts through the paramotel in a single showy sweep, and when we stepped on it moved us down slowly, like products on display. I wouldn't have minded if there hadn't been several dozen people in high drag at the bottom, sipping cocktails and watching us descend. Just before we reached the main floor I thought I saw neon flashing: NIGHT'S SPECIAL FEATURE, but there were people clumped in front of it, tossing off drinks and laughing; as I squinted, trying to catch the rest, a new group came in a flurry of jewels and draperies so I never did see.

I don't know, I might have gotten to like the place if the management had stayed out of the act. The cocktail lounge was crowded with the rich and the chic and the sleek, all of them wearing beautiful tans, with minimal clothes that had cost a fortune. There were a handful of Japanese and even more Arabs, who stayed covered in their white burnooses, Europeans and Americans so rich they could afford to keep on looking like high school kids no matter what their age; there were people from every corner of the world but they were more alike than different, uniformly taut and slim and beautiful, and the unifying ingredient was money.

Four fabulous women converged on me and cut me off from the Fentons, working on me with silky fingers and velvety voices; they said I had been wonderful in the jungle and at the time I didn't even wonder how they knew because at the time I was feeling warm, appreciated, bemused because all the time my admirers were humming and chattering ("safe at last," "tell us all about it," and "oh you poor baby"), their eyes flickered over my chinline and down my throat toward the area south of the snap on my coverall and as they touched my cheek their tongues curled and they were grinning as if they knew something I didn't know.

They were saying things like, "Adorable," "less rough diamond than I thought," "imagine, lost in all that jungle," and, "I'd like to get lost in *his* jungle," when the one with the glitter on her eyelids and the glitter heart low on her left breast separated herself from the others and said, "You were terrific in the pigmy village," so that I turned, fast, and said, "How did you know that?"

Which is when the management made itself known. The girl in the white body suit had been assigned to me. The next thing I knew she was between glitter heart and me, and if she was expressionless before there was no mistaking her expression now, it meant: ah ah, look but don't touch. She said, "Why Mr. Castle, you don't have a drink. Mr. Castle has come a long way today, and if you'll just excuse us for a minute, I think he needs a drink."

Glitter heart said, "Why don't you get it for him, hon?"

"As you know, all our drinks are special."

"I don't want a . . . "

"Rags won't know what to fix for Mr. Castle until he puts his hand on the tailortron."

Glitter heart tried to follow us. "I just love bodily chemistry."

My girl in the white body suit just said, "Back soon," and she had us halfway across the room before anybody could follow. All along the way there were people turning and smiling, reaching out as if to touch me but she just smiled like a crocodile and kept them off with her eyes.

I said, "You're pretty smooth."

"Put your hand there, on the handplate."

I did, it glowed, and the bartender handed me a specially tailored drink. I pretended to taste it.

"Wonderful. Thanks very much, uh. What shall I call you?"

"You can call me 1047A."

Once she was locked in place she never left my side. A new group formed around me, a couple of sheiks, several women with diamond eyes, an American who obviously preferred boys; I thought maybe we would flutter eyelashes in code and I would let him lure me into some dark corner where I could extort the truth from him right before I broke his heart, or else I could waltz away with glitter heart who had rejoined us, lifting her head and flicking her tongue, but I had the idea that any information I got from glitter heart I would pay for in spades, clubs, diamonds, she would feed on me until there was nothing left. I was more or less trying to decide between them: which might know more, which I could afford, when I understood that I wasn't going to get a chance with any of them because 1047A was too good at her job.

She put herself between me and all comers, expert as a casino dealer, answering this question, deflecting that caress, making sure that everybody got a chance to talk to me and nobody got too close. Her opposite number had the Fentons in a little phalanx in a corner, with the kids perched on the edge of a table while Dottie and Fred stood on either side, beaming and accepting congratulations as if we had just conquered Everest with our bare hands or rounded Cape Horn in a canoe. The whole scene was so chi-chi and civilized that I wanted to jump on a table and start swinging, yelling, *Hey wait a minute everybody, wait a minute, wait.*

"You're not drinking your drink."

"Ooops. I spilled it."

"I'll get you another. Put your hand on the tailortron."

She gripped my wrist and when I didn't drink the fresh

drink she said, "What's the matter with you anyway?"

Too good at her job. "Maybe I'm too far from home. Right, 1047A, right?"

"What does it matter? Relax, go with the flow."

"I will, babe, just as soon as somebody tells me where it's flowing. I don't suppose you would . . . "

"Don't hold your breath." She smiled through her teeth at an inquisitive African, who was gorgeous in feathers and sharks' teeth. "Mr. Castle has been through a terrible ordeal, Chief, you'll have to forgive us now because he's a little tired."

"I'm not tired."

"It's going to be a lot better if you just go with the flow."

"Wait a minute." Wait.

"What did you say you did at home?"

"I'm a holomaker." She was looking through me so I added, *"Manqué."*

"You haven't made it."

"Not exactly."

"And you have a woman friend?"

"Some. Nobody special."

"But you still want to go home."

"Right."

"What's the point?"

"Why can't I split if I want to?" I caught a flicker in her eye and I decided to press. "Look, there's something you aren't telling me."

"You are at Happy Habitat, isn't that enough?"

"No dammit, it isn't."

She closed her fingers on my arm. "I think you'd better be careful what you say here."

"Why in hell should I?"

She lifted her other hand without opening it. "You'd just better."

I thought I might as well test the boundaries. "What if I start yelling right here and now?"

All she said was, "Try it," and then she opened her

hand so I would see the hypodermic bug. One move and she would slap it on my rump.

"OK," I said, "OK."

She knew she had me so she relaxed and began fielding questions from one of the sheiks. I pretended to drink my drink and got busy with the bowls of shrimp and wheels of brie and assorted cocktail nibblies, and when she wasn't looking I stashed some crackers and a wedge of cheese in my coverall because I figured this food was probably safe. I was throwing down peanuts and thinking what the hell, what if I just got drunk on this tailortron special and went back to the apartment and finished off that buffet, why shouldn't I be stoned and happy like everybody else? What difference would it make? It made a difference. I looked at the Fentons, they were laughing and glowing with no concept of what was happening, if they even guessed they didn't care. I couldn't do that. I could not let go until I knew more, and maybe not even then.

Besides, I didn't want to lose touch with my head.

"Drink your drink."

I turned fast, so it sloshed all over. "Oh, sorry. Oh look, 1047A, I got you all wet."

Which is how I happened to miss the press conference, when Fred and Dottie told all about the wreck of the cutter and their bravery in the jungle and the flight from the pigmys and the battle with the water buffalo. Then the interviewer asked them how it felt and Fred did a complete number, after which the bar picture faded and we had a photomontage with voiceover and film clips about Fred Fenton up until his life had been transformed by the wreck, they intercut that with reaction shots of Dottie and Fred, who were looking flattered and happy with the show, while I whirled in front of the wall-sized picture in the empty apartment, yelling, "Where did they get those film clips, how did they get those photographs." I was lunging at the screen with a chair, still in touch with my head but just barely, I may have heard the hissing sound but I didn't heed it because I was about to swing the chair and smash the picture. "How in hell did they get all that stuff on you?"

I guess it was gas; the next thing I remember was waking up on the floor with the chair on its side next to me, both of us sprawled where we had fallen, me listening to the Fentons coming in. I was trying to be steely and controlled. I wanted to rally them for an escape but none of the words would come out in the right order; before I could get any of it out Dottie had put a hand on my forehead: *poor Boone* and she was shuffling the kids off to bed while Fred said, "It's OK, kids, Uncle Boone just had a few too many."

"I'm not drunk, you bastard, they gassed me."

He was standing over me. Don't be ridiculous."

"Fred, don't you think all this is a little strange?"

"I saw you down in the bar. Getting drunk." He was sauntering, looking up into the corners of the ceiling: for monitors? I wanted to think he was checking the place out, maybe he was even coming to his senses, but he had his hands behind his back and he was whistling.

"I said, don't you think this is a little strange?"

When he turned to me then he was not the same Fred I had seen on the picture wall, giving the grand press conference; he looked alert, more troubled than I would have given him credit for, and he was shaking his head.

"Fred?"

He was writing on the back of a matchbook:
KEEP IT
FOR OUR OWN SHOW.
WE ARE BEING RECORDED.

"Well I'll be damned."

All he said was: "Pull yourself together. Think of the kids."

I muttered, through my teeth (" *What are you going to do about it?"*)

105

(*"Wait till tomorrow, demand an explanation."*)

I said, "Sure, Fred. (*You knew all the time?*)"

(*"Suspected.*) You OK, Castle?" Was this the same Fred?

"OK. (*You knew all the time and you didn't tell me?*)"

(*"I didn't want you to blow my cover.*) Going to bed, Castle. (*I think this may be a very good deal.*) You'd better turn in too." He gave me a dark look that didn't make any sense to me and went into his room.

I felt around the walls for a switch or rheostat that would douse the living room lights but I couldn't find it. I finally gave up. When I headed down the hall the lights went down behind me. I turned and went back in. On. I ducked out and back in, just to test it. Out. On. I tried to sneak up on it but it was too fast for me. I gave up and went to my room. Once I had stripped and brushed my teeth the bedroom lights began to dim; by the time I got in bed they were low, but no matter what I did they would not go all the way out. I thought I heard a hissing sound and I put my head under the covers and breathed what air had collected there before I uncovered it again. I lay for a long time and when I thought whoever was watching would assume I was asleep and lay off I slid out from under the covers and got up. As soon as my feet hit the floor the lights came up. I did the staggering-to-the-bathroom-in-your-sleep impression as convincingly as I could and went back to bed, covering my head while they piped in the anaesthetic gas. After that I lay for a long time and then lifted my head, waiting for my eyes to get used to the dark. Then I stood up, on the bed this time, so the trip mechanism wouldn't bring up the lights. I thought I had a better chance in the dark. I felt along the head of the bed without knowing what I was looking for, and then I walked the perimeter of the mattress, listening hard, because I heard something, I could not be sure what. Then my eyes picked out a moving shape and I jumped back and almost fell off the bed because I could see another figure circling.

Oh. Right. The mirror wall.

I waved at the figure. It waved back.

I lifted my right foot. It did the same.

It was only my reflection.

It's only your reflection, Boone, OK?

I didn't know why, but it was not OK. My heart was still rattling and I couldn't stop staring at the mirrored figure. There was something about it. No. There was something behind it. I thought I could see through it, and if I could I saw something moving behind the mirror, and if there was something moving behind the mirror, the whole thing, what bothered me, snapped into place.

"You damn bastards."

I jumped off the bed and plastered myself to the mirrored wall, pressing my face so close my nose was mashed flat. As soon as I hit the floor the room lights had gone on but it didn't matter. That was one-way glass, not a mirror, and when I cupped my hands around my eyes to shut out the light I could see just fine.

I could see right through it.

The first thing I saw was somebody sitting, staring at me. He was staring hard, moving slowly from left to right, rather, being moved along in a little seat like somebody in a fun ride at the fair. It was a sheik with a drink in one hand and a program in the other, when he smiled I could swear I recognized him from the bar. When I looked again I saw he was only one of a whole row of people, all clamped into little moving seats and riding by like paying guests at the fucking Futurama, and when I banged on the wall with my fists and started raging a couple even smiled and waved. I picked up a lamp and started bashing at the glass but when I stopped and pressed my face close I could see they were applauding: just what they wanted, apparently, so I stopped. I tried standing without doing anything, which worked better. A couple of the clients yelled, I could see their mouths stretching even though I couldn't hear anything, and glitter heart went by shaking her fist. If I shielded my eyes and looked down the wall, to my right, I could see the wall of Dottie and Fred's room coming out at a slight angle, Dottie and Fred behind it, in the bed, the chairs curving to take the spectators along past it and out of the exhibit, and if I looked far enough to my left I could almost make out, did make out, could see, oh my God. Damn. There was a sign, dayglo and bordered in flashing lights:

TONIGHT ONLY
BOONE CASTLE
DISCOVERS HIS PLIGHT

The least I could do was warn the others.

I had forgotten about the anaesthetic gas.

Outtakes

"I'm sorry to get you all together so early in the morning but this is an important week for us, and if we are going to keep things running smoothly we are going to have to keep abreast of developments and plan for contingencies. I know some of you are still a little sleepy so I have provided coffee and poppers at every place. As you know, Monday marked the opening of the third and next-to-last phase of the master plan for Happy Habitat, the introduction of the live exhibits, pinpoint hiring for ticklish positions and an intensified effort to assemble talent for the core group. I have asked you all to prepare interim reports for evaluation because this particular phase of the operation is crucial. We'll hear from Cynnie first, on accommodations, then Dante on hiring; Twink will bring us up to date on the Oldies but Goodies, Gayle will give us crowd control and then we'll have a report on the live exhibits, with special emphasis on audience response. You have a question, Corky?"

"What about Phase Four?"

"You'll hear about that when the time comes."

"We can't keep working in the dark, Dearest."

"I'm afraid you have no choice. Now, Cynnie, will you begin?"

"The new accommodations units are in operation, with

potential core-groupers located in units 480, 500 and 501 on the top floor of the paramotel. You can look in on them via monitor if you'd like. The security and removal elements have been checked out in case there are refusals."

"And those are operative?"

"They're the same kind we have in use on the Fenton Family exhibit, they have been stress-tested and when the time comes they can be activated from the control room."

"The guests are happy?"

"They see no difference between their accommodations and the others. They like the complimentary grass and booze and flowers, the cleanup crew reports some heavy tipping, so I would say on the whole the response is positive."

"Excellent. Now, since Cynnie has brought up the matter of the core group, we'll move on to Cort."

"Wait a minute, Dearest, there are a couple of personnel matters that need immediate attention, and I . . . "

"Dante, you will wait your turn. Cort?"

"Yes. The two we have earmarked for the core group are a hydroponics expert from England, no immediate family and no real desire to return to the British Isles . . . "

"I thought you had spotted three."

"The hydroponics man, the Indian biochemist and the computers person. To tell the truth we've had to phase out the computers person, he's proved too heavily sybaritic and erratic to be useful in the long-term operation so we're not making the offer. We're concentrating on the other two."

"What does the Indian have to offer?"

"Energy. He found a new source and struck it rich. The new source is . . . the new source is . . . "

"Why are you laughing?"

"I'm sorry. His new source of power is cattle dung."

"What earthly use . . . "

"Well, to begin with, I think we can turn his talents to

112

our own needs, but I would have to confess that even if he never goes near the lab he's going to be useful."

"Explain."

"He's the richest man in the world. He keeps it in gold."

"Ah. Yes. Well, that makes sense. How do you plan to proceed?"

"Cynnie and I have checked out the rooms, and everything is in readiness. Of course if those two do not accept our offer, we will activate Plan B."

"Excellent."

"*Now, if you don't mind . . .* "

"All right, Dante, it's your turn."

"The recruiting operation is going along smoothly enough, but in taking this new class of employees we have opened the door to a few problems that I don't think we can overlook."

"You're going to have to amplify."

"Yes. The new advertisements have been more than successful, we are swamped with applicants, all prepared to do anything we ask, we even have some volunteers for the true-life adventures in case the Oldies but Goodies get used up too fast, but there is a new factor that develops when you begin to hire people in this category, something you don't have to deal with when you are using recent college graduates from the middle class. Now I tried to point this out before we ever entered this phase and you all chose to ignore me, but sooner or later we are going to have to deal with it and I think you had better confront it now."

"Dante, will you get to the point?"

"All right. When you hire the criminal element you get discipline problems. We've only seen the tip of the iceberg so far, but I am afraid . . . "

"You're going to have to spell it out."

"We've only had one incident so far, a woman criminal who damaged two of our regular people because she didn't like her assignment. We are maximizing her violent tendencies in a new assignment and so far so good, but I do think that when you begin recruiting people who will do anything you create a volatile situation in which . . . "

"If you can't manage your own department, Dante, I'll assign somebody who can. Twink is next."

"Don't say I didn't warn you."

"I don't want to hear any more. Now, Twink."

"As you know, we have incorporated our Oldies but Goodies in the real-life adventures for some time, they are as anxious for excitement as any of the other paying guests, and we have always managed to cover neatly for your occasional heart attack or accidental death. We have experienced very little difficulty sliding into the new life-or-death option offered our paying guests, but there is some question as to when our senior citizens begin to note the increased rate of disappearance. I don't know what will happen when they put two and two together, but it's something we are going to have to keep in mind. Enrollments and revenues are stable, at the moment we are managing to keep ahead of the demand factor and as long as Scenario keeps its requirements within reason I think we are going to manage very nicely."

"That's Corky's department, along with continuity."

"For your information, I'm doing the best I can. But that still doesn't . . . "

"Thank you, Corky. Now Gayle on crowd control, after which we will hear from James. Gayle?"

"The response to the new developments has been very good. This is going to double our revenues, most of our paying guests have been adopting the luxury options wherever possible, so long as the supply holds out I think we can cash in on this new wrinkle in a big way. Most of our clients are willing to pay through the nose for the life-or-death option and some are requesting the million-dollar holofilm to take home as a souvenir. At the moment we have only one technician, but I think we are going to have to think about expanding the filming operation. There is, however, a certain fly in the ointment, a potential for failure that we are going to have to recognize."

"You could have had the good grace to tell me first."

"Sorry, James, I thought the group should know. It's about the Sheik Ahmed. Jimmy, if you'd rather that I did this privately . . . "

"It's too late now."

"All right, I'm choosing him as an example of, now I know I'm overflowing into your territory, James, but it illustrates a possible weak point in the operation, one we're going to have to face. Now I don't know whether we can meet it simply, by permitting more total involvement on the part of the paying guests while they are in the environments, or by removing them by one degree, on the principle of the less you see the less likely you are to be disappointed, but this is not the last time we are going to see the problem and I think we had better decide. I personally would opt for the live exhibits at one remove, like the Fenton Family arrangement, in which the paying guests can look but not touch, because as long as you let them mingle you are going to have the kind of problems I have described, yes I mean the real-life adventures, we are heading for trouble."

"Words of one syllable, Gayle."

"The sheik wanted to bring back his Memphis belle. When we wouldn't let him he cracked."

"Where is he now?"

"Infirmary. We're sending him back to his room shot full of happy gas, with one or two things in his head rearranged. No matter what else happens, he'll think he had a wonderful time. My point is, this is troublesome and costly, and we can't keep doing it."

"Hey Gayle, what if we let him have her?"

"Corky, you know as well as I do there is too much margin for error. The facelift scars alone would give it away, and if word got out . . . "

"I say give the public what it wants. This is James's fault, for not thinking through the environments."

"Thanks, Cork. I trust you understand that I am working with extremely volatile ingredients here, I cannot possibly . . . "

"Enough recriminations. Let's see if we can handle this by indirection. Just give us the facts, James, without editorial comment if you please, and we'll move from that into a rethinking of story lines."

* * *

"My dear Simpson, what's the matter?"

"Oh. It's you. Menahmumum."

"Mahadevan."

"Manumnum. I didn't mean for you to catch me this way."

"Tears are no disgrace, Simpson. Tell me, what has brought you to this sorry state?"

"Well, Manumnum, I went back to Marathon."

"Ah, good."

"No. Bad."

"But why?"

"All those beautiful boys I told you about?"

"Yes, my friend."

"Ah, I thought I could spend the rest of my life chasing them and then I caught one, and now . . . "

"I thought this was what you wanted."

"Not what I wanted. Not it at all."

"Ah it is the old story, anticipation vs. realization."

"Not on your life. It was an Oldie but Goodie."

"No!"

* * *

"You ought to see the Fenton Family, they're a riot."

"I must have missed them, I went to the Cuban cockfight after the parade."

"You can ride through now and watch them getting the news. I mean to tell you, they're a scream."

* * *

"Mari."

"Yes, husband."

"I wonder if this may not be too much for you. Too stark, what is happening to these poor people on the life-raft."

"No, I am interested, I like them, I wish to stay and perhaps, husband, we can effect a rescue."

"I do not know if that is one of the available options."

"This is so exciting, watching the survivors struggle for survival."

"Yes, Mari, but you must promise me one thing."

"Anything, husband."

"If their story becomes too ugly or violent, you must promise me you will let us move on."

* * *

"Now mind you, I *liked* the prehistoric setting. Men bashing women, for a change, dragging them off by the hair, but I wouldn't want to spend much time there."

"I noticed you're back early. You barely stayed through the prehistoric dawn."

"They were having such a good time, dragging those women off. I was tempted, but . . . "

"You were afraid it was conduct unbecoming an executive."

"Not exactly. I was afraid the caveman was going to bash me to get his woman back."

117

"I thought you came for violence."
"I don't intend to be on the receiving end."

* * *

"Oh, Fred, what a wonderful opportunity."
"The attendant just finished explaining, Dottie. I could hardly wait to wake you up."
"We're really going out over all the airways?"
"We're going into every home in the civilized world—on a slight delay, of course, so Control can edit out anything that's not becoming. Dottie, we're going to show them how an American family lives."
"Oh, Fred. Fred, do you think we're interesting enough?"
"A man of my caliber? A wonderful sensitive woman like you, with two lively kids who have their ups and downs? We have everything to offer."
"I, ah, wonder, do you think we ought to have a fight or something?"
"Not just yet, honey. Let's just let them get to know us as characters first, you know, the day-to-dayness, we can get into the heavy stuff later on, as it comes up."
"What shall I do?"
"If I were you I'd comb my hair for one thing, and then, I know, I'll get the boys up and you can make breakfast. We can probably do a thing on, ah, breaking the news to them, how well they take it, you know. Crêpes are showy, why don't you make crêpes?"
"Oh Fred, I'm so nervous."
"Just be natural. Make it good because all our friends at home are going to be watching, to say nothing of my associates, and what I want them to see is, well . . . "
"Fred Fenton, man of history."
"Yes, dammit, if you want to call it that."
"And we're supposed to be honest."

"Absolutely honest."

"Well, all right. To be frank, Fred, I didn't know about this whole vacation when you first sprang it, I didn't think I wanted to go anywhere with you at all, not even Happy Habitat. As a matter of fact . . . What's the matter?"

"Not so fast."

"I thought you wanted me to be honest."

"I do, honey, but the world is watching. Let's just take our time."

"If you say so. The world, imagine, what an honor."

"I think they have a lot to learn from us."

"Oh, Fred, it's kind of embarrassing."

"Don't give it another thought. We can give them insight, emotion, if any of them learn a little about their own lives by watching us, why then we will have made a significant contribution, it's going to be worth any petty limitations . . . "

"Limitations?"

"Well, we have to stay within camera range, which means we're, ah, more or less stuck here for the time being, but it's going to be worth it, Dottie, we're going to go down in the history books."

"I don't know, Fred."

"There are going to be talk show interviews, your face will be on the covers of all the major magazines . . . "

"I'll have to get my hair done."

"And at the end they're going to give us our own prints of every foot they shoot, and it will be our work this time, I won't have to depend on that stupid Castle."

"It sounds wonderful."

"What's more, our expenses are paid for as long as we stay here, even if it's six months."

"Hello, everybody, I am Dorothy Fenton, née Jaggers, and I . . . "

"Keep it natural."

"Six *months?*"

"As long as it takes. Think of the contribution we are making, the fame, we're going to be celebrities."

"I don't know if Boone is going to like this."

"Fuck Boone."

* * *

" . . . and Operating Theater, which turns out to be the most popular, especially with our older paying guests. We simply remove the damaged Oldies but Goodies from the real-life settings and recycle them wherever possible. We saw to it that last night's patient was only partially anaesthetized and then let one of our oil barons administer the *coup de grace*, putting the patient under for the duration, after which our surgeons repaired the battle damage and for good measure took out a tumor the size of a Bartlett pear. As a special feature we let the highest bidder come onstage and close."

"James, that's very exciting."

"Which brings us to the live exhibits. We have, as you know, added the life-or-death option to the real-life adventures and we have in addition the two new, spontaneous and unrehearsed exhibits, and I'd like to report that these last two have been enormously successful. The Fenton Family is drawing them by the dozens, they started building an audience when we were broadcasting their adventures in the jungle, and now everybody in the place is signing up to ride by for a closer look. I should add that we have ensured their cooperation by telling them that they're being simulcast, we have taped a loop of the family sleeping in case they decide to check the monitors, and the cover story is that the show is going out on a delay. The others are flocking to watch the crew of the X-9 in the liferaft situation, they were discovered in an advanced stage of starvation with impending death by dehydration, and we were able to render them unconscious and remove them to our tank without risking discovery. The success of these exhibits accomplishes two things, it takes the pressure off Scenario, and, to speak to the problems Gayle raised, it tends to distract malcontents who want to return to the preceding day's adventures, which is just as well because, as you all know, none of the settings can stand too much close scrutiny."

"Excellent."

"With these successes in mind, Dearest, I am wondering if you will authorize the necessary funds for more live exhibits. They have the advantage in spontaneity, plus the subjects are more durable than Oldies but Goodies, they can stand up to more punishment and if you'll excuse me for saying so, Twink, when you get up close they look better. I think we fell into a good thing by accident and I would like to capitalize on it by arranging more crashes and maroonings in this area."

"That makes sense, James. Write out a report in full and I'll get back to you."

"Wait a minute. The Fenton thing is working now, but how long can you count on it?"

"Corky, I would appreciate it if you would mind your own business."

"I'm Scenario. This is my business."

"All right, if you want me to spell it out, the television ploy is working very nicely, and we plan to follow that with Discovery of Entrapment. Then we're going to move on into Attack by a Masked Burglar, followed by Villain in our Midst, where we arrange for one of them to turn psychopathic and they won't know which."

"You're leaving something out, Jimmy. How are you going to play out Discovery of Entrapment when Castle already knows?"

"That's being taken care of Corky, he's being removed."

"What are you going to do with him?"

"Ice him for the time being, Dearest. Then we'll see. If I

thought we could swing it I'd start an escape plot, but I haven't worked out the tracking technology. He's a holo-maker so we may be able to use him otherwise. They all want pictures to take home to their friends."

"What makes you think he'll cooperate?"

"If not there's always the Inca sacrifice, but that's the least of our problems. Right now I have to figure out how to approach him."

"Thank you, James. Now, if there's no new business."

"Dearest, you've forgotten me."

"Not now, Corky."

"Now. It's my turn. We've been working in the dark for years now, when are you going to take the wraps off Phase Four?"

"Ours not to reason why, Corky."

"The hell with that. What are we doing all this for? What's the payoff, or are you scared to let us know?"

"James, Dante, if you'll take Corky to his quarters?"

"Wait a minute. I want to know the facts."

("Corky, we don't want to hurt you, but."

"Take your hands off me."

"Sorry, Corks but we have to do what she says.")

"Thank you, boys. That's better. Now if you'll take him away."

Boone Castle

I was awake for a long time before I could move. I lay there listening to Dottie bang on the door and ask wheth-er I was up yet; I heard her trying the door, and I thought I heard her strike a high note of anxiety but at the time, even if I had been able to talk I wouldn't have known what to say: Don't mind me, save yourself, this is a trap? That I would like to answer, but my throat was stuck? To stay away from strange sheiks and never, ever undress in

122

front of mirrors? Later on I heard the kids calling but the anaesthetic they had piped into the room left me laid out flat, not moving, unable to speak, funny: not really caring, at least not at first. At first I couldn't figure out where I was, or what I was looking at that was this beautiful blue with little white clouds scudding across it. Maybe for a minute I thought I had waked up in hog heaven or in an open field somewhere but that was only for a minute. I guess my brain was laid out too; it took me longer than it should have to figure out that the blue sky and clouds were some kind of back projection on the putative ceiling of my socalled private room. I couldn't for the life of me figure out what was going to happen next. Maybe Dottie would get worried and come back. When it got to be cock-tail time and I was still in bed she might have Fred break down the door and I could signal with my eyes, the only part of me that still moved. Once they got the message they would hoist me on their shoulders and use me like a battering ram, splintering doors with my head as we lunged for freedom. Death before dishonor. Anything was better than lying here.

When help came it wasn't through the door. It wasn't exactly help, either.

There was a slight hum and the mirror wall slid aside; I couldn't turn my head but if I worked at it I could cut my eyes and so I saw it moving along the track where it inter-sected the ceiling. The next thing I knew somebody was giving me an injection and massaging my wrist. I found I could turn my head.

"Are you all right?"

"Hem. Hram. Hey, did you hear that?"

"Your voice is back. The rest will be along soon."

I got my first good look at her. "I hope so."

"Your poor wrists."

From where I lay she looked beautiful. She was red-headed, with one of those wild manes that bounced even when her head wasn't moving, and she had what looked like a terrific body underneath all those veils, she looked like a fugitive from a harem. The jewelled collars went all the way up her neck to cover her throat, the veil kept parts of her in shadow and the voice was a little pebbly but at the time I was too excited to pay much attention.

"Where did you come from?"

She ran her hand along my cheek. "And your poor face."

"Who are you working for?"

"When we get out of here I'll have time to kiss it, but now . . . "

"Why are you wearing that crazy costume?"

"Shhh. We're escaping."

"I don't know if I can walk yet."

"Please, the caliph . . . "

"The what?"

"His men are everywhere, they are just waiting." Her lips were sliding along my cheek, her breath was not exactly what I expected.

I managed to stand up. "What are you, one of the acts?"

"Please. No. I have to help you, together we will escape. The caliph is going to . . . "

"What is all this crap?"

"I am his favorite." She was hustling me toward the gap in the mirror wall. "Together we will escape. Hurry, there isn't much time."

She was a phony, what kind I wasn't sure, I couldn't be sure where she was leading me but at least the mirror wall was open partway so wherever we were going it was OUT and I couldn't afford to hang around and wait for another dose of anaesthetic gas. I held back for just a second and then, feeling her nails cut into my wrist, I followed her, noting out of the tail of my eye that the old plush chairs were still rolling past, and some of the audience was applauding.

Before I could think about that, she had pulled me around a corner, beyond the sight lines. We could see the audience but they could not see us.

124

"Hurry." She was pulling my arm. "Hurry my dear one, we're almost there."

The next turn took us into a service corridor where the squad was waiting. There were four of them, all in black uniform. There were three boys, one girl, at least I guess that was a girl, the body was right but the face was tougher than any of the rest.

"Goodbye, my love."

"What?"

"This is where we must part."

"But you said we were escaping the caliph."

"I brought him, sir, according to instructions." She wouldn't let go my wrist. "Can I do the rest of the story with him?"

"You can pick up your partner for the Escape from the Caliph plot over there, by the monitor's station."

"But I like this one."

"Forget it."

She was lingering, trying to run her fingers down my cheek one last time. "But this one is so . . . "

"You can't separate us," I said, thinking fast. "This is the woman I love."

"Not for long," the squad leader said. "Eleanor, are you going quietly, or . . . "

"But sir, I . . . "

"Or am I going to have to . . . "

"I love him. Oh!" One second she was stroking my cheeks and in the next she was flapping and swirling all her veils at once, trying to cover her head because the red mane separated from it when the squad leader yanked, there were a few tufts of scraggly white hair underneath and underneath that a bumpy, naked scalp, I had an instant flash of repetition: my dream encounter with the tiger. "My dearest." The Oldie but Goodie was backing away from me, trailing veils and tears, "Forgive me for deceiving you."

"Cheer up," the squad leader said to her, "your partner for the Escape from the Caliph plot is just as cute, once you start running you won't even notice the difference."

By that time she was halfway down the corridor, still sobbing with embarrassment, looking terrible without the wig. "It's all right," I shouted, wanting to make her feel better. "I thought you were sensational."

"Luce, go after her." The squad leader gave orders in a clipped voice. "See that she gets that wig on straight before she gets to her next assignment."

Which left the three of us, the guys in the squad and me. "Look, guys, if it's a good runner you need, I would be more than happy to . . . "

"Forget it, Castle. You can't be trusted."

"I gave a good show in the bedroom last night, didn't I?"

"Up to a point. Frankly, you're a bad risk."

"Is that why you gassed me?"

"Partly."

"That woman. This rescue."

"Continuity needed a smooth way to remove you from the setting."

"You mean cut me off from the only people I can trust."

"The truth is, you weren't functioning in the family plot. The front office wanted something with a little more pizzaz, so we had to remove you."

"You bastards."

All he had to do was touch his belt. I thought my head was imploding. "As you can see, struggling only makes it worse. Enough?"

I got up, nodding. By that time the woman guard was trotting toward us. She saw me wringing my ears and I thought I caught a flicker behind the eyes, something going on there, that wasn't with the others: recognition, or something remembered, but by that time the other two had me by the elbows and they had me part way off the ground, waiting for their orders.

I tried to kick a few shins. "Bastards, bastards." I might as well have been a small animal, or a spunky midget.

"Put this one in the Chateau d'If for the time being, see that Costume sends up the right rags this time, something in period."

"Wait a minute," I said. Two goons had me by the elbows. "What are you doing?"

"I'll check with Scenario and get back to you." The woman guard had come closer; she was shifting from one foot to the other, waiting for the squad leader to pay attention, which he finally did. "Well, Luce, mission accomplished?"

"Not on your ass. That was an Oldie but Baddie. Konked out before I could get her around the corner." Her attention was wandering, so that by the time she finished her report she seemed to be talking to me. "Heart, I think."

"Continuity is going to have to . . . Luce, are you listening?"

Maybe it was paranoia; I got the idea she was staring into me. I looked at my hands, still on frontwards; checked my crotch.

"Hey, Luce."

"Huh?" she said. "Oh, right. Continuity. Continuity is clear. They had a replacement ready before the body hit the deck."

"Well done."

"So this will go into my fitness report, right?"

"Right." The squad leader raised his hand and the goons jacked me up and started dragging me to a scooter.

"So why not let me handle this one?" Luce was saying. "Let me show the company what I can do."

The leader shrugged. The two stiffs let me go. "OK, it's all yours."

"Right," she said, and that grin was really sinister. "Right right." When she gave you that look, you moved.

So I ended up in the scooter with the tough lady. I tried to keep track of the geography but there were a dozen different levels and at some point we drove onto an

127

elevator platform and there was no way for me to be sure which way we were moving. I coughed and she touched her belt and knives went through my ears.

"It's all right, I'll go quietly."

"You bet your ass you will." She was muttering under her breath, I think it was: "I don't need this."

"What?"

"Shut your hole." Was that a wink or did she only have something in her eye?

The corridor narrowed and we went on foot. She clamped her fingers on me and straight-armed me against the wall, frisking me with the other hand. God she was ugly.

"I'm clean."

"Can't be too sure."

"What the hell is going on here?"

"Don't ask me, I only work here."

"I thought this was Happy Habitat."

"What you see is what you get."

"What the hell is that supposed to mean?"

She clouted me on the ear. It was the last straw; I pulled out of her grip and hit her with a stiff left that didn't even rock her. She just grinned at me and then she stuck a hypo bug on me and I went out.

The Chateau d'If was more or less as you would expect. The cell looked real enough, I got a sinking sensation, and when I mastered it and stood up I felt even worse. I was in the rags, right enough, I was in a place where nobody would hear me rattle the bars or shout for help and from the looks of the place I might as well be trapped three hundred years ago in darkest France. There were your classic withered arms reaching through the bars in the oaken door opposite mine, but when I called the arms didn't move and there was no answer. There were handfuls of white hair stuck in the wood of my own door, along with dried blood and there was the classic plink plink or was it drip drip of some terrible unidentified

128

moisture falling somewhere just out of sight. I was sure those were real slugs oozing along the walls and that was probably the rustle of real rats in the straw underfoot but I took hold of myself because I knew no matter how real it all seemed, I hadn't come to it in any real way.

I had not been dragged past a gallery of crazed captives and down crumbling stone steps, but instead had been popped in through a sanitized hole in the back wall, if I felt the stones I could find the place. Behind it I knew there were all those miles of efficient-looking tunnels and brilliant technology, and above ground there were the merry-go-rounds and silver arch of the world's most famous playground, but I could not for the life of me reconcile my idea of Happy Habitat, as advertised, with what had happened to me here, any more than I could figure out what all of that had to do with all this. In spite of all the authentic detail this was not the real Chateau d'If, which meant that this could not be the real end of the longer continuing novel I am living, which meant it had to be the real something else—but what? If I could just figure out what that something else was, get a handle on it, I might be able to figure out how to escape.

I went through what I would take to be the traditional reactions to imprisonment: astonishment and rage, reconciliation, a cold-headed survey of the situation, a search for ways to escape. The door was solid, and I had nothing sharp to use to work on it, and even if I could get the bars out of the opening it wasn't big enough to push a rat through. I thought of setting the straw on fire, but the first heap I made bared cement flooring and there was no guarantee that guards would come before I'd burned myself to an ash. I had at the back wall with a slat from my prison cot but all I managed to do was splinter the wood and take off an inch or two of the moss. It was the moss that tipped me off. It felt funny and when I rubbed my thumb and fingers back and forth it did not disintegrate or smear but came away in a neat clump: plastic. I stood, considering, and when I moved it was to comb the place, looking for the eye.

After a while I saw it moving. The camera was concealed in a mass of spider webs in a high corner and when it moved to cover me light glinted off the lens.

So I was still in the show.

"All right, dammit. Show's over."

I lay down on the cot and turned my back to it. My pallet was foam rubber but I didn't blink when I found out, and when I found the chocolate bar inside the pillowcase, I didn't take it out. No more pleasing the audience. No more anything that would divert them even for a minute. They could rot in hell before I would entertain them. I was going to turn them off by being boring. I was going to keep control of my damn fears and they could look elsewhere for satisfaction. I would leave off the escape attempts and I wasn't even going to let them see me eating. If I had to piss I would sidle over to the corner and stand with my back turned so they couldn't see. I would keep it boring so they tired of watching and when I was pretty sure nobody was watching I was going to find a way out and take it. Meanwhile I would triumph by stultifying them.

Or I thought I would until I found the note. It was stuck in my boot and I couldn't be sure whether it was real or only part of their hoked-up story. I wasn't even sure exactly how it got there. The lady guard? It read:

STAY LOOSE AND I'LL COME FOR YOU

Evaline

Last night I thought I had made peace with this place. Freedom for security is not a bad tradeoff, I am out of the kids' hair for good and all; I have done everything to keep my looks and my independence, and if I have lost the latter, well, I still won't be a bother to anybody back home. So maybe they will drag me off in the end, I'll go wherever Ashby went, Ashby, whom I have not seen since, but that won't be so bad. At least it won't be boring. And if I have to die? Sudden death beats your lingering illness any day, you can go out with a smile. Meanwhile, if the party is good enough, that should be sufficient.

Was, until I met Val. We came together in the Plaza and it all changed. I was out there dancing, when this great golden-haired swinger took me by force. He was, yes, beautiful by dint of effort, years of exercise and self-denial, just like me: brave, like me. He whirled me out into the middle of the dance and said, into my ear:

"Be careful if you can. Stay alert, and you will survive."

"Do I want to survive?" His arms were strong and I was whirling, thinking it might not be bad to go out like this; one minute I would be in the arms of a handsome man and the next I would be gone, like an extinguished spark.

He spun me so quickly it took my breath. "You're strong, like me, you have the guts to make it. Dance, and be merry too, this is only the beginning." He was warning me: about what happened to Ashby? "There is life after this."

"Tell me how you know."

"Because I've been there, and survived." His arms clamped against my back and his lips brushed my forehead in a way I loved. It took me back to all those foolish, hopeful dawns when life was still ahead and sudden warm touches were a prelude, not phases in an ending. We danced until there was no more music and when the others drifted out of the square we were still dancing. When the music stopped he pulled me into a doorway and we sat with our backs against the wood and looked out at the broken glasses and scattered cap containers, the shredded flowers and abandoned veils, the ruins of the party.

He said, "There are no bugs or cameras here. I think we can talk."

"Why did you choose me?"

"You looked so . . . " He was embarrassed by what he almost said; instead he said, "You looked as if you could go the distance."

"What do you want from me?"

"I want to leave here. I can't do it alone. Tell me your name."

"Evaline."

"Evaline, do you know who I am?"

I looked at him more carefully, trying to strip the years. "Valentine Stone. I thought you were dead. Oh, I'm sorry."

"Only to my backers." He looked into the dimness. "I thought I would never make another movie, but then this place . . . Ev, I want to show you something about this place. Will you come with me?"

The pressure in my ears was so great that I had to yawn. I could hardly breathe for excitement.

He misread me and got up to go. "If I've made a mistake about you I'm sorry. I'll take you to your room."

My ears were roaring; I exploded into words. "Wait. No. Take me with you."

His smile blazed. "I thought you'd come."

I let him put an arm around my waist and draw me along. I had a sense of stepping out of bounds, the possibility of alternative endings. Each step made me stronger, we were almost running. We came to the wall that separated the Golden Acres section from the rest of the place and we ran along it until he showed me a hole he had made at the base. "I survived one of these, that I'm about to show you. The staff were going to finish me but the audience said no.

"They liked me, they wanted me to survive. Now that I have a following the management will keep using me until I buy it, one way or another. Let me show you."

It was hard getting through the hole in the wall. We came out in a stand of bushes and lay on our bellies. We were looking at an empty field and as we watched a group of people in medieval costumes came through the trees on the other side like something out of Ivanhoe, laughing and smoking dope in mirrored shades even though it was night. They surrounded a flabby man in a loincloth with a spiked belt, patting him and urging him on. He removed his wristwatch and stepped into a ring of light. Someone said, "Now," and it began. His opponent was pushed into the light, puzzled and blinking but beautiful in a leather breechclout; he was about to strike a muscle builder's pose when somebody handed him a mace and chain. Before he even knew what was happening, he was fighting for his life. It was long, ugly and bloody. At the end the flabby man in the spiked belt kept swinging the mace again and again while his fans laughed and chattered and applauded; he kept on even though his opponent was already dead.

"That was one of us who died," Val said quietly, and led me back through the hole in the wall. "They use us up to please the paying guests. I have notes on all of it, I want to make a film . . ."

"A holo."

"All right, a holo that will expose this place. I have all the material I need and I want you. I want. Ev, there's something I want you to do."

We were at his room by that time. He took me into the bathroom and pulled the shower curtain to shield us from the mirror wall, after which he hung a towel over the camera eye, grinning and winking so they would think we were just about to make it there on the floor, and wanted privacy. Then he took the lid off the toilet tank and showed me the sheaf of notes rolled and sealed inside a plastic bag, the set of instaslides. He was going to take them back to his studio and make a feature that would put an end to this. They had sent him here in the first place, a living monument with no credit rating, no backers, nobody willing to use him on a feature; he had to come because he had no alternatives. After the first couple of weeks he was cast in an adventure and defeated a Nubian in front of a delighted audience. The astonished attendants cast him again, in the Avalanche Disaster, and after he survived to claim the snow queen they understood they had a star. They were going to keep on casting him until his heart gave out and he was killed. On each job he learned a little more and now he was ready to leave.

"I saw you and I wanted you to come with me. If I don't make it, I want you to carry on alone. Ev?"

"Oh Val, I would do anything for you."

We lay together quietly, I let him hold me and I thought: We are of an age, we both have scars behind our ears and our bones are frail and our flesh tight through sheer force of will; if we were together we could both let down together; if we could be together none of it would be quite so bad. I didn't know whether we would escape, whether Val even had a plan, I could only guess where it was going to end but for the time being I could be his and he mine in the old ways, kindred hearts feeding on promises, and in that hour I was happier than I had been in all those years of wild dancing with beautiful boys who despised me. I remember thinking: Oh God, if we were only young, and at the beginning.

His mouth was close to my ear. "Don't hope."

"I know better."

"At least there's this."

"Oh Val, I love . . . "

He put his fingers to my lips. "Not now. If we get out, then maybe . . . "

The next morning they came for us. The people on their chaises on the terraces were supposed to think they were taking us for saunas and rubdowns or a brisk dunk in the hot springs, I guess we were too, but we knew better. They had the hypodermics ready, in case we struggled, but Val waved them aside and then he turned to me with such a look of love and pain that I wanted to hold his hands and kiss him until he stopped trembling. He said, "Remember, if I can't go, you know what you have to do."

"You have to make it," I said, silencing him with my lips.

Then the attendants called and we went quietly. We went through costume quickly; they already had my measurements. First we had to pass the medical and then we went through wigs and makeup, at the other end we were transformed. Val looked gallant in tattered guerilla · clothes and I was dressed as an angel of mercy in a uniform with a starched apron with a red cross on the bib. Briefing gave us our instructions: do what comes naturally, defend yourself any way you can unless the assailant is a paying guest. You will identify them by the gold wristlets. You may do whatever you can to escape if he attacks but you must not hurt him, even if it costs your life. (Val whispered, "It wouldn't do you any good—they all have safety shields." "Then how can we survive?" "We're one up on the others. We want to live." "Oh Val." "It's all right, I'm going to take care of you.") They moved us through Briefing into a monorail car with the others who had been plucked and costumed for the great event; we went through tunnels and onto a loading elevator, and at the top they spilled us into Armageddon.

I can't remember, don't want to, will never forget: the noise and horror and blood. There was fire everywhere, the sky was brilliant with exploding shells. We were fleeing over a rocky plain. It was terrifying, but at the same time my blood rose because I was in the middle of a movie, something better than a movie because real; there would be no going to the ladies' room or walking out if I didn't like the way it was going, there was risk and exhilaration and the giddy feeling that life was taking me instead of me dragging it; whatever was going to happen would happen no matter what I did, it would keep on happening until it was over and willy nilly, like it or not, I was a living part of it.

"Oh Val."

"Stay with me."

Together we were brave, we were wonderful. We backed away from the enemy, fighting every step; if any of them were wearing gold bracelets we pretended not to notice, and fought brilliantly. We were separated from the others by that time, backing down the hillside to a burned-out tank. We were going to hole up until the battle was over, would have, too, but at that moment, when the air was filled with the screams of the wounded and the shellbursts had reached a crescendo I heard someone shouting:

"Stronger music. Louder death."

After that everything changed.

In the next second there were people charging down on us, explosions everywhere, and in the same moment I saw a gold bracelet flash and an arm hurling a grenade; I saw all this at the same time as my dear Val saw the grenade flying and leaped in front of me, catching it in his chest as his arms and legs flew like the points of a star and he exploded with it, going out in a burst of light. The last thing I heard was someone shouting, "Now that's more like it."

Then I might as well have been dead.

So I turned out to be a survivor, because I looked dead. They must have collected me when they started cleaning up the set after the scene was over because I woke up in the Infirmary, pretending to take pills filled with enough dope to put me out for days. They asked if I remembered anything and I said no I didn't, the shock had been too much, and when their backs were turned I spat out the pills. After they took me to my room I lay awake, remembering everything.

In late afternoon I crept into the courtyard, clinging to walls like a spider with toothpick legs, and I finally made it to Val's room. They had already finished cleaning it for the next arrival, but when I went into the bathroom the plastic roll was still inside the toilet tank, Val's script. I hid it in my front, touched his pillow once and crept back to my room. I lay in bed for a long time, with the script firm against my bosom, and tried to think. I was not going to survive another real-life adventure, and right now, for the first time in a long time, it seemed important to survive. For the first time since I could remember, I had responsibilities.

Maybe I slept; when I opened my eyes again it was morning, and I thought I knew what to do. I could stay out of the action by refusing to look the part. Nobody wanted an old person, so I went in the bathroom and hid the screenplay, and then I washed all the pretty color out of my hair, after which I undid my makeup and the hooks behind the ears, that keep the face from sagging, and slipped back into the crumpled Infirmary robe. I went out on the terrace and popped my caps because I had to keep feeling good, it is part of the plan. Then I sat there leaning back with my feet up, looking hideous in the early morning sunlight, waiting to be noticed.

It didn't take long. The neighbors were offended but respectful because there but for the grace of cosmetics, and the wig . . . I smiled and waved; they gritted their teeth and waved back. The attendants tried to make me go inside because I was depressing the others, but I just grinned and waited until I was damn sure I had been seen. Then I took my sweet time going inside.

I said, "One false move and your other customers are going to catch on."

"Behave or we'll put a guard on you."

"Anything you say," I said, because by that time I was too well-advertised to be removed. I went back to bed. By that time the other Oldies were lining up outside my door, begging leave to make sympathy calls, and I thought: why not let them, as long as I have company nobody is going to come in here and drag me away. I have to hang on, I have to survive.

For the first time I have something to live for. I am, at the moment, planning my escape. I will take Val's screenplay back to his old studio, there is a covering letter in the front that will get me in, they will make his feature and the world will know. For the moment I am gathering strength. I lie here collecting extra caps from all my visitors and biding my time, fulfilling the first part of my plan.

Kaa Naaji

And so I have something to live for once again; having through my own skill and perseverance lighted all the lamps and fueled the dynamos of Mother India, having reaped all the praise and fame and wealth the world has to offer and having found it stale and flat, a mere handful of chaff thrown into the jaws of yearning, I have at last found my heart's desire and given it a name. That name is love, oh yes, and I shall find her.

My heart starts after the Amazon in black whose face flamed across my consciousness last night, when they took Ahmed. She is seared deep in me, a want there is no erasing. What's more I think she is real. If this were part of the program designed for me by the most gracious management of Happy Habitat I should have her by now, but I do not. I stalked her this entire day, I have followed her like a faithful dog and at every turn she has repulsed or managed to elude me. Very well, then, she is not employed to please me. She is not one of their hired *houris*, programmed to please. This means my chase is real, her flight is real. I have no promise of easy fulfillment this time, and so I warm to the chase and I am glad. I was not meant to have her any more than poor Ahmed was meant to have his Magnolia; our love has escaped the ingeniously designed boundaries of Happy Habitat, and if this is so then it is a much more valuable thing than any of their magnificent jungle rescues or ravishing nights in a seraglio: not a commodity bought and paid for, but the object of all striving, a happiness to be earned.

I awoke wanting her. I went to the window to see pink dawn spreading over the empty plaza, so neat and clean-swept that last night's parade seemed less than a memory. I had to wonder whether that had really happened to Ahmed because I felt weak and lazy, almost hung over, even though I do not touch either grape or grain. Do they put something in the lemon squash? I drank much coffee from the urn by my bedside and when I was able I went out into the corridor to explore.

The attendant was at my elbow at once, holding it hard.

"Mr. Mahadevan. What are your plans?"

"I wish to see my friend Ahmed, and then . . . "

"Perhaps you want to join the group going to the battle at Sebastopol, they'll be assembling in the Parabola Room in twenty minutes. Or you can wait until eleven and drive an ambulance in the Spanish Civil War."

"No thank you. I shall wander in the park." I shall find my love.

"That's child play, Mr. Mahadevan. Now our cavern tours . . . "

"Why can I not do what I want? Am I not the paying guest?"

The attendant was polite but showing impatience. "You signed on for the real-life adventures. That's where the real excitement is."

And, I thought, the real money for your management. I thought I would like to as you say get shut of this person. "I have had enough of real life for the time being, thank you. Now, if you don't mind . . . "

The attendant at the door to Ahmed's suite must have expected me. He stepped aside and let me ring. As I wait-

139

ed for the sheik's bodyguards to admit me I remembered the night in its entirety: Ahmed's removal, the guard's hand on my shoulder, the strange lassitude that overcame me at a time when I should have been searching the stones for the trap door, trying to recover Ahmed and find the woman of my dreams, for she was real. The only thing that was not real was the indifference with which I had turned my back, humming, "Good Night Sweetheart," along with the band. How had I been drugged? Was Ahmed all right? As his bodyguards opened the door I feared the worst but as it turned out he was safe in his own bower, sleeping away. I thought it would not be so bad to dream what he was dreaming for he smiled so in his sleep that I myself smiled to see it.

Alas for me the day was empty. I could not even relax on the swan boat ride along the moat outside the fairy castle because I was staring hard, straining for a sudden flash of black in the greenery or sunlight glinting on fiery hair. When a program counsellor met me at the end of the ride I asked outright:

"If you wish to make me happy, find the woman I love." I described her carefully and the villain denied that there was anyone by this description in all of Happy Habitat. He tried to distract me with promises of orgies on the mini-Riviera, and when that did not draw me he offered the crew of the X-9 in survival circumstances, but each time I shook my head. At last he seemed so downcast that I quickly promised to sign up for two real-life adventures tomorrow, just to cheer him up, so at last he left me alone to search for her.

When I went to the main building, the pussy boy in the yellow uniform tried to turn me away from the desk. "Black uniforms? Perhaps you are talking about the Gestapo Revels."

"I do not know any Gestapo. I think this woman works for you. She was one of your, how shall I say this, your police."

"Police? Why Mr. Mahadevan, why would we need police?"

"I . . . " I was remembering Ahmed, smiling in his sleep. "Do you not need someone to keep order?"

I did not like the way he looked at me. "This is Happy Habitat, Mr. Mahadevan. Everything is in order."

"The sheik. Last night."

His voice became metallic. "The sheik had one too many."

"How did you . . . " Kaa Naaji. Fool. Be quiet. I made namaste and backed away quickly. "Ah yes, of course. Perhaps I too have had one too many."

I went from the desk to join the others on the balcony, and I tried to ask this one a little, that one a little, but they were too preoccupied to speak; each one moved in a buzzing cloud of desire. Marva brooded over her long-lost ripper, could today's Ernest Hemingway approach him in virility? The Japanese couple bumped foreheads, fixed on things to come, and Simpson—alas. The desk have told Simpson that he must forget Marathon and give himself to the pleasures at hand or they will pack his things for him and send him home, never to return. I suggested that he spend the day with me, in Papeete or at the Aztec sacrifice, but he turned his face to the window and would not speak to me.

So it was that I was alone when there was a ruckus in the pavilion, the bushes parted and I saw her. I recognized her at once, she may have seen me too but she only grabbed the fellow who had started the ruckus and pulled him into the ground. I ran to the spot and fell on my knees; there was a faint outline in the grass, a hidden door. So it was true what had happened last night in the plaza, and I was right; she was one of the police. But why did they need police?

To stamp out discontent, perhaps, but I knew there must be more. I had to find her so I could learn the truth. I began to rove, looking for places where she might reappear, searching for signs of discontent or disagreement because her group would come to stamp it out. I watched for heavy drinkers and when one became ugly her group appeared; poor Simpson had his heart attack in the plaza, and I was there, memorizing the outlines of my love's body, surmising the face under the mask, feasting on the beauty of her auburn hair. I wanted to push my way through the crowd and speak to her but she had Simpson over her shoulder in a trice and they disappeared into the ground. There was a contretemps at the Satyriosel and once again I saw her; this time she saw me: did her body stiffen with desire? I might have moved closer to claim her but there was a steely hand on my elbow, yet another program counsellor. He steered me away.

"This is a particularly good time to see the Fenton Family."

"The Fenton Family?" I did not know if I recognized this fellow; most Anglos look alike to me. "What of Boone Castle. Will he be there too?"

"Step over here."

"But I wish to be free today, I . . . " The fingers tightened on my arm. "What are you doing?"

"You almost fell. If I hadn't grabbed you, you might have been hurt."

"Of course." I knew perfectly well he was forcing me. We moved into a chamber at the base of the paramotel and onto a moving sofa; it embraced me and we started going up, into a velvety tunnel that frightened and excited me by turns; along the inky walls were holos of adventures in other parts of Happy Habitat, battles and orgies and the parched inhabitants of a liferaft bobbing up and down, up and down; music marched to a crescendo as our sofa moved up a final grade and past a flashing neon display with the Fenton Family names. Then we were poised in front of the living room and there were my friends Fred and Dottie, talking most seriously, and I knew from the way she stood, with her belly protruding,

142

and the way he delved into his ear with his little finger that they could not see me. It was exciting but it made me feel guilty.

"Do they want us to watch?"

"Never mind."

"And Boone Castle. Where is Boone Castle?"

He said a most mystifying thing. "Take care and you won't have to see him."

"I don't understand."

There were the fingers on my elbow again; the sofa had hesitated long enough and now we said goodbye to Fred and Dottie and started the ride down. "Tell me how you are enjoying your stay in Happy Habitat."

I knew what he wanted to hear so I said, "Everything is most ingenious." I also knew he would not answer any of my questions and so I said, "What's more, everything is so organized, so beautifully run."

"Good, good." He looked so pleased. He lowered his voice, saying, just as we got off the sofa, "How would you like to have a special part in it?"

"What do you mean?"

"I can't tell you anything more right now. Just remember that I spoke to you, and that I offered you a special part."

"You have not told me what part."

"I have my orders," he said. "Think about it, and you'll find out when the time is right."

"Wait, I have questions. What has happened to Boone Castle?"

"Maybe you'd like to spend the day in Sebastopol, or at the Spanish Civil War?"

"Another thing. There is a woman."

"Or on the mini-Riviera with the companion of your choice?"

"I believe she is one of your police."

"Old Moscow in the winter?" He was considering me. He said, sharply, "We have no police."

"But I know . . . " I was aware of a hard slap on my kurtha pajamas, a sting, and then . . .

I woke in my room. It was night and there was somebody in white moving in the dark. I sat up in fright, Hsst, but a hand on my mouth silenced me. "Quiet, it is your friend Ahmed," he said, and I said, "Acha. Ahmed, there is something wrong."

"Never mind. I have come to leave a message with you, in case."

"In case?"

"I am going out beyond the pretty places, where no guest has ever been. I am going to find my beloved Magnolia, my Ashby, and escape."

"Shh. They may be listening." I leaned closer and whispered: "Ahmed, your bodyguards will never let you go alone."

"They are all sleeping," he said. "I was fasting to purify myself, and so I escaped sleep. You understand."

"Acha."

"Plus there is also something in the air."

"I will go with you."

"No, I need you here." He put his axe-blade face close to mine and said, "You are the only one I can trust, Kaa Naa Mahadevan, even though your ancestors and mine did battle for centuries. You and I are friends."

"Yes, we are friends."

"And if I do not return, Kaa Naaji."

"Yes, Ahmed."

"You will be alive to tell the tale."

And so without wanting to I understood. "Yes, Ahmed, but they may not stop at removal if they catch you. I have seen them work and I fear for you."

"It does not matter, I am going to find Ashby, my Magnolia. I have found out that they keep her with the old people, I do not know why."

"And if you cannot find her?"

"By Allah, I might as well be dead. But you, Kaa Naaji, you will take my story to the world."

144

"What if there is no way out of here?"

"I think you will find one. I am a great sheik but you, you are a scientist."

I was struck with great humility. "Ah, I fear I have not acted the scientist. I have been a fool, a worthless sybarite . . . "

"If I fall, Kaa Naaji, you will spring up in my place."

"But you are going to be all right, my friend, tomorrow you will tell your adventures over tea."

"I do not think so, my friend. Goodbye."

"Oh Ahmed."

"Tell the tale. Promise."

"By all that is holy. But Ahmed . . . " I did not go on for he was already gone. Instead I sat in the darkness, thinking I would stay awake until my friend returned, I must keep the vigil for Ahmed's sake, but in the next moment there was a faint hissing, as of gas, I must not be in my room the next time night falls because, I must not . . .

Luce

So we took the Arab guy out of the scene that first night in the plaza, there he was scrambling and slobbering after one of the Oldies but Goodies, "Magnolia, my dearest," and she was slobbering and trying to scramble to him. I can tell you that kind of thing doesn't look so good to the rest of the paying customers, and it is that kind of thing that me and my squad are on the job to prevent. Nobody is unhappy here in Happy Habitat, nobody ever gets drunk or bothers anybody or messes up, we are Cleanup and Removal and we're the ones that have to see to it. The only trouble was, I was beginning to get the idea that I am the only one that gives a damn about their work, which is rotten unfair when you think about it, because all those candy-faced twits that don't care at all get to go up topside and work with the public, while I am stuck down here.

After we stashed the Arab guy we were off duty for the night, we all got a fistful of goodies to pop and snort, not my idea of a good time. The rest of them, all they think about is kissy-lickies and making it on every available surface and taking enough junk to keep them spaced out to Sunday, maybe the idea is to keep everybody flying so nobody asks questions, well that doesn't work with me. I stuck the stuff under my pillow and lay back in the rack and thought. What frosted me was that the ones that cared the least were getting the best jobs. When it got to be morning it would be them that got detailed to Central Plaza, they would rinse the guck out of their mouths and go out there to meet the public with their beautiful bodies and their great American smiles, they would hobnob with the jet-setters and the power people and make their impression, while I bust my ass with the dirty work and got stashed below for the simple lack of physical beauty. If they thought I was going to let that stop me they were dead wrong. First thing the next morning I went out and volunteered to work overtime. I was going to show them.

The first job of the day was getting this guy out of the Fenton Family setting, and all right, it threw me off. There was something about the way he looked, not squashy, like Norman, but like he could, what, be something to me. I did a dozen other jobs that day but I would have to confess I was not one hundred per cent with it because that Castle guy's face kept getting in my way. That thing I used to look for—was he it? No time for that now, Luce. Castle, get away.

Plus there was another thing that slowed me down, and kept me from making my best showing. I was being watched. I was getting up topside a lot by that time, all removal jobs. Somebody yelling Shit Crap Shit in the middle of the Bavarian garden, some old guy having a heart attack. You have to take them out before the public notices. A quick hypo in the butt and it's off to the Infirmary. The next shuttle home, if retraining doesn't work. The customers get everything they want, right? That kind of thing takes first-class management. It's like they are building a house of cards or a bridge out of crystal toothpicks, one false note and it goes smash.

So I was doing my job, going around with the squad, but no matter what scene we came up into I had the creepy feeling there were eyes on me, I could feel them drilling through my back. Then on the last job of the day the crowd parted like the Red Sea and I saw him: little brown guy in white pajamas, looking at me with melting brown eyes, it was enough to make you puke, I wanted to knock him down and make him stop.

But there wasn't time. We were taking out this drunk and disorderly, and it was not your ordinary case. Orders from headquarters: Handle with care. First thing was he was wearing a uniform a lot like ours, but silver, with a diamond dog collar, and he had come up in the middle of the Nymph-and-Satyr carousel. He was running backward on this jewelled merry-go-round, waving his arms and yelling, "Phase Four, Phase Four, don't any of you wonder about Phase Four?" The clients were trying not to notice, riding along on those sapphire snakes but there he was, in a minute he was going to fall under one of the snakes and ruin everything. We had to filter through the crowd and onto the moving carousel without attracting much notice, we got the drunk out without ruffling a lock of that silver hair and we took him down the hatch. I shouldn't have looked back but I did: there was the little brown bastard with the cowflop eyes still watching me so I gave him the finger as we closed the hatch.

One look and you knew this Drunk and Disorderly was special. We did not dump him in any of your usual places, either. We loaded him into a scooter but we were not heading for the Infirmary. I kept track of elevators and levels and turnings because we were going someplace

147

new, and I knew it was going to be important. At the bottom of the last elevator ride the corridor widened out and the light changed, the next thing I knew the floor had turned into old-fashioned brick, pretty soon there were artificial trees and shrubs coming up on either side and we came out into a row of house fronts like the ones you see in pictures of old-time New York City. It was wild. We took the guy to the last door in the row and left him. Damn, there were real geraniums in the window box.

I said, "Don't we put him inside the door?"

"No. They don't want us to see any more."

I said, "Some kind of big deal, right?"

The detail leader just shrugged.

"I mean, nobody else gets this treatment." I hummed a little, tra la, oop shoop, to throw off suspicion, and I took a look back. The door had opened, and there were hands taking him in. I said, "I just thought he might be Management."

"Management shmanagement. Who gives a shit?"

Me. I. I did. This might even be the heart of the operation.

Did I get a chance to follow up on it? Hell no. We reported back to the desk and got sent to clean up the bodies in one of the Oldie but Goodie massacres in the Spanish Civil War they had drummed up for some sheik. You have never seen such a mess. There were shellholes in the Permaturf and the bodies were so thick you had to hold your breath. I schlepped a few bodies and was going back for more when I found them; two old parties, sprawled where the explosion had flang them, and the old lady was still alive.

I should have left her for somebody else. I had her head in my lap the whole way to the Infirmary, and I was so cool that nobody from the detail knew how much it shook me. She was out of it, I mean altogether, but she couldn't stop talking, the poor old thing was burning up with love. "Val, my darling. Why did we meet too late?" She had on

148

this nurse suit that was a wreck; his blood, I guess. "Oh Val, why couldn't I have died with you?" Even with the smudges and the scars behind the ears from all those lifts she was, surprise, beautiful, burned from the inside out by the guy she loved. I had handled his body: big, with this handsome head, this shock of silver-gold hair, she was raging to get to him, I had to hold her down.

She was an *old* Oldie, I could tell by the way her arms and legs flopped, those bones were probably hollow, but here she was with the one great love that I had never had, I held her in my arms and I was thinking: All right, lady, if I'd ever had it, I would not be here in this uniform. There was a fire running from one knee up through the heart, I guess, and that guy in the dungeon kept coming back to me, snapshots flicking in front of my face. Get away, Castle. No time for that now, Castle, get away.

Then we were at the Infirmary and she was coming up, hand over hand, from whatever hell it was where she had been wandering. She didn't ask, Where am I, she just said, "Val." Now when was the last time I met somebody that they were all I could think about? Castle, get away. What I knew right then was that I had spent a long time chasing after success that didn't even know I was chasing, and here was this poor old broad that had succeeded at the one thing that she cared about: she had been loved.

When I got back to the dorm I popped a couple of uppers to take my mind off it. By that time the dorm had filled up with people sleeping in twos or threes, reeking of whatever they had been wallowing in, there was going to be a lot of ass-dragging on the job tomorrow and your fresh-faced crowd movers weren't going to be quite so pretty because it was going to take them a long time to pull themselves up from the flesh pits, it was damn depressing. I went to sleep in spite of everything. Damn that old lady with her lover, that she was ready to die for, damn all the squashy love stuff that I have tried to keep buried, that she had raked the flesh away from and left exposed. I began to dream. In the dream I was going along the wind with this dream person, I was barefooted and wearing gauze and flowers, laughing like a damn fool because I had found *him*, whoever he was, that I could love. Couldn't afford that, not Luce Finley, shook myself awake and sat up straight with my back getting stiff and my flesh cooling until the last shreds of that damn dream had floated to the ceiling.

Which is how I happened to be on the scene when they called for an emergency work detail, they needed a crack quartet to go to the perimeter.

There were four of us: two guys in black hoods, one other woman, hooded and skinny as a long distance runner, and me. We were fast, mean, deadly, piling into the skimmer, kicking it into high gear almost before the elevator spilled us on the surface. We zoomed along empty streets. There were no paying guests in the street, nobody hanging on the lampposts or sleeping it all off under the shrubbery; I mean the place was deserted, which made me wonder if they just turned everybody off when it got to be night.

The only people left were us, and one or two hundred guards who gave us the nod from doorways as we passed. It was spooky. There were lights in all the doorways and street lights at every corner and twinkling lights outlining all the buildings, but when I looked at the long curve of the paramotel I saw there was light crashing out of the lobby and nothing coming from any of the bedroom windows; it could have been a giant birdcage that was covered for the night because there was nobody out but the guards and us, humming along in the skimmer.

We went from the plaza into a little woods and from there into the war set and from there we went through real-life adventure settings: full-scale jungle, medieval courtyard, concentration camp. We were going fast by that time, homing in on a signal from the perimeter, but as it turned out it didn't matter how fast we went we were already too late because as we came out of the Malaysian rain forest and covered the final open space where searchlights raked and automatic skimmers circled, the alarm shut off because the emergency was already over. The sheik or whoever it had been was plastered up against the electronic shield that surrounded the place, sizzling and already flatter than a flounder, with a smaller shape next to him, burned out and already disappearing into ash, so that all I could make out was the tail of a big skirt with scorched bows and flaming ruffles.

"Removal reporting. Subject terminated." The other woman in my detail had punched several numbers into her belt and now she was in voice contact with Dispatch. "Request instructions."

"Let him burn out, to eliminate problems with disposal."

I looked back at the shield. There was nothing left but two outlines in ash.

"Accomplished."

"Return for report and drafting of telegram."

She was raking the shield with her light, looking for other outlines. "I thought he had a retinue."

"Still iced in his suite."

"What are you going to tell them?"

"We'll turn it over to Scenario. Right now, return and report."

"We're on our way. Back on board, everybody. Finley. Finley?"

Oh I turned pretty quick and got on board fast, so she could not be sure I had been doing what she had caught me doing: staring into the darkness beyond the shield, at the spot where her light had flashed for just a second. I thought there might be trouble but my guess is she didn't know what was beyond the shield, or that there was anything beyond, but I had seen it, or thought I saw it, and when I got into the skimmer I closed my eyes and tried to bring it back, checking for after-images. Either I saw it or I

151

didn't: shapes out there in the dark beyond the shield, outlined for just a second when her light raked them. If they were there at all they looked like domes or spheres or blunt noses poking up out of a crater, not rocket noses, I don't think, but something rounded, featureless, something I was going to have to find out about because they were not part of anything I had seen so far, at least not the surface operation, which meant that they had to be—what?

Boone Castle

I didn't like jail. I was thrown back on my own resources in a cell identical to the one Edmund Dantes risked death to escape in the novel, or was that the movie, and I didn't know what to do. Sure I wanted to get out, but the damn thing was I wasn't sure exactly why; I didn't have any basically compelling reasons like true love or honor or revenge, the things that made your Count of Monte Cristo plummet into the sea and swim for miles and climb out on the rocks to crawl to freedom. There was no one terrific lady waiting, mine are interchangeable; I had no job to go back to, hell, I didn't even have one real reason to go on. The world I came from more or less ran out of higher motives somewhere along the way between then and now and instead everybody is more interested in staying safe and feeling good. This place was not bad, ersatz straw pallet was comfortable and the food was good. If I cracked out I might end up back in the ring with the lions, bleeding to death in three colors for thrill-crazy tourists. There was another thing. They, whoever they were, might want me to escape; it might be part of the show.

All right, one last thing. The terrible truth was, there was no place I wanted to go. I was lying on my (artificial) straw pallet considering all these things when the old man broke into my cell. At least I think it was an old man. I sneaked a look at him. He had backed through a hole in one corner and he was shoving the stone slab back in place. He was too true to life in his tattered prison garments, with the wooden sabots and the straggly white beard; I didn't like the looks of him.

He said, "At last, my efforts have been rewarded."

I lay there with my back turned.

"Twenty years of digging, and nothing to work with but a miserable wooden spoon."

I didn't say anything.

"Twenty years with nothing for company but spiders and the prison rats, nothing to feed on but my memories. Twenty years of bread and silence . . . Are you asleep?"

I didn't say anything.

"Friend." He started shaking my shoulder, trying to get me to turn over. "Friend, why have they put you here? What terrible crime have you been accused of?" After a long time he said, querulously, "I know you're awake."

I was damned if I was going to feed him lines.

"Perhaps they have cut out your tongue for speaking against the throne, but you could write notes, you could at least make motions. Please?"

I waited.

"Quickly, we must exchange knowledge before the guard comes. Come through my tunnel and we can make our escape."

I could feel him hanging over me, trying to stare into my face, but I kept my eyes shut and tried not to twitch.

"We'll hide in the tunnel, when the guard comes in to find out where you have gone we'll rush him and get away." He was snuffling with excitement. "Ah but the cliffs are high and the waters thick with sharks, my friend, we may die on those rocks, or drown . . . "

I willed him to go away.

"Dammit, you're supposed to say, 'Anything is possible.' "

Not me. I was giving nothing. I lay like a stone.

He shook me harder. "'Anything is possible.' Go on. The least you can do is look at me." He poked me a couple of times and then gave up. "This isn't the way it's supposed to go."

I don't know what he expected me to say.

As it turned out, nothing. He was talking to the hidden microphone. "Some vacation this is. Half a mill and he won't even say his lines." He poked me with his toe. "Some prisoner you are."

A voice came over the intercom. "Perhaps you would like to use this opportunity to take out your aggressions, Mr. Kayerts."

"I am not an animal. If this is the best you can do for me, I'm taking the next cutter back to Amsterdam, and I want back every penny I've paid so far."

"This is only the beginning, Mr. Kayerts. We have other adventures planned. In fact if you will go back through the tunnel you can begin the other plotline we have prepared."

"I want you to know I am very unhappy."

"Don't worry, Mr. Kayerts, nobody is unhappy here for long."

What about me?

I wouldn't speak, I was damned if I was going to show myself, either to my friend the dissatisfied customer or the eyes of the monitor or the audience, if there was an audience, either live or watching from the comfort of the cocktail lounge. I had the suspicion that if I wanted to alter my circumstances all I had to do was show a little cooperation, start playing along with whoever fed me lines, or else initiate a little plot myself and my situation would change. They would, what, write bigger and better scenes for me, find a place for me in the organization, I would be their good boy or white hope, at least I would get out of this damn cell, but I had decided early on that I was tired of playing according to other people's plotlines or dancing to their tunes, so I thought: fuck it, and lay still. I was being so still that I was going to start rattling with muscle spasms in another minute, when I heard my friend the customer turn with a resigned sigh and start stuffing himself back in the tunnel. I was relieved, but at the same time I wondered how long I was going to be able to lie there playing dead before reaching the point of diminishing returns. I might even starve to death lying there with my teeth gritted and my back to the camera, and even if I did I would be a show; they would come in every once in a while to dust me and the studio audience could tune in and watch me decompose. I thought it over and after the customer pulled the rock back in place, I rolled over and sat up.

"All right, what do you jerks want?"

There was somebody at my cell door in five minutes.

The conversation was perfunctory. I was to go with the technician, I was to take the holocorder they supplied me out on a job and if I did well, I would survive. If I tried to escape, I would not. It was as simple as that. We went out the front way, down a long dank stone hallway, past all those oaken doors with the slits and the withered hands reaching out, I still didn't know whether those arms were real, and if they were, whether they belonged to masochistic thrill-seekers, who were paying for the privilege, or genuine captives, like me. At the top of the dripping stone steps the door opened on a bright and tidy corridor, lined with office doors. We took a scooter into an elevator and emerged in the equipment sector. He checked out a hand-held holocorder, beautiful, light years ahead of the one Fred had provided for me, which was the most sophisticated on the market.

"Do you know how to use this?"

"Do you know who you're talking to?" I took it from him and settled it on my shoulder, running my fingers over the meters and switches. It was lightweight, stripped-down, smooth. "Where did you get this?"

"It was developed specially for us. When we get to the

scene you're going to frame up what I tell you, and shoot when I say."

I thought I would probably do as I damn pleased but I said, "Sure."

We took another elevator directly to the surface. We came up in the middle of a high hedge maze, within earshot of a hell of a battle. The hedges were so high that there was no seeing over, so I followed the technician around the bends, wondering what would happen if I just brained him with the holocorder and took off. I would get lost in the maze was what would happen, and furthermore I wasn't going to hurt that holocorder because it was a gorgeous piece of equipment, and when I did break out I wanted to take it with me. The maze gave way to a hedge-lined avenue, which brought us closer to the sounds of musketry and war-cries, the *thock* of arrows and an occasional thud, which I think must have been the sound of a tomahawk lodging in somebody's skull.

When we got there, there were only two people left standing, a man in buckskins and a coonskin cap grappling with an Indian who looked as if he might have been recycled from our jungle adventure. The Indian was slight, but stringy, with a cocky look and a fighting style I liked. His opponent was slow, hawking and rattling in frustration as they fought. The technician elbowed me.

"Start shooting."

So I lined up the holocorder and caught the rest of the battle. It looked pretty good for a while, because the Indian got his second wind, and for a minute I thought he was going to win. It looked as if our pioneer was just about to get his, either from the forearm pressed against the windpipe or the knife the Indian had at his back. Just then the settler broke free, and as the Indian let go he wheeled and gave him a feeble push. I distinctly heard the puff of a silenced weapon just before the Indian crumpled.

I put the holocorder down.

"What are you doing? This is good stuff, keep shooting."

"My picture. You quit taking my picture."

"That Indian was deep-sixed."

"Davy Crockett here got him."

"Bullshit, I saw it."

"I got him," the pioneer said, smoothing his buckskin shirt. He had fat cheeks and a big belly, he looked much too clean and well-groomed to be a pioneer at all and there was something else the matter with the picture: he was Japanese.

"He was shot and I saw it."

"No such thing, I killed him with bare hands," Davy said, wiping them on his tailored frontier pants. "And now, please, you will photograph me with trophies." He turned to the technician. "You will help arrange victims, please."

"Certainly." Damn if the technician didn't fall to, lugging Indian and settler corpses out of the stockade to make an artful pile for our oriental Davy Crockett to pose with. "You understand there will be an extra charge for technical assistance during filming."

"Is worth it," said Davy. "Please. I will stand here."

"Wait a minute," I said, "aren't you a little embarrassed?"

The technician turned so I could see he had his hand on his weapon. "All right, Mr. Iwamoto, we're almost ready."

"What is vacation without pictures to show friends?"

"Wait," the technician said. "I have an idea."

"All those killings . . . "

"Friends will be impressed," Davy said. He let the technician drag his last victim out in front and together they laid him out with one knee raised to give height to the composition and both arms stretched above his head as if he had died in the middle of a frontal assault.

"Fine."

"Wonderful."

Davy put one foot on the body and raised his tomahawk.

"Just a little to the left," the technician said. He angled the Indian's head so the 'corder would pick up the death rictus. He backed off and said, "There."

"Shall I smile?"

"You look good just as you are. Good, fine, you're doing fine. This is going to look . . ." He turned to me. I was just standing there. I put the holocorder down. "Why aren't you ready?"

I said, "I think you'd better take me back to jail."

When I woke up there was somebody else with me in the cell. He rolled over in the straw when I came near and his face was alight, but I was not at all sure I was glad to see him. Last time he delivered me to the guards at the edge of the jungle, just part of the show, I guess, and this time there was no telling what he was up to, lying there in the straw with the blood dribbling from the corner of his mouth. For all I knew this was part of some larger plot like the adventure in the pigmy village, a new kick to keep the little bastard entertained. "What are you doing here?"

"Alas, I do not know. But you . . . "

"None of your damn business."

"Boone, my friend." He said the first out loud, because he had already figured out that there was a microphone somewhere in the cell. "Ah, my sandal," he said, loud, for whoever was listening, and then he bent over and pretended to mess with the strap. He was whispering. ("*You have heard, perhaps, of the Man Who Knew Too Much? I think I may be he.*")

("*Not on your life. It's me.*") I matched his whisper even though I didn't know what made him any different from Davy Crockett, back there at the frontier. I said, aloud, "Let me help you with that shoe."

"Thank you, my friend."

(*"Some friend you are, selling me down the river to those goons in purple suits."*)

(*"A thousand pardons, Boone, how was I to know?"*)

We were still pretending to mess with the sandal, which was pretty funny, since he was barefooted. (*"Perhaps together we can escape."*)

(*"How do I know this isn't just another one of your comic book scenes?"*)

(*"You are going to have to trust me, Boone."*)

That was not going to be as easy as he might think. I just shrugged and then waved at the gargoyle carved in a high corner: the camera. He nodded and we both moved out of camera range. Although the gargoyle was fixed in place I could see the camera eye glittering in its mouth; it was trying to locate us even as we crept along the wall. When we reached it, he scrambled onto my shoulders and pried open the gargoyle jaws, which turned out to be plastic. He made it disgorge the mike and disconnected it with my Swiss Army knife. We both knew better than to tamper with the camera so I let him down and we meandered back along the wall and into camera range, Kaa Naaji smoothing his nightshirt and me shaking my trousers so that anybody watching would think we had been taking a piss. Then we both flopped on our pallets with our backs to the camera and feigned sleep. With the mike out of commission, we could talk.

He said, "We work well together."

"What's next on your dance card, escape?"

He said, "You do not trust me."

"Not exactly."

"None of this came out the way they promised. I came here to put an end to being alone and now . . . We might as well be enemies."

"I don't know what you thought you were doing back there in the jungle," I said, "but I know what I thought I was doing. I thought I was trying to escape."

159

"How can I explain what they promised me? I should have known that money does not buy anything, but Boone . . . "

"Customer. You're nothing but a fucking customer." I was thinking of the Jap.

He looked embarrassed. "When you are truly lonely there comes a time when you will do anything to end it. Anything."

"But you must have known this was a fake."

He said, with a certain dignity, "I thought for a while they might maintain an acceptable illusion. What else is left for a scientist whose work is over at thirty? If you must know, I was buying hope." He was getting defensive. "I suppose you came here for some higher reason?"

"You asshole, my cutter crashed. I'm a prisoner."

"Forgive me." His face changed. "Our adventure. I thought it wasn't real. No. I thought it was real and you really needed me. No. I did not know whether it was real or not and at the time it did not matter, I simply enjoyed . . . "

"Who the hell did you think I was?"

"Forgive me, I may have thought you were one of the help." He shook his head. "You understand, I was so sure it would end happily."

"Turns out you were wrong. We're locked in here and they're really watching. Or maybe that's what you ordered, you half-assed two-bit . . . "

"Stop. Please. I would never order your unhappiness."

"You ordered the jungle."

"I never knew at what cost. Oh Castle, somewhere, somehow, we have crossed the line."

"I wish I knew where the line was." Things were blurring now: distinctions between me and him and the Fentons; who were guests and who were prisoners? Maybe he was really a prisoner, like me, and maybe the next stanza would have the two of us making the slide for life.

What if we thought we had made it, we broke out gasping and the studio audience cheered?

Kaa Naaji was saying, "Perhaps I had better tell you about my friend the Sheik Ahmed."

I was looking at him hard, trying to decide what were the differences between him and my Japanese Davy Crockett, whether there were any, but the harder I looked at him the less I knew. "OK," I said at last, "go ahead."

All right, so Ahmed had come to tell him about the big escape attempt, and that was the last thing Kaa Naaji remembered. Did that mean he was on the level? I did not know. He looked really troubled, but was that part of the show? "Why did they try to prevent him?" he said at last.

"Maybe they didn't want him to see her up close." I was thinking of the one that died on me: the wig, the scars behind the ears.

"Perhaps, but it was all he ever wanted."

Poor bastard; if he got up close he would see what she really was. I said, "There are plenty more where she came from."

"Not for Ahmed, he was in love. Do you know what it is like, to be obsessed?"

"Not exactly." Why was that embarrassing? He was *crazy*, while I . . .

"It is to be both brave and frightened, to have blood that runs both hot and cold, to be enflamed by the sight of someone, even the thought of her, and to be rendered miserable by her absence." His head was rolling on the straw. "It is . . . "

"Hey, take it easy."

"Ahmed was like a storm whirling in my room, a cyclone, he was going to escape with her or die in the attempt."

"And you don't know whether he made it."

"We both knew when he left that he wasn't going to make it."

"Then what was the point?"

"There. You see, Boone?"

I was getting mad at him. "See *what?*"

He looked so smug. "You do not understand love."

"Fat lot you know."

"Yes," he said, picking at the straw. "Fat lot. Boone, I think Ahmed and his beloved are dead."

"If we could get out maybe we could . . . " I thought twice and shut up. For all I knew the little bastard was proceeding according to a script.

"I am not prepared to leave yet, even knowing what I do." He looked at me with a mixture of expressions. "I must stay in Happy Habitat until I can find her. Boone, I am in love."

"Courtesy of the management, no doubt."

He shook his head. "This is my thing. Mine. Will you break out with me and help me find her?"

"Why should I do anything for you?" I let him dangle. I thought I probably did trust him up to a point and even if I didn't it was going to be less boring than spinning out my days in this cell. When I thought he was just about to fly into pieces I said, "OK. Look, I probably ought to show you something. It may be our ticket out." I rolled over slowly, for the sake of the camera, and fished out the note I had stuck in my boot. "A woman guard laid this on me when they first put me here. What do you think?"

"STAY LOOSE AND I'LL COME FOR YOU. What does this mean?"

"It means we may have some help getting out."

"You say a woman guard gave it to you."

"Don't get excited, I don't think we can count on it."

"That's not it." His voice leapt. "Castle, my beloved is a guard also. Perhaps this is she."

"Not a chance." I remembered her face and laughed. "This one looks like a bullfrog on a bad night."

"Then she can't be the same," he said. "Mine was beautiful."

'I don't care, it may be a way out."
"So you intend to wait."
"Kaa Naaji, I intend to go back to sleep."

Evaline

Imagine me getting old, me that fought so hard against it. What did I think I was going to get if I stayed young? I guess I thought all along that there was a great big block party going on somewhere without me, if I looked hard enough I might stumble into it, but now I don't know. There probably never was one and if there was I don't want that now. All I want to do is go where Val went, wherever it was, and if it is not oblivion after all, then he and I will be together forever and that will be a very nice surprise. But first I have things to do.

Meanwhile I lie here gathering strength for the escape, and people come. The attendants don't like it because the pretense is that we are all always young here at Golden Acres, and I no longer look the part. Why are all the Oldies but Goodies drawn to me? They have been coming all morning, I never thought there would be so many. I used to see my own kids getting old and want to turn away, but now that I have become that which we all ran so hard and paid so much to escape, all the others want to come and look at me. As they talk they finger my infirmary robe and when they get up to go they all find ways to touch my hand. Do they think that just because my hair is grey I know more than they do? Do they think the sliding wrinkles and the water collecting in my eyes make me wiser, or am I getting old *for* them, instead of them? Maybe I am a sacred object they can touch to ward off things.

Blanche was the first. She looked in my face and said, "My God, Evvy, is that you?"

I said, "Who the hell did you think it was?"

"Oh Evvy, you let it happen."

"What's the matter with that?"

She said, "Don't die."

"I'm not about to."

"That's what Ashby said, she left last night with that Arab who wanted her and now . . . She gave me something to hold, Ev, she thought I could give it to her family, but I would never . . . "

I said, "Shh." They have darkened the mirror wall so none of the audience will have to look at me, but there are still microphones. She was pressing something into my hand: a packet, a letter with Ashby's wedding rings.

"I don't know what you are planning, but if you go, will you take these with you?"

I nodded and now I have one more thing to hold. I looked at her standing there in her bikini with the glitter shrug; lord she looked pretty but I knew how much had gone into it, the lifts, the pills, the exercise and starvation and I thought, none of that matters, we are both of us going to end in the same place. I said, "I'll do what I can."

She said, "I don't know what is going to happen to me."

I pressed her hand and she slipped several caps into mine.

When she left the others came bundling in, all old and tricked out in their glitter suits that they kept pulled tight over tits and ass, they said, "I hate seeing you that way," and each one slipped me some caps, maybe they thought if I popped them I wouldn't have to look like this. I thanked them all and stored the caps in my bra. They were more comfortable talking to each other and I looked at their tight faces, their smooth bellies and wondered why they bothered, what kept them from seeing the differences between their bodies and the bodies of the attendants, that were truly young, and then I looked at the attendants, their stupid unlined faces and I thought: I

164

wouldn't swap. We don't know much, but when we were young we didn't know *anything*.

The old men were quieter; they didn't mind as much, maybe they looked at me and saw their mothers, or maybe they saw themselves.

One said, "I heard from my kids today."

I said, "I haven't heard a word from mine, not since they . . ."

"Sold you down the river?"

"Yes. No. Partly."

When he smiled I could see that his eyes were watering, same as mine. "That's all right, you're not the only one. We've all had our turn, I would just as soon make it a good show." He had on a flying jacket and a scarf, like Errol Flynn's in *Dawn Patrol*, he was just about to fly. He looked snappy, brave. As he got up to leave he said, "I don't know if you should have let yourself go."

I couldn't let him know I had a plan. I just said, "What's it to you?"

"You, um, uh." He was trying to find some way to spare my feelings. "What will people think? I mean what happened to your, um."

"Resort wardrobe?"

He snapped right back. "Your pride."

"Oh," I said and I stared at him then; I stared hard. "I don't know about you, but I still have my pride."

I could see his face changing, light dawning. "You mean, make them take you as you are."

"Or not at all." Then I made a mistake; I pulled him closer and told him part of it. "If you're ugly they won't make you work."

"You mean no more flying?" He meant: no more dying. "Shhhh."

It was already too late; they were listening. I thought: what the hell, and told him anyway. As he left he was humming the end of that song they sing in the flight room, "Hurrah for the next one that dies." I guess I knew he was my last visitor but I didn't care, by that time I had collected enough caps to last for days, and by the time the caps are gone, I will be too.

The management set a guard on me.

Brute young thing she is, plain and big-bodied, strong enough to win battles and fight our way out of here, but she is being paid to keep me here. I think I remember her from somewhere, yesterday morning at the Spanish Civil War? If she knows me she won't acknowledge it, just sits there tilting back in her chair with her thick red hair hanging and her boots set against the foot of the bed. She keeps her weapon on her knees and looks over it at me, filing her nails. Lying here in the bed I think: I am never going to get out past that. I try a little something.

"They must think I'm pretty special."

"What?"

"Assigning somebody like you."

"What's that supposed to mean?" She looks ready to spring either way: she can be flattered or she can slap me down.

"You're too important to be stuck in here with a poor helpless old lady, unless they think there's something to be afraid of."

"Never mind what they think." She is squinting; she doesn't know what they think.

I say, "You must have better things to do."

"Maybe I do," she says, "but I'm the only one they can trust to do the job."

"Some job."

"They're all spaced out to Sunday down there, no discipline in this place. Whole operation is going to hell."

"Do we dare hope?"

"Shut up," she says, and raises the gun to make it stick.

I am already calculating. How to win her confidence? Can I get her to leave me for a minute, or turn her back so I can make my break? I have no idea what she is thinking, tilting back like that, whistling through her teeth. The muzzle is moving slightly and I see it is not carelessness on her part but rather she is taking my outline. What does she see? My eyes, that are still good; the bony structure; the body that remembers love? She is measuring, trying to figure something out, and then I don't know whether her face is changing or I only imagine it; she is thinking hard. What? If I can find out, it may help me make my escape.

"Was that you yesterday, in the Spanish Civil War?"

"What if it was?"

"I guess you and that guy were really in love." She runs one hand along her hair and it is a gesture I remember: one of my own, before an assignation.

So I have a clue. I roll my head on the pillow and murmur Val's name.

"What did you say?"

"Nothing."

"I heard you, you said his name."

I am filled with him but I say, "That's no concern of yours."

"Maybe not," she says, "but I don't like it."

"Why not?" It reminds her of something she doesn't want to think about; some source of weakness. Can she be in love? I lower my voice, trying to be confidential. "What's bothering you?"

She stirs the covers with a dart and snaps, "Never mind."

I leave her to think for a few minutes and then I begin again, partly to see what she is made of, partly because it eases my heart to talk. "Have you ever loved a man so much you would do anything for him?"

She squints and ducks her head. There is a curious flicker in her eyes as she says, "You might not know it to look at me but I am married." Pause. "Was married."

"And you would die for him?"

"Not exactly." Yes, her big face is touched with a look of regret.

So I have her. "Then you haven't lived."

"Wait a minute," she says. "There is somebody that I

would . . . that I. Dammit to hell I don't have time for that."

"A handsome-looking woman like you." It is not exactly a lie. She has the look of one of those old-time figure-heads, wooden and chunky, strong. "It's too bad."

"You don't think I'm, uh, ah . . . not up to standard, I mean, the management . . . " She is blushing.

"You have a lot of potential." I want to be kind.

"I've got my career to think of. No time for that. It saps your strength."

"My dear, career isn't everything."

This time she hits back. "It lasts longer than good looks."

Aha. "But not as long as love."

I pretend to sleep, knowing that I have left her to think about him, whoever he may be. I guess it is too much for her; she sighs heavily and lets her feet drop to the floor, clank. I say Val's name once more, to keep her thinking and when I open my eye a crack I see she has raised the gun; she is just about to fire, anything to shut me up. She barks: "What do you mean, it's too bad?"

"Simple. You look made for love."

"Shut up." She sends a tranquilizer dart through my sleeve. I know enough to pretend it has hit me; I start and fall back, listening as she punches in to Central and tells them she has me out cold and is going for a break. This is all I ever wanted. I loll on the pillow while she inspects me, breathing heavily into my face. She lets my limp arm drop and gives the bed a pat. "Now don't go 'way."

I don't know who she thinks she loves or where he is but I will bet eight dollars she has gone to look for him.

Boone Castle

Kaa Naaji. What does he want from me?

I get this feeling we have backed into an empire movie,

Gunga Din or something worse, or else the basic comic book setup from the dawn of superheroes, I am supposed to be the big man in this case and he is going to be my sidekick. We will go everywhere together, we are supposed to be friends. I am supposed to help him crack out, fighting shoulder to shoulder if necessary, and together we are going to go in search of his fantastic woman, prying her loose from the clutches of, what, the management? just in time for the great escape. There is this problem: I don't want to be anybody's hero. Furthermore I cannot shake the idea that this is one of their storylines, being played out for somebody else's satisfaction. What's in it for me? A day's occupation, maybe, a little tinny applause. I don't necessarily want to turn my face to the wall but I would like, just this once, to sidestep what is expected.

I seem to remember him shaking me and me turning over, diving back into sleep. I woke up at last because I couldn't help it; my back hairs were crawling the way they do when you know there is somebody watching you breathe. I rolled over and there he was, squatting patiently in the straw, just waiting.

"Perhaps now," he said.

"Now what?"

"It is morning. Let's escape."

"I don't know."

"Perhaps you think it is too hard. My friend, nothing is too hard when you are in the right."

I yawned and sat up. As soon as I did he started talking, filling the cell with his plans until they crowded me, cluttering up the straw. "I don't know what you think you're doing."

He was burrowing in one corner of the cell, hacking at the mortar with his Swiss Army knife. "Trying to get out."

"You don't even know if this is real."

He sat back on his heels. "Of course it is real, my friend. This bruise on my arm is proof positive."

"It could be makeup."

"Oh come on, Boone. At least give it a chance."

So we tore up the place. Between us, we tried everything: prying at the bars, calling a guard so we could trick
him (nobody came), playing out a murder-suicide for the
camera so we could jump the cleanup squad (still nobody
came), rattling our cups against the bars in hopes of
arousing the other prisoners (were there any?), prying at
the back wall with belt-buckles and fingernails. Nothing
worked. I had a nagging suspicion that we were doing all
the right things to please the management or was it the
studio audience, and if there wasn't an audience there
was still Kaa Naaji. Even after everything we'd been
through I couldn't shake the idea that we were in one of
his prepaid Dial-a-Plots, but there he was ripping his
fingernails on the fake rocks and urging me on like a
trouper, so who knew? I didn't know anything any more,
and after we had finished setting fire to our straw pallets
and stamping it out when that didn't work either, I told
myself this could conceivably be the real thing, because it
didn't come off according to design, like the rescue from
the pigmy village or the killing of the water buffalo. It
didn't come off at all.

Nothing happened.

"We must be doing something wrong." Kaa Naaji was
fretting. "There must be something we have missed."

I watched him try each of the possible exits without
success and found it strangely reassuring. If he was for
real after all, maybe we could really escape. I could find a
way to dismember the camera and use the innards to
make a handy weapon or a torch that might work on the
hinges. If nothing else, taking out the camera would bring
the guards, we could jump them and get away. I had devised two or three alternate designs, I was on the verge of
having to get up and get started; Kaa Naaji was musing on
his pallet, when the back door to the cell popped open
and we both stood up.

There she was, as advertised in my note: the big old funny-looking guard who stashed me in here and stuck the note in my boot, she was standing in the opening with this big grin on her frog face; I was about to turn to Kaa Naaji and say, I told you it couldn't be the same lady guard, but I didn't get the chance because people were saying. "I told you I'd come," and "I knew you'd come," and rushing forward with their arms out at which point other people were supposed to melt into them except nothing was working right because Kaa Naaji was barreling into her like a half-assed Romeo at the same time that she was pushing a hand into his face and heading for me.

So there we were in the morning light, at least I think it was the morning light: he was, I was, she was—that brute lady, scowling and turning those headlight eyes on me; the glow was embarrassing. She was advancing with her arms out, crunching over the straw like an updated Godzilla with those beams trained on my face and I was thinking: boy, got to dim those. Kaa Naaji was inching up to get as close to her as he could, if he was really lucky she might accidentally step on him so he would get to touch her after all. She didn't even see him, she just stood there waiting for me to fall on her neck and when I didn't she stuck her chin out and snarled: "What's the matter with you?"

"What?"

"I—thought you would . . . " (she was so embarrassed she was angry) "be glad to see me."

"Hell yes I'm glad to see you." I tried to sound businesslike: just us chaps together. "What's the plan?"

She fell back a step, accidentally mashing Kaa Naaji. She brushed him off and he looked at her adoringly. "Plan?" Her chin started shaking and I was pretty sure she had come in here without any plan, beyond clamping those arms around me and the two of us falling down together in the straw, which was out of the question because I wasn't playing and furthermore there was Kaa

171

Naaji, languishing at her elbow, the extra wheel. "I thought you needed me."

"Hell yes, we need help getting out."

"That wasn't what I had in mind." She was getting mad. What was I supposed to do, carry her off to some damn bower? It was scary, looking into her face and seeing exactly how much she expected. Another time, in another year, hell, maybe even last week I would have made it with her because that was what she expected, never mind what I wanted, it would just be easier than having to play the scene, but I was done doing what was expected just because it was expected and besides I couldn't do that to Kaa Naaji, who was about to faint from woe and unrequited love.

I said, "Look, whoever you are . . . "

"Luce Finley."

"Luce, I'd like you to meet a friend of mine."

"Little creep."

"You might get to like him, there's more to him than you might think."

Kaa Naaji touched her arm. "If you will let me try."

She swung like a turnstile, catching him with her elbow. "Get away."

I couldn't stand his naked crazy pain, it put me back in all those old movies I had to look at for my dissertation, with the sidekick who never got the girl. Maybe I could deliver her to him as a going away present. I needed both of them for the escape. "It's going to take three of us to do what we have to do."

She couldn't quit scowling. "I guess you're right."

"Beware."

"What?"

He didn't have to say it again. By the time Luce and I had turned to see where he was pointing, Kaa Naaji was grappling with the guard who had plunged through the opening in the back wall. The two of them were rolling in the straw, the guard cursing and trying to get at his weapon and the crazy little Indian all arms and legs, twining around him and ready to fight to the death. Luce aimed her own weapon at the tangle and when the black-clad rump rolled to the top of the mixup she fired.

Kaa Naaji kept on struggling even after the guard went limp. I tapped him on the shoulder. "It's OK."

"Have I subdued him?"

I said, "He's out cold."

"And I did it?"

"In a manner of speaking." He was looking from me to Luce, who was putting away her weapon. He needed praise so I said, "Hell yes, you did it."

"Not bad for one reared in the tradition of passive resistance."

"You were terrific. Right Luce?" I glowered until she answered.

"Have it your way," she said grudgingly. "Now, are we getting out of here or not?"

"All three of us?"

She looked at us. I straightened his funny-looking shirt and brushed him off, trying to make us look like a united front. Finally she said, "Yeah, shit. All three of us," and the three of us ducked through the hole in the back of the cell.

The corridor looked like all the others; I had no way of knowing how many cross-hatched above and below us, or where any of them went, so I picked a direction at random and started to run. I was just hitting my stride when Luce grabbed my shirt.

"Wait up."

"Got to hurry. The guards."

"What guards?" She shished me.

I realized I didn't hear anything. "Where is everybody?"

"I think they're running out of guards. The ones I saw

173

are all too busy puking and snorting to do any work." She saw Kaa Naaji blanch and said, "Pardon my French. Truth is, they're short staffed."

I was thinking about all my maneuvers back there in the cell. "So there were no guards in the Chateau d'If?"

"Only the one I iced."

"Wait." Why did that make me mad?

"Practically everybody there is stuffed."

"What about the monitors?"

"Who watches?"

I thought about those holiday sightseers riding past the Fenton Family. Voyeurs. Rich bastards. "You mean nobody in power."

"Think what you want." She started off at a right angle from the course I had chosen, and as I went along behind her I found an old thought repeating, sour as a belch.

What if this is all part of their game?

I said, "How do I know you're not one of them?"

"What in hell's the matter with you? What do you want?"

"I want out." I thought: *That isn't it.* I was remembering the Fentons, stashed like puppets in a box; I was remembering the selfstyled Oriental Davy Crockett, the so-called Indians he had shot, real blood; I was thinking about the way I had been manipulated, gawked at, jerked around and used ever since the cutter crashed and I said, "I want to get out and put an end to this."

She stopped cold. "End it? Man, together, we can run this place."

"I wouldn't be caught dead."

"Run it. You and me. From the top."

"Luce, real people are getting hurt."

Kaa Naaji had been touching my arm. Now he gave it a jerk. "My friend, you are about to be one of them."

I turned and saw that he was right. Behind us in the corridor there was a dull beam approaching; as I watched it got closer and separated into headlights, bearing down on us. I just stood there, starfishing in the approaching light, but Luce was already in action, shoving Kaa Naaji and me into a doorway and lobbing a grenade. As it exploded she hurled herself into us, throwing us all into a niche as smoke puffed in the corridor and the lights went out.

I said, "Where are we?"

"Guard's station, they'll never look for us here."

There were sounds in the corridor outside: outraged yells, drumming feet. "I hope you're right."

"We'll lie low until this blows over. Then we can get moving. You and me."

"What makes you think I'm going to help?"

"You have to if you want out." She went on slowly. "You can forget about blowing this place up or whatever it was you had in mind. You can play it my way or we won't play at all." She made swatting noises in the dark. Kaa Naaji yipped. "Get your hands off me, you little creep."

"Shut up, they'll hear us."

"Then tell your little friend to keep his hands off."

Luce

I thought when I got him in the dark he might forget what I looked like and go on smell, feel, good old personal magnetism, we were all three crammed in the guard's niche at such close quarters that all I could think about was how close we were, I couldn't keep my mind on anything. I thought maybe he would be feeling likewise but all the bastard wanted to do was sit there pretending we weren't touching and talking about ways to get away. So we sat around listening to the guards' feet rushing just outside the door and batting it back and forth, putting together what we knew, which wasn't much, while he kept asking tough questions and I kept finding it harder and harder to answer because all I could really think about was him and how all my dreams were going glimmering, all that hard work and scrambling for the top, and all because of him.

Then I thought : OK, Luce, you are the guard, you are the one with the weapon, you are not going to throw it all away just for a fresh-faced jerk but maybe you can get this jerk to go along with you. He keeps trying to get me to say that once we break out we are going to get to the heart of the operation and end it, blow this place off the map, which just goes to show that men are all weaklings in the long run, but I guess if you really love a person you are willing to tolerate a little mush. I let him think that is an interesting idea because I figure we are in this together and we might as well get as far as we can together, but I also figure when it comes to a showdown I will win out, when we get to the front office or the nerve center or whatever it is I will say, Boone, here are the keys to this place, I am giving it to you on a platter. All right, won't he love me then, and isn't he going to be grateful? I don't know, wish to hell I did. I say:

"Together we can run this place." I will make him think he is fucking King Arthur.

"Together we can blow it off the map."

I lay back and think for a minute, and when the answer comes it surprises even me, because the echoes go back for generations. I say, "We'll see."

Doesn't he just draw in his breath then.

Better say something to lull him, give him a role he can fall into. We can be enemies until I hand him this place on a plate. "I think you had better play along with me." My voice gets even harder. "I am the guard, remember?"

"I guess I owe you one."

I can feel the currents going through my belly. I come on tough. "Keep it in mind, right? If you don't I will turn you in "

"You can't afford to."

So I have him. "But you can't afford to find out the hard way."

He doesn't argue. Now I know we are in it together.

Meanwhile the little Indian is crawling up my back, I can't stand another minute in the closet. I say, "I can't stand another minute in this closet."

When we crack the door and peek out, the hallway is empty. If there were any guards they are gone now, at least I think they are. We are all out in the open, stretching and blinking, when the drumming starts, guards approaching in a flying wedge, a tight unit that comes down on us with weapons and nooses.

Think fast, Luce.

The companionway. I manage to gather both of them and shove them into the niche and get them started up the ladder.

Boone says, "What about you?"

Oh, do you mean it? Really? I am about to melt again when I realize what a damn fool thing this is, it was sex that brought down Samson and a couple of million other people, one kind word and I am ready to forget what I am doing.

"Get your ass up there," I say, and I give him a belt to remind myself who I am. "We're going to be safer on the surface."

"How are you going to . . . "

"I'll hold them off. I've got grenades."

"Wait a minute."

"I'm OK," I said. "Get going."

Outtakes

"Once more into the breach, dear friends, and my apologies for calling you all together so early, but as some of you already know, things are not going one hundred per cent according to plan, and there are a few matters we are going to have to discuss."

"Hi, what's going on?"

"Sit down, Corky. You're late."

("And hung over, too, you're a disgrace to the uniform."

"Shut up, Gayle.")

"Now, as I was saying, I do want you to know that we have things under control, but it's never too soon to face facts, and it has always been axiomatic here at Happy Habitat that, if you deal with contingencies in time, they will never become emergencies."

("What's going on?"

"What rock have you been under? She's been talking about the escape.")

"First, I want to congratulate you *all* on covering so magnificently and now let's see whether we can find a way to turn all this to our advantage. Now . . . "

("What's she talking about?"

"If you hadn't been stone drunk you'd know. A guard broke into the prison setting and took out one of Jimmy's

181

live exhibits, that Boone Castle, along with a paying guest, a live one."

"Why not just let them go?")

"Corky, if you have something to say, say it to the group. You know as well as anybody here why we can't just let them go. You might as well know that the paying guest is a leading scientist, one we had earmarked for Phase Four."

"Who blew it?"

"If you want to know what I think, I think it was Jimmy's error, him with his damn live exhibits. Hubris."

"They're raking in a fortune, Dante, and I'll thank you not to try to shift the blame. Where were you when that guard took off?"

"Children. It's too late for recriminations."

"If you'll allow me, Dearest, I'd like to follow this through because it touches on an important point. I'll tell you exactly where I was, Jimmy, I was trying to get my staff together, and I'll tell you about that. When I took over the expanded staffing I thought I was going to have a staff to work *with*, but no matter how many I process we are always short-handed because you and all the other empire builders are bent on expanding without once looking into the matter of means."

"Now Dante, if that concludes your report . . . "

"Wait a minute, I'm not finished. There are not enough guards to go around. By the time I've finished staffing all the traditional surface operations, that made the name and fame of Happy Habitat, I am hard-pressed to staff your undercover operations, plus which Jimmy here has been stretching the limits of his live exhibits, siphoning my people off, in addition to which . . . "

"Wait a minute, Dante. I only have two live exhibits going, that is, in addition to Operating Theater, which simply uses patients who come to us via illness or accident or exigencies of plot. What's more the crew of the X-9 in real-life survival conditions have all contracted some plague and are dying off so in a short time I am going to be left with the Fenton Family, which means I am going to be down to one. One, that is, plus whatever we can get going with this new escape, which I personally think we can turn to our advantage."

"If you want to know what I think, I think that would be playing with fire. I think we ought to snuff them and let it go at that."

"You would say that, Corky, because you don't want to cover. Now as I suggested earlier, these live exhibits are pulling bigger crowds than the rest of the operation put together, and with that in mind I think we ought to cash in on this escape. If we can put cameras on these people, make tapes to replay later, I think we can clean up. If we can locate these people, we might even get the audience to where they're going to be . . . "

"That's the trouble, Jimmy, nobody knows for sure because Dante doesn't have enough staff to keep track."

"Corky, stop hanging crepe. Dante can handle it. Right, Dan?"

"I can't Jimmy, and that's the truth. The riffraff you've been recruiting just can't do the job."

"I don't understand, Dante. I gave you carte blanche."

"Yes, Dearest, and I think that was the mistake. As you all know, all recruiting for the surface operation has been from the front ranks: honor students, Misses America, but when we entered, ah, the new phase in the operation, we had to go for a different type."

"People with nothing to lose."

"Precisely. Now, I guess we are discovering that these people who have nothing to lose really don't give a shit."

"Dante!"

"It's the truth, Dearest. They don't care about money or advancement, they are heavily committed to self-gratification at the expense of the operation. They only care about themselves. How can you give orders to people like that and make it stick? If you want to know the truth, unless we solve this problem and solve it soon, we are all going to hell in a handbasket and that's the truth."

"Enough. I will appoint a committee to look into the long range problem."

"I'm saying this is an immediate problem. We have this problem now."

"At the moment, Dante, we are going to have to deal with the matter at hand."

"And I'm trying to tell you we don't have the means."

"We are going to deal with it in any case. Now children, the question at hand is, are we going to stop this escape or are we going to cash in on it?"

"I think it's going to bring us nothing but trouble."

"I say Corky is begging off because he doesn't want to write continuity."

"I side with Jimmy. Corky is bugging out."

"Wrong, Gayle, Corky knows as well as I do we don't have the staff. I vote that we snuff them."

"And write off all that extra income?"

"Better safe than sorry, Gayle."

"I'd like a show of hands now. For letting it run? Against? Thank you. I'd say the group is more or less evenly divided, which, I suppose, means that as your leader's deputy I am to cast the deciding vote, and in doing so I want you to understand that I do not only represent myself in this matter, I am also speaking for *him*, for whom we are doing this, and I think *he* would want . . . "

"Yes?"

"I think he would want us to go ahead."

*   *   *

"Oh Fred, that was nice last night. Are you sure the cameras were off?"

"Positive. And even if they weren't . . . "

"Oh Fred."

"Don't be embarrassed, sweetie. The poor world has little enough pleasure, and if we can set a good example, or raise a few spirits along the way . . . "

"I suppose you're right."

"Of course I'm right, and furthermore, when we go home, we get to keep the wardrobes, plus they are going to give us prints of every foot of film . . . "

"What if we don't get to go home?"

"Don't be ridiculous. We're going to go down in the history books. When we get home we can write our experiences, and spin off that into books about our thoughts on life. Now give me a kiss."

"All right."

"That's better. What's for breakfast?"

"Scrambled eggs."

"That's wonderful."

"On English muffin halves."

"What else are we having?"

"Ham, and grapes to begin. Look Fred, real grapes."

"Imagine that. I don't think I've ever seen . . . "

"Hi, Mom. What's for breakfast?"

"Scrambled eggs."

"Scrambled eggs, yeugh."

"Jack, get your hands out of the grapes."

"What else?"

"Ham and English muffins."

"Then why can't I go ahead and eat my . . . "

"Because the table isn't set."

"Hi Mom, what's for breakfast?"

"Scrambled eggs."

"Scrambled eggs, yeugh."

"Can't I fix *anything* around here without somebody going yeugh?"

"Do I have to eat mine?"

"If you want any grapes."

"Hey, Mom, what's for breakfast?"

"I already told you, I . . . "

185

"Hey, Dottie, don't cry."

"I'm sorry, it's just nerves."

"Your face is getting all blotchy."

"I'm sorry, I just can't . . . "

"Don't cry, honey, remember, they are watching."

"Oh . . . Fred . . . for a minute I forgot. Yes, all right. Does my hair look OK?"

"You know you always look beautiful to me."

* * *

"Chalmers, the skipper's dead."

"He can't be."

"He is, I just felt his pulse and he's . . . well . . . "

"I guess I should have known."

"What are we going to do?"

"Pull yourself together, Jake. We have to carry on."

"But Chalmers."

"Steady, Jake. It's what one does."

"Right, stiff upper lip, steady on."

"Jake?"

"Yes, Chalmers?"

"I'm afraid it's just you. You're going to have to carry on."

"Don't die, Chalmers. Please don't leave me. Promise."

"I'll try to hold on."

"How long have we been floating on this godforsaken raft?"

"I don't know, Jake, when people started dying I lost track."

"I'm so *hungry*."

"I must be dying. I've stopped being hungry. Jake . . . "

"Yes, Chalmers?"

"There's something you ought to know."

"Yes?"

"Back there, when the food ran out? I was hungry, I

knew I was starving, Jake, I kept looking around at them, I thought we might . . . you know."

"You mean eat them?"

"Only the dead. How can I forgive myself?"

"Chalmers, don't torture yourself. All that is gone and done with, and if it makes you feel any better to know it, you might as well know that you're not the only one. Even the Captain started looking good to me, all that meat on him, but I have pushed his body overboard and so . . . But look, this is going to have to be our secret, Chalmers, yours and mine, and if we ever get out of this and back to civilization it's going to have to stay our secret, we're going to have to swear to keep it to ourselves. Maybe we'd better swear right now, we'll make a pledge and seal it, Chalmers, silence to the . . .

"Death?

"Chalmers?

"Chalmers!

"Oh my God, Chalmers, what am I going to do?"

*　*　*

"Oh look, Wataru, poor man is all alone now on the raft, how very very sad. Perhaps we can have a copter come in and save him."

"Ah, Mari, I am checking the terminal and I find rescue is not one of the options on my card."

"Not at any price? If it is money my dearest husband, I wish to save him, no matter what the cost, I will turn over to you the contents of my numbered Swiss bank account."

"Is not money, Mari. Rescue is not one of the options, not at any price."

"Oh Wataru, how sad. What a sad ending for such a happy holiday, to see the man who we have been watching in such suffering. My darling, are you sure?"

"Only choice left between shark attack, quick and merciful, or boredom and loneliness, the drinking of sea water, madness and subsequent death. Mari, what shall we?"

"Please, my husband, he has been so brave, can we not have him commit hara kiri?"

"I have checked my card, Mari, that is not one of the options."

"Sharks then, my love. The last of the crew of the X-9, sailing with the dead. Oh Wataru, I do not like this show."

"Sharks, then, Mari. I shall order it at once."

* * *

"All right, Dearest, why have you called me in?"

"It's about the drinking, Cork. In front of all those people, after all the pains we have taken to keep our existence secret to protect our secret plan."

"You ask me to work in the dark and then you wonder why I want to go out and get drunk with the ordinary folks?"

"You know I can't tell you anything about Phase Four."

"Then you had better look the other way when I get drunk. Eight thousand facets to the operation, and I am supposed to keep track and write continuity. That Ahmed thing was bad enough, and then Simpson, planning his heart attack . . . "

"What have you done about Ahmed?"

"Told his retinue he died of plague. I even got Jimmy's people to scrape the ashes off the shield, so they could take home some cremains . . . "

"Excellent."

"But this escape thing. The flyers, the animated previews, half the time I can't even keep track."

"Nonsense, you're doing fine."

"Bull crap he is."

"Dante! I thought I told you never to bother me here."

"Sorry, Dearest. Emergency. One of the Oldies but Goodies is on the loose."

"You'd better get on it, Cork."

"Can't you see I've had it? Now get off my back."

"Dearest, I think it's time to end it."

"We can't, Dante. Pa would never . . . Besides, we need the revenue."

"But that's four runaways. What if they get together? What if they really get away?"

"Nobody has made it out yet boys, so relax."

"We've never been pushed to the limit before. My staff isn't up to it. Do you realize what could happen to the operation if these people really make it out? They could bring the roof in on us."

"I can't terminate, not without *his* permission, and you know how he is . . . "

"Dammit, *he* got us into it, him with his grandiose—it's damn well time to bother him."

"All right, boys, I'll try."

* * *

"Wonderful lunch, Dottie. Dottie, there's something I have to . . . "

"I'm so glad you enjoyed it, Fred."

"Darling."

"Oh Fred. This whole experience has made such a difference in our relationship—even with the cameras. Oh Fred, when we get home . . . "

"Ah, Dottie, about home . . . "

"What's the matter, Fred? What are you getting at?"

"The doors won't open. I can't get them to open the doors."

"Why we can leave any time, it's in our contract."

"Oh Dottie, I'm not so sure."

* * *

I told you we should have saved our money for the Out of this World Extravaganza instead of coming *here*. Or we

189

could have gone to Lawton's Lamasery, vacationed with the Dalai Lama."

"You said you didn't like Tibet."

"Maybe, but all these deaths are just tacky, it's all so, I don't know, it's just a flop."

"Madam, please, we want only happy customers here. Come into the consultatron and we will make up a program that will satisfy your every . . . "

"Forget it. I want my money back."

* * *

" . . . *to the land of fulfillment beyond all fulfilling . . .* "

"Stevens, what is this thing?"

"A messenger brought it. I think it's from Happy Habitat."

" . . . *power over life and death.*"

"Well get it out of here, I've heard nothing but bad things about that place."

* * *

"Oh Wataru, if this is the land of heart's desiring, why am I so sad?"

"Perhaps, my dearest, this place is not all it is cracked up to be."

* * *

"The Fenton Family was really boring today."

"I don't know, I kind of liked it."

"Tomorrow let's watch something else."

* * *

"I told you never to bother me."

190

"This is an emergency."

"Dearest, you know I have to conserve my strength."

"You can't possibly know what I've gone through for you."

"Stop crying and get on with it."

"First it was the kids, and now the customers are getting out of hand, the reservations have dropped off, and oh . . . "

"How about the live exhibits."

"That's what I've come about. We've sold secondary rights to the Survivors of the X-9 and the Fenton Family is being syndicated and now we have a new thing going, the Terrible Threesome escape, except Dante says now it's the Fearsome Foursome, and oh, Pa . . . I'm scared to death they're going to get away. The audience potential is enormous, but oh, Pa, I think we ought to terminate."

"I'll think it over."

"But Pa!"

"You heard what I said."

Boone

When I last saw her she had dropped into a crouch at the bottom of the ladder and was firing around a corner. I thought I ought to be down there helping, mixing it up with the guards, but she wasn't having that, she said she was going to be OK.

She was, too. By the time she came panting up the ladder Kaa Naaji had found a lemonade fountain and by brute force wrenched it loose from its moorings. As soon as Luce cleared the hatch and sprawled in the grass we took the fountain, which was in the shape of a spurting conch shell, and dragged it, pipes and all, to stuff it into the opening. I could hear the first guard up the ladder sputtering and cursing as the stream of lemonade reached him and then a series of shouts and thuds as the thing broke loose from its moorings and crashed down the hatch, taking everybody with it. We locked the hatch cover and lay back in the grass.

I said to Luce, "How long do we have?"

"Not long enough."

The grass we lay in was perfect, every blade like every other blade. The hedges in the park were holding hands like marching children and above us the trees spread more like umbrellas than living things. If that was sky and not a dome above us it was also flawless; there was even a light breeze. There were neat little walks paved with bits of colored glass and if I rolled on my belly I could see a water fountain like a flower and at a distance, gigantic bunny-rabbits making laps for people to cuddle in. It wasn't real countryside or even my idea of country but someone else's concept, your ideal countryside, everything placed just so—for what?

We were in the country of an imagination that I didn't much like because it presupposed something about me, that I would be pleased by it, impressed; all those artificial plants and flowers were saying, *look at all the trouble the management has gone to for your pleasure, see how much we care, for you. Now do as we say.* Yeah, shit, but wasn't it Hitler who made those terrific roads? I knew all that order and comfort was supposed to make me happy and peaceful, all that nature suppressed, but I knew I wasn't safe. For the moment I stayed where I was, trying to catch my breath and figure out what we had come up into—which part of Happy Habitat this was, and where we could go from here.

Luce was saying, "We can't stay here."

Kaa Naaji's voice melted all over, like caramel. He said, "As you wish."

What was he doing? I turned my head and saw that he was sitting up and looking at her, he was ready to spend all week sitting there in the deep grass watching, never mind who saw, he was going to sit there grooving on her militant profile until a guard spotted him and blew his head off, if he thought that was what she wanted it would make him perfectly happy. I yanked his arm. "Get down." Luce said, "Never mind, it's too late. They're coming."

I parted the long grass and looked where she was pointing. At first I didn't see them at all. All I saw was a rinkytinky band coming along the avenue, everybody happily thumping and tweeting, and behind them I could see a Chinese dragon weaving in the street. The parade was surrounded by a crowd of carefree vacationers waving New Year's Eve rattles and fuming sticks of punk; they had on funny hats and everybody looked drunk and giggly, so swept up in the parade that I was sure the whole thing was going to pass us by.

Then Luce grabbed my arm, hissing, "The feet, the feet."

She was right after all. It was an epic Chinese dragon, all silk and banners and glits and gaudy paint, and the people running along beside it were innocent enough, happy customers all capering in their resort wardrobes without a care for anything but the music and getting their money's worth, but when I looked down I saw that the ones going along underneath the spangled backcloth of the dragon, swaying underneath the brilliant silk, were something different. They were not kicking or dancing or cavorting, there was nothing aimless or carefree about them; instead they were all marching along in lockstep, black legs and booted feet tramping with grim purpose, the great red-and-gold head was already angling in our direction and we were going to have to clear out fast before the whole thing turned and began moving toward us or else it would bear down on us like an express train and we would be slupped into the belly of the dragon and spewed out in little pieces without any of the holidayers even noticing.

"Now," Luce said, and as the marching band left the

street and clumped over the flower border, tootling down on us, we took off, doubling our speed in the first three paces because we could hear the bandleader giving orders so that his band and the dragon both started double-timing after us while the partyers tripped and giggled and bumped into each other and trotted along laughing, puzzled but still jolly, more or less game and trying to keep up. We almost lost them as we rounded a corner that took us out of the park and into what turned out to be the Piazza di San Marco but somebody saw us and the whole parade made a hairpin turn and came after us. Even the dragon managed to wedge itself between the topiary elephants, scrunching down to make it through the fence beyond and then roaring out into old Venice, so they were after us again, but by that time Luce had reached something I recognized as the Campanile, but half-scale, and I had a quick flash of our last stand, we would be plastered to the thing, impaled on the dragon's horns. Then she turned to face me with a black look, saying, "In here, it's our only chance," and she slipped into a doorway that shouldn't have been there, dragging me and Kaa Naaji after her.

At first it was only dark; then as our eyes adjusted we could see that we were not safe inside the stones of Venice after all, we were trapped in a plastic mockup supported by a wooden scaffolding. Outside the dragon was already beginning to twine around the base and the rest of the crowd was helping push so the Campanile was rocking just a little, in addition to which somebody was chipping away at the plastic in one place, trying to make a hole to put a weapon through, which was less alarming than the shouts about burning us out. The rocking and the chipping stopped while somebody, and not necessarily somebody on the staff, it could have been one of those half-wit insatiable thrill-crazy tourists, got everybody to collect sticks and rags and pile them around the base of the Campanile while somebody else, and I still do not know whether it was according to orders or by popular demand, while somebody else went off for kerosene and somebody else started asking around for a match.

By that time Luce had discovered the ring in the stone floor, which wasn't real stone either, and she was yanking at it, cursing and groaning and trying to get it to come up. Kaa Naaji had his arms around her waist and he was pulling too. When I grabbed him to help give leverage I could feel him trembling, he was fleeing for his life but at the same time he had his arms around her, I got the idea he was going weak from the warmth and that she wasn't pulling as hard as she might ordinarily because she couldn't stand his arms on her, so I tightened my wrists against his belly, hard enough to hurt him because he had to keep his mind on what we were doing or we were never going to get out.

The din outside was getting louder. I could hear the thump of wood being piled against the base of the tower, voices were rising and there was the rush of feet as the crowd grew thicker but above all that I could hear another sound so alien that for a second I didn't connecf it with what was going on and when I recognized it, I didn't want to believe it. It was a mechanical voice, the hawker with the bullhorn, amplified and electronically hyped to carry over several hundred yards, advertising and gathering a crowd. "Only two more minutes to flashtime, ladies and gentlemen, watch the Terrible Trio try to make its last escape, be on the spot as the flames engulf all, for an extra consideration you too can hold the torch . . . "

I looked at the back of the little creep leaning in front of me, pulling with Luce, I said, "You little bastard, if this is one of your master plots."

He didn't even hear; he was breathing in and out, making little sobbing sounds as he yanked on Luce, who was yanking on the ring.

"It would serve you right if I let go."

"*One*," Luce was saying.

If I let go, I thought, would the director walk in and end it? "You little bastard, did you do this?"

"*Two*," Luce said.

"Do what?" I had pushed Kaa Naaji instead of helping pull and he was wild, saying, "Do what? Do what?"

"Turn us in." Outside a shout rose and I heard a thump as the Campanile caught fire.

"*Three.*"

"How could I possibly?"

"I don't know, you little bastard, but we're back in the show."

"*Heave.*" Luce leaned back, throwing all her weight.

"Nothing, my friend, I did nothing." He threw himself back at the same time as Luce in one final effort and I fell back with them, our combined weight did the trick this time and the hatch popped open at the last possible second.

In the nick of time. "Or was this all a crummy show?" I was raging, when Luce went down the hatch I dragged him over and shoved him down, I didn't care how deep it was or how he hit. "Is it?" I don't know what I thought I would do next, slam it on the two of them and rush outside to face the crowd or cross my arms and wait to go up in smoke, but by that time the flames were melting the plastic, the fumes were terrible and to escape them I had to go on down the hatch.

At the bottom we lay in a heap, gasping. When I could talk I said, "Did you hear that up there? We're in the show again. Somebody wrote us into the fucking show."

She rolled out of the tangle. "Well it wasn't me."

I sat up and looked at her: the wild eyes, the crackling hair. For all I knew she was enjoying this. "It could be you, you took their money, you're wearing their uniform."

"Me risk my own ass? Hell no." She looked at Kaa Naaji, who was sprawling where I had thrown him, trying to

196

decide if he was going to be able to get up. "There's only one paying guest here. For all we know he ordered this."

He sat up. "What?"

She was on her feet and standing over him, she may have been ready to kill him. "You, you little bastard. I'm talking about you."

Then damn if I didn't hear a new voice saying, "Wait."

Evaline

As soon as she left I got out of bed and found what I could to wear: my Lurex glitter pants that still fit, a leathrex jacket the guard had left behind when I stampeded her, maybe she thought when she found her man he would like her better in just the jersey and for her sake I hoped he did. I pulled on my old dancing shoes and wound a scarf around my head, leftover vanity or was I only thinking the grey hair would give me away? Then I went in the bathroom and fished Val's screenplay out of the toilet tank and lashed it to my middle with a pair of pantyhose, zipping the jacket over it so that anybody who thought they were going to get their hands on it would have to get me first. After that I stopped and looked hard into the mirror.

It was the first time since I let down.

Old, I was thinking: *that's what I really look like. Old.*

All right, I am old. I was thinking: *At least I can be what I am.*

Yeah, it was not so bad. Being young was never really that much of a gas. Parts of me looked better but they never went together right, I was never glamorous or beautiful, I was never any of those things everybody thinks they want to be and maybe nobody ever truly is, I was young all right, but I didn't know *anything*.

I was thinking: *I don't know that much now but at least I know what I am.*

What else did I think about? Dying, for one thing, what happens after; if there was a place and I got to it, which part of me was going? Would it be the dumb one in the young body or the old smart one in the young body or the old in the old or only a part of me that has been the same person ever since the time when I first started to think and remember? I remember being on my hands and knees under my crib, crawling in the bits of a broken mirror; I remember what it felt like to be looking out of my head then and I know I am that same person. If there was a place and I got there, what would it be like? Would I be stashed in one corner with my folks whose child I will always be or do I go to another with the late father of my boring children and wait for Herb and Sybil to arrive, or do I get to be with Val, whom I love as I have loved no other? Would it be something else, everybody one, so all this would be immaterial? What will I look like then? Would I like it, would it be boring, would I be scared? All right I couldn't believe it all just stops we care too much there is too much of it, that isn't finished, there is a place, what, I will go.

I thought: *You had better stop maundering and get your ass out of here.*

So I took a dinner knife and went to work on the door. I poked at the seal through the crack. No alarms went off when I slit the seal; nothing happened when I tried the knob and when I opened the door a crack there was nobody outside waiting to jump me so I had to wonder where they were. There was nothing but me and the open door. Out in the courtyard a bunch of new arrivals were whooping it up and across the courtyard I could see a couple of attendants stoned as skunks and falling off their chairs. Nobody saw when I zipped across the courtyard and through the trees to . . .

What?

I didn't know where I was going. I went along through a little grove and twice I thought my heart was going to give up because there were these shapes in the bushes but one turned out to be a lifelike Smokey XXXIV, with its jaw moving and no sound coming out and the second time it was a mechanical Bambi, broken, which didn't matter because there was nobody there to see. I crossed a clearing where there was a campfire surrounded by mechanical animals: skunks, squirrels, bunnies, a guinea pig or two, even a couple of deer. I knew if I went and sat on a rock in the center they would all cock their heads at me and beg me to tell them a story and together we might be able to go back to the hut where the seven . . . and then the prince would . . . I remember taking my kids but we had to leave in the middle because my daughter Edna got scared and would not stop screaming, the little bitch.

Still no guards, not even any signs, there were no attendants and I didn't see anybody taking tickets or selling refreshments or taking care; they weren't taking care of me, either—as far as I could tell I was alone with nobody following, either they had lost interest in me or they knew how my story was going to come out and they had written me off. I came out of the woods and into a phony stockade fence. I went along until I found a part that gave when I pushed on it. It was a door and when I came out on the other side I was somewhere else.

Downtown Oz.

Toyland?

Freedom Land?

For a minute I thought I had come into a gigantic playroom. I was surrounded by huge toys. Oh I recognized the big landmarks all right, the green glass boomerang where everybody stays and the silver arch; I even knew the big center fountain from all the pictures of Happy Habitat, all the holos, the magazines and telefilms and postcards from rich friends. It was Happy Habitat all right and the thing about it was that nothing looked like what it was.

I suppose that's part of it. If you put people in with a lot of big toys maybe they don't have to face reality, they can be kids again. That must be why so many pay so much. I knew I didn't have much time, I had to get out while I still could, but coming out between the two bushes, the boxwood panda and the boxwood elephant, I felt like a little kid. Everything that grew was cut into the shape of something else. There were tigers and alligators and a Spanish galleon, and everything was blooming. There were drinking fountains shaped like jacks-in-the-pulpit; I stepped on the lower petal of one and water came out the top. There were no lampposts, only palm trees that glowed even though it was morning, and there were no fences, only rows of flowers holding hands. I got next to a giant toadstool and saw that it was a computer terminal, with the day's attractions flashing in purple and a keyboard so you could punch in your desires; people were going into restrooms in the belly of a giant purple panda and people were getting dope out of a fluffy kitty's mouth and there were other people buying ice cream from the center of a gigantic rose. Afterward they lolled among the petals, licking their cones. I saw a fuzzy little black dog whirring along the sidewalk and I thought: how cute, until I saw that he was a vacuum cleaner, busily sweeping the walks whether there was anything on them or not, and as I watched he rolled over and bumped against a four-foot pelican, waiting to be emptied into its beak. The benches where I stood were all soft brown bears with wide laps and sweet faces and I sat down in one because I was exhausted and, I don't know, a little weepy because in my weakened condition the bear seemed so soft and nice that I wanted to bury my face in her furry bosom and be a little girl again. Everything was so *pretty*. I thought: whoever they are that made all this, they must be nice people because they have made it so nice, perhaps they have made some kind of amnesty with their pretty little flowers and their sweet-singing birds.

I knew the bear wasn't real and nothing in this part of the park was real and as I snuggled in her lap I began to think that maybe what I was running away from wasn't real either and I had no real reasons to be afraid, it had been a bad dream, that's all; the bear was humming a lovely song and I could feel her soft breath on my cheek, coming and going so sweetly, but just before I went to sleep I felt a flicker of panic, a razor-sharp moment of recollection: Val. The Spanish Civil War. That wasn't real either but the blood and pain were real, my God, Val's death was real, I started up but before I could get off the bear she licked my face or I thought she did and that's the last thing I remember.

When I woke up it was much later; the light had changed, all the holidayers had gone off somewhere—to lunch or a siesta? I was more or less alone there, curled up in the bear's lap, but I was not precisely alone because when I straightened and tried to put myself back together I saw there was this bunny on the grass in front of me, sitting up on its hind legs with its ears cocked and its eyes glittering. I said, "Awww," and when I bent to pat it, it said, or the microphone in it said, "Unclassified guest."

"Why, I just stopped for a little nap."

"Identify yourself."

It was so cute I said, "You know me."

"Insert credit card for identification." It lifted its paws and there was a little slot in its belly.

"I don't . . . "

"Credit card. Credit card."

. . . have a credit card. I tried to face it down. "I left it in my room."

"Guests have cards attached to wrists. Please insert."

I got down from the bear's lap, keeping up a line of patter to make the bunny think I was on the level. I explained that I had my card, of course, it was inside my jacket here and if bunny would only be patient I was going to unsnap my sleeve . . .

When I got up close I grabbed it and before it could do anything I took it and I stuffed it into the mouth of the nearest pelican. I could hear a bell go off as the vacuum tube took it away and when I turned I saw a pair of attendants leaping the candy-cane hedge and moving in my direction so I started running.

They were closing on me, I think they would have gotten me and if they had I don't know what they would have done to me but we came around a corner next to the entrance to the Love and Death ride, that we all know from pictures of the silver arch, the shrieking crowds, and of course there was a dense line waiting, sheiks and their ladies, industrialists, an entire crowd of the rich and the beautiful all waiting their turn on the ride. The attendants slowed down and I did too, getting my breath and taking it as slowly as I could because I knew they wouldn't dare try and grab me here where the paying guests could see because it is so nice here that nobody wants a scene. I strung it out for as long as I could and as I did something came up, over in the band pavilion, some minor disturbance, so the two of them took off and for the time being I was home free.

Or thought I was. I had gone some distance before I was aware of a sound that followed wherever I went, that stopped when I stopped, it was tiny but pervasive. I looked to the right and left, making sudden stops and quick turns, and finally saw it: nothing big, nothing frightening, it wasn't even a person. It didn't matter what I did, it was going to stick with me and it wouldn't make a scene or alarm anyone because it was tiny. What's more it was adorable, one of those long-haired guinea pigs with the little golden eyes, it could have come out of the cute little circle of animals back there in the woods but who did it think I was, Snow White? Wherever I went it went; it followed relentlessly, stopping whenever I stopped, sitting up on its haunches and looking at me brightly, always safely out of reach.

I waded an ornamental pond and it swam after me. I jumped a hedge; it scurried through the roots. I picked up another stone and it rolled away. I climbed a tree and it waited underneath. I had been going along with my eyes on the path, watching the little thing and trying so hard to lose it that I hadn't paid much attention to where I was going. I was aware of the crowd getting thicker and I saw how clever the little thing was because it had brought me in a circle so that I was not on my way out at all, I was back at the foot of the Love and Death ride, trying to look like just one more person in the line. There were attendants heading my way; my guinea pig guardian was rolling toward my ankles now, I don't know what kind of poison it had in its teeth but if it didn't get me the attendants would, I was going to have to act fast so I did the only thing I could:

I jumped the line.

I pushed my way through the last rank of waiting customers and jumped onto the platform, where one of the purple-suited loaders was leading a languid boy toward the last seat in the last silver car on the Love and Death ride. I rushed them from behind and pushed into the seat just as a starter somewhere up ahead lifted his arm and lowered it; the ride started just as I snapped the safety belt and the bar clanked down over my lap. The loader and the wronged customer were huffing and chattering, the first guards were coming up on the platform and everybody started after me just as there was a whoosh and a whir and the string of cars was sucked into the opening. The next thing I knew everything was black and my car had begun the long climb inside the giant silver arch.

Maybe I should have let them catch me. This was worse. I lay back, panting, as we went up inside the arch, with holidayers in front of me laughing and jabbering and lifting their hands as blue and silver lights started flashing; the entire tube or corridor went from black to silver, with mirrors refracting flashing lights at so many angles that I lost all track of up and down long before we reached the top, and at the crest I didn't know which way we were coming at it or which ones were my hands and at the moment at which we passed the crest I lost track of everything except the pressure of Val's screenplay, the only thing that kept my heart from crashing through my ribs.

From the outside the silver arch looks safe and beautiful, the glittering emblem of whatever it is they are trying to sell at Happy Habitat; looking at it you would not imagine it could contain the zig-zags, the drops, the spirals that took us in, out, over, under, all the way out of ourselves before my heart choked me and I passed out. Nobody could conceive of the mixture of sound and light that bombarded us or the jangle of movement or the violence of the final drop that must have snapped the neck of the rider in front of me because I came to at the end of the ride to find our car slowing down at last and myself looking directly into her dead face at right angles to the back of the seat. The unloaders spotted her at the same time. They sent a pair of attendants to get her out quickly while they led the happy survivors to the swan boats, loading them for the ride back into the sunlight, keeping up a patter that would keep them from looking back and discovering the corpse. The attendants lifted her out and hurried toward a side door in the mirrored grotto and I took advantage of the confusion and followed, slipping into the tunnel behind them just as the guards pulled up in their launch, setting all the swan boats bobbing, and leaped out. They landed at a dead run, heading toward the empty car where I had been but by that time the mirrored door was already closing behind us so all they would have seen was the glittering reflections of light off the rippling water.

The two who were dragging the corpse heard me coming along the tunnel behind them and looked back.

"What's that?"

I said, "Nothing." I scraped and tried to took small.

"Who are you?"

"Special mission." I tried to smile.

The tall one said, "Don't you think we ought to . . . "

I said, "Oh, no. Certainly not."

"Let's get back to the party," the short one said.

They gave me a last look.

I grinned. "Don't mind me."

"This might mean trouble."

"Come on," the short guard said, "you're no fun any more." They heaved the body onto a conveyer belt and left.

I went in the opposite direction, going carefully at first. After a while I went along faster because there didn't seem to be any guards except for one, who was asleep at his desk. I saw a couple from a distance but as I went along I had the feeling that I had come aboard a ghost ship, if I could find my way to the bridge the wheel would be swinging aimlessly, there was nobody at the helm, which should have cheered me but instead left me depressed and fearful because I had no idea where I was going any more, or which way was out.

Then I heard shouting and thuds ahead, sounds of people quarreling, and as I came around the last corner I saw two men, a small one and a big one who, for a split second, made me remember Tiger, those hands, and there was, Lord, a guard, not just any guard, the one that I had sent out of my room and for a second I thought things had not turned out so badly, because she had found her man. But she didn't seem happy, or fulfilled; instead she had her hands around the little man's neck, I think she was going to kill him, he was looking choked and miserable, as if he wanted to die if that's what she wanted, the whole thing turned my heart over and I hurried into their circle, shouting:

"Wait."

Kaa Naaji

Oh, *oh.* If only I could get her to love me I could die, and happily; I could bear to go on living if I could earn the trust and good wishes of my friend Boone but so far she has repulsed my gestures of love and turns aside my good wishes, my giant, inexorable woman, and my friend Boone believes I have brought them to this pretty pass. So as we fell in a heap in the tunnel underneath the flaming Campanile I could see Boone starting up in a mixture of outrage and mistrust but at the same time Luce had reached for my throat and was trying to throttle me.

"My beloved." Yes, it was hard to speak under the pressure of her fingers but I gasped out the words, the best I had to offer. "If you want me dead then I will die for you."

"Hey, Luce, take it easy." That was Boone. "Maybe he didn't do it after all."

I gave my all. "I will do anything you want."

"Watch out, you're going to kill him."

"Who gives a damn?" Ah, but at the sound of his voice she had lost concentration, for I could feel her fingers loosen as she was ineluctably drawn to him. We jerked back and forth in a terrible tangle: her, Boone, me, and then I heard other footsteps in the corridor and a new voice, a woman's, most piteous: "Oh stop, please, this is terrible. Whatever you're doing, stop."

She looked into my eyes one last time, my implacable dearest. "You little creep."

"I did not bring this upon us." My eyes were bulging, my voice rasping. Did she even hear?

There was the new voice. "Oh stop, you're hurting him."

"You." My beloved turned in anger, forgetting me as she did so. "How in hell did you get out?" Her fingers loosened and I fell to the ground; as soon as I could breathe again I sat up and looked at the new person, an old, old woman in battle dress, entreating Boone to help her, while my beloved said, through gritted teeth, "That's my jacket, you old bitch."

She turned us a face like a shriveled pansy, faded and beautiful. "I'm sorry, I had to take what I could."

"Can't talk now," Luce said. "Got to go."

"Wait, please. I need your help."

"Boone, are you coming?"

"Give her a minute," Boone said.

"I'm telling you, that old broad is nothing but trouble." My Luce was trying to turn us, but when Boone would not follow she said, in anger, "Are you coming or not?"

"Just hold it," Boone said, and let the old lady draw him aside.

And so Luce paced the corridor with an impatience that tore my heart: does she reject my best love because she yearns for Boone? The thought is too terrible. I tried to draw her attention, saying, "You know I did not order the fire in the Campanile."

"Shut up, I'm trying to hear."

But Boone had bent his head close to the old lady's, they were in a secret world, leaving my darling and me more or less alone. I opened my heart to her. "You know I would not do anything to cause you unhappiness."

"Shut up." She gestured toward Boone and the old lady. "Can't you see I've got troubles enough?"

They were approaching. "Luce, this is Ev, she's got something important she's trying to take out of here."

"That's a line of crap."

"Luce, we're going to have to trust her."

"If we take her along, we're not going to make it."

Then Boone looked at her and said, simply, "It's all of us or nobody."

"Oh shit." She was shaking her head. "Oh shit."

Boone looked at her. "We can't do it without you, Luce."

Then I can tell you she would have done anything for him. Her grin lighted the entire corridor. "Son of a bitch."

And so we set out, with my beautiful tough lady leading the way through the labyrinth.

"I don't know if they're still tracking or not," she said, "but down here at least we've got a chance."

Boone said, "They'll never think to look for us down here."

The old lady went along stoutly. "As far as they know, I'm dead and gone."

"Ah, my friends . . . " What was I going to tell them? That we were overconfident? Wasted breath for I had no, what is it the politicians say, no credibility. Still . . .

We were entering a new area and there were indeed signs that there had been somebody here before us: leaflets littering the floor. I wanted to cry a halt but did not for I was along on sufferance, and knew it; I dared not try their patience or my luck. The heaps of paper on the floor were getting thicker and so I picked up one anyway, and began to read. It was much worse than I had thought.

My spirits sagged. Here we were going along into what we thought was terra incognita, and here was the fine hand of the management: brochures, advertising our escape and headlong flight. I groaned in desperation and then took a closer look, marveling at the technology that enabled them to appear so quickly and be so quickly obsolete. Perhaps the technology was not so wonderful after all; the ink was smeared and these leaflets were hopelessly out of date.

Instead of bugling our flight through the tunnels, that we were now embarked on, instead of billing the addition of the old lady, these poor folders headlined our adventure in the Campanile in three colors, begging the customers of Happy Habitat to join in our death in the conflagration back there in the tower.

SEE THE TERRIBLE TRIO GO UP IN SMOKE
For an extra consideration you can light a torch

Aha, I thought, this is old news indeed. A good sign. These leaflets are good for nothing more than yesterday's newspaper—lighting fires or wrapping yesterday's fish, for we have escaped this one and what's more we are no longer a threesome, we are four.

"Boone, we are ahead of them."

He ran along, ignoring me.

"Acha, we are escaping."

"Shut up and run."

Not three, four. Beyond control of the management. Proof that I could not have ordered this. Proof of my honesty.

I called again. "Boone."

If I could get him to look, just for a minute, he could see that I am, as Boone would say it, on the level.

"Boone, this is none of it my doing."

"Shut up, Kaa Naaji."

"But I have proof."

"I said, shut up and run."

"Luce, my dearest lady."

She turned on me and snarled. "Get away."

"But we are in a new chapter."

"Shut up and get away."

I put out my hand and tried to make Boone look at me but he turned with a look that made me tremble. I persisted. "You can trust me now, I have proof."

"I bet you do."

"Ah, Boone." I groaned aloud. Even in Agra I did not experience such terrible loneliness. These two suffered my presence barely, the man I most admire, and the woman I love. They both believed I was to blame and nothing was going to shake them. Oh. They thought this was my doing as was the business with the water buffalo, a rich man's caprice, and I could not make them see the difference between what I had unwittingly arranged, which was indeed a false business, and this, in which I was even more helpless than they. I thought of all the hopes that had brought me here and I thought: *You see, Kaa Naa Mahadevan, you cannot buy and pay for happiness, for friends,* and then I thought: *You knew before you came that one cannot buy happy endings.*

True, but one hopes for happy endings in order to be able to go on.

Yes. I must always try again.

I ran along after them, saying, "Please trust me."

"There there."

"What?"

"Whatever it is, it can't be that bad." There was the poor old woman who had joined us, running along beside me with a gallant determination, even though I could see her breath was coming faster and faster and she had put one hand to her tender side. She could not keep up with them either but she looked ready to die trying; her jaw bounced with every step and she was gasping, and yet she could see my distress and she was doing her best to console me, even as we ran.

"Dear lady, they think I have betrayed them." I could see she was losing strength and so I slowed down to make it easier for her, and when she faltered I gave her my arm, half supporting, half pulling to help her keep the pace.

Her voice was gentle and what she said was astonishing, for she seemed to be able to peel back the layers and understand what I was feeling. "Sometimes it's hard—" she gasped but would go on talking "—to make people see you—for what you really are."

"Dear lady." She turned such a sweet face to me that I asked her outright: "How can I prove myself?"

"You don't need to prove yourself to me."

It was like water falling in the desert. "Oh thank you."

"I can see you're not like that." She leaned on me in complete trust and I found myself smiling as we went along.

So we ran along together, Boone and Luce had not looked back to see how far behind we lagged and because the old lady could not keep the pace there was a widening distance between us, and when guards in black hoods came lunging out of one of the side tunnels, I could see we were cut off.

"Do not fear, dear lady, I'll protect you." I put her behind me and prepared to fight with whatever I had left. They were many, and they were approaching fast.

"No," she said. "Save yourself."

"I must protect you."

"Beat it, there's still time."

The guards were huge black shapes, fast and ferocious. "I will save you," I said, and hurled myself into their midst.

I do not know what happened after that, exactly, except that there was loud shouting and much blood. I heard their breath and the sounds of blows and I went down in a tangle, we were fighting, and when the guard directly on top of me went limp and another lunged, raising his arm, I shielded the old lady with my body and waited for the final blow.

It seemed an eternity. Still I waited, frozen. There was only blackness, silence.

"It's all right." That was a voice I knew.

I opened my eyes.

"I said, it's all right." It was Luce. They had come back for us.

"You do care."

She would not look at me.

When I got to my feet I saw that the guards were all dead or stunned: Luce's work, and Boone's, and most of the blood belonged to me. I staggered.

Boone reached out to support me. "Are you OK?"

I took my hand away from my arm, and more blood came. "It is nothing." "He almost bought it," the old lady said. "He was trying to save me."

I looked at Boone, hoping. "You can see that I am really in it now."

He was scowling: dislike for me? "Kaa Naaji. God."

"Perhaps now you will believe I am not a traitor?"

"Don't even say that." He was shaking his head in regret, and, ah, I heard it joyfully, his tone was one of remorse. "We should have stuck together, but, dammit, I thought. . . . "

Luce was saying, "Don't trust him."

"I know what you thought," I said, and I did the American thing, I offered my hand. He took it and shook it, in a pledge of trust, so that I nodded, satisfied. "But now you know it is not true."

Boone Castle

So I had been wrong about the Indian after all, I was pretty sure I had, and sooner or later I was going to have to find a way to make it up to him, but there were other things getting between me and that. Survival, for one. That and the way things were happening. I looked at them in turn: Kaa Naaji, with his wounded arm, the old lady, binding it up. Luce. I shook my head, saying, "I don't know what's going on but somebody has arranged all this, and somebody is keeping track of us."

Ev said, "Does it have to be one of us?"

Kaa Naaji said, "The last leaflets had us dying in the fire. Maybe they have lost track."

"But those guards came from somewhere." I shushed him. I wanted us to be quiet because I heard something. There was a sound, an extra voice in the corridor; I had heard it the whole time we were prying the guards off him and the old lady and I heard it now. I shushed everybody so I could try and make out what it was saying, and trace it to the source. That was not hard to do. In the doorway the guards had come out of, there was a deserted guard's station and in it there was a monitor, making beautiful pictures even as we discovered it. They looked innocent enough, your holidayers on the Zugspitz in hypercolor, followed by a montage of people dancing intercut with intimate shots of open heart surgery.

Luce said, "Maybe we're next."

"Shut up, maybe we're not."

"We interrupt this program . . . " So there it was, the voice of the announcer running along underneath the pictures of the happy holidayers and the real-life drama and the ersatz orgy; this was the breathless television voice that brings you news of wars and executions, railway disasters and victories at the Superbowl; it was vibrating with passion and charged with air from the belly, communicating a sense of danger and adventure to all the ships at sea and all the happy customers and all the people safe at home:

" . . . to bring you a bulletin from the Terrible Trio, who as some of you may know from our last bulletin have become the Fearsome Foursome; the four have fought off a squadron of Cleanup and Removal staff and now they are binding their wounds in preparation for a renewed attack on the surface, they . . . "

"The hell you say, mother." Luce threw a chair at the screen, smashing it right in the middle of a closeup of a circus parade with people laughing and dancing around a gigantic clown head.

" . . . probably emerge around the shark-infested waters where the crew of the X-9 died so gallantly," the voice said anyway. "There is still plenty of time to get over there folks, so pick up your tickets from the nearest programmer and rally on the banks in time to get costumes and spears so you can be in on the action. Will the Indian inventor win his lady love?"

Kaa Naaji said, "That's *me*."

"Will the old lady make good her exit from the enchanted kingdom?"

Ev said, "Oh my God."

"Can the runaway prisoner and the renegade guard find happiness? Come along, come on along, and if you can't come along, stay tuned."

"Shut your *hole*." Luce's voice was rising in a mixture of rage and high hysteria. She beat on the monitor with the chair until the right tube popped and it was silent. Then she turned to me and said, "What are we going to do?"

"I don't know."

I didn't like any of it. When we went down the hatch in the Campanile there were only three of us and I was ready to think the chase was over. Then the old lady turned up which made four and it still wasn't over; we were still on the run with them advertising our escape at every turn, which meant they were still on top of us, so that I was beginning to wonder whether what we were doing would ever have any real ending, that we could point to and say *There*, or whether I was damned to spend the rest of my days in this ostensible fairyland, frazzled and hungry and always out of breath because I was always on the run. I had my doubts about everything we had done so far and I had my doubts about giving up. If we gave ourselves up, would it be over? Maybe that would show them, they couldn't use us if we wouldn't play, but I could already imagine the capture and the execution scene, the stakes and the hoods, the final cigarette; the four of us would be lashed to the stakes, choking out a few appropriate last words before the drumroll sounded for the delectation of the assembled paying guests. It might be worse if the firing squad let us have it with blanks; I didn't for a minute believe they would thank us for the performance and turn us loose; they would make us get up and grin and start over. For all I knew we would be recycled to escape again and run again and be captured again. And again. So I had my doubts about outrunning them; I even had my doubts about the old lady. She seemed earnest enough but she could be a plant laid on us by the management, the thing where the story editors come to a certain part in the plot and say, This needs complications. Maybe she was ours.

I looked at her: are you on the level?

Luce said, "What's the matter?"

"I don't know yet." I looked at the monitor, at the others, at her. I said, "If they're so damn good, why haven't they nailed us?"

"Maybe they don't want to."

I nodded because she was confirming my suspicions. "You mean we're on the air for good now."

"Like it or not."

"Camera fodder."

Kaa Naaji said, "I think we'd better have a plan."

"Shut up." Luce almost hit him. "Don't you know this whole damn place is bugged?"

I nodded and made scribbling motions, reaching around for something to write with, anything to write on.

Damn if the old lady didn't scratch a notepad out of the pocket of her leathrex jacket.

Luce said, "My notepad. What in hell are you doing with my jacket?"

"I didn't think you were going to need it."

"What's that supposed to mean?"

"I thought once you found your lover, you . . . "

"My lover." Luce spat next to my foot. "Keep the damn jacket. While you're at it you might as well give him the damn pen. Clipped in the zipper pocket."

I took it and wrote: WE'LL WORK IT OUT BY NOTE.

The old lady took the pad from me before I could write any more. She wrote: IF THEY EXPECT A, WE'LL DO B.

I answered: IF THEY THINK WE'RE GOING UP, WE GO DOWN. WHO ARE YOU, ANYWAY? I handed her the pad.

THINK OF ME AS A FELLOW TRAVELER. She thumped her chest. I HAVE SOMETHING IMPORTANT TO DO. Her knuckles made an interesting thunk.

Luce yanked the pad away from her. THIS IS STUPID, she wrote. WE'VE GOT TO GO SOMEPLACE THAT ISN'T BUGGED.

I said, "There isn't any place."

SHUT UP AND FOLLOW ME. She showed the note around: to Kaa Naaji, to the old lady, to me. Then she added, ARE YOU WITH ME? They each nodded in turn. I looked at her and as I did a new monitor flickered into life, a plate in the ceiling this time. The picture was us. The voiceover began:

" . . . and now, the Fearsome Foursome meets its fatal finale."

We got up fast.

When the Chinese dragon materialized at the corner we did not turn and flee, which was probably on the program, nor did we swarm up the nearest ladder to emerge near the wreck of the X-9, as advertised. We didn't stand and fight, either, although I had an impression of cameras grinding as we turned to face the thing. Instead we let it come down on us and as it did it filled the tunnel, all red and gold and flashing lights, the mechanical jaws opening and shutting to show curved metal teeth and the dark faces of the marchers underneath. We let it come down on us, standing our ground in the face of all that power and noise, holding fast even as the nostrils let out sparks and jets of smoke, and just before it was too late we rushed the head, dashing into those fake teeth and at the last second veering, two to the right and two to the left so that we rushed on past the teeth and down the corridor, grazing the whiskers as the head thundered on in one direction and we ran in the other. We went so fast that it was a couple of minutes before the marchers behind the eyes caught on to what we were doing, and it took even longer before the ones marching along under the spangled body cloth got the message from the ones marching under the head, who had seen us and figured out what we were doing but figured it out too late to stop. By the time all the

216

parts of the thing had gotten the message they were squawking and bashing around under the fabric and the wire frame because it was too close in the tunnel for them to get out from under the dragon body without ripping it and getting tangled in the ribbons, and it was too late for them to turn around.

We were following Luce now: heading down.

She took us down several levels, into a huge dim place that was filled with Plexi cubicles and festooned with rags. From the ceiling dark shapes hung; I thought I saw an ancient Fokker, suspended from ropes directly overhead, and at a distance a Model A that had been used in some extravaganza and then hoisted on pulleys to be stored until it was needed. As nearly as I could make out we had escaped the guards, there were no voiceovers and no sign of the Chinese dragon.

"This is Costume," Luce said. "If they haven't replaced me we're home free."

The old lady was lingering, looking through the Plexi. "Look at those *gowns.*"

Luce just said, "Look at those poor freaks."

There were people behind the Plexi, clubfoots and hunchbacks and microcephalics all sewing or pressing or sorting; one dwarf looked at us without interest, holding a spangled strapless gown up to his barrel chest and changing focus at once so he could catch his reflection in the Plexi. If the others saw us they didn't care. Luce pulled us into a cubicle at the end of the corridor; it was littered with smashed equipment and hung with filmy cloth in candy colors.

"Can you imagine," she said. "They stuck me in here. Me."

The old lady said, "Any fool can see you have too much class."

Kaa Naaji said, "I will make them suffer for their blindness."

"Damn right," Luce said.

There were food trays overflowing the work table and costume capsules scattered around. A couple had cracked open, spilling soft garments in candy colors. Some of the food on the trays was moldy but the bread and fruits were still all right so we divided them and sat around on the floor, eating without talking, storing it up, I guess—not running, not being watched, being quiet for once. We leaned back and looked at the vaulted ceilings, the ranks of cubicles.

After a while Luce said, "When I ended up here I thought I was finished. They promised me a big deal job and then stuck me in the back room."

The old lady had picked up a negligée and was holding it up to her cheek, like somebody trying out a color. She caught her reflection in the Plexi and stopped. "They made us all hope for better. I guess no matter what you say you're selling, you're really making people think they're buying happiness."

"So they say," Kaa Naaji said.

She sighed. "I guess when you come right down to it, promises are only promises."

I said, "They didn't promise me anything. I think."

"My friends, if you had seen their, what is it, *promos*, you would understand what they are selling." Kaa Naaji waggled his head and his voice lifted. "They are selling hope. Alas, they could make you believe in anything."

"Yeah, right," I said. "What are we supposed to believe in now?"

"Each other." The old lady looked right at me. "Us."

Luce was sounding strangely throaty. "You'd better believe the old lady, Boone."

What was there about it? All those people turning to me, those leaflets, the voiceover in the halls. I still didn't know why I was there or who was running the show, maybe I thought I was being managed, because I dug in my heels. "For all I know not one of you is on the level. For all I know . . . "

"Shh. Don't." The old lady touched my arm. "We've come a long way already. We're going to make it now."

Luce said, "You've got to admit, we're doing OK."

Kaa Naaji said, "Dear lady, you were very brave with the guards, and once again with the Chinese dragon."

"It was nothing." She was trying not to look pleased.

The old lady touched his hand. "You were pretty good yourself."

He saw what she was trying to give him and said, "Dear lady, it was my great pleasure."

"Call me Ev." She turned to me. "Oh Boone, what are we going to do now?"

I turned my hands and looked into the palms because I didn't know the answer.

"Yes, Boone, you have brought us this far . . . "

"*I* brought . . . "

"Yeah, right," Luce said. "Now we can't go much farther without knowing what are the plans." For reasons I could only guess at she was handing the whole thing over to me, looking at me so hard her eyes almost crossed and willing me to say: what? "So what are the plans?"·

"The plans . . . " I really did not want anything beyond immediate relief from being watched, wait, I did, I wanted it to end, but what I really wanted was for somebody to take it away and end it for me. Later they could come back and tell me about it. When I looked around at them I saw that there wasn't a one of them who could do it. The old lady was too frail to go much farther without help, I could see her wilting by the minute; there was Kaa Naaji, nursing his arm, too torn up by love to keep his mind on anything, which left Luce, who was too crazy to be trusted. She would fight like a demon for what she thought was right but I could study her for the next hundred years and not be certain what she thought was right, or whether it would be a good thing or a bad one.

Which left me.

I did not want the responsibility.

"My friend . . . " Kaa Naaji did not want it either; he wanted only her love, and to stay friends with me.

"Boone?" The old lady. What did she want? To complete her mission; whatever it was, she was burning up with it.

"Boone? Hey!" Luce was glaring at me, waiting. What did she want? Maybe better not find out. I could see she *wanted*.

So there I was, the Great and Powerful Oz, without a clear idea of what to do next, without even a pasteboard bag of tricks to parcel out to cheer them, I had backed or fallen or been drawn into something I could not necessarily control, didn't even want, all because of my, all right, tragic flaw—*because it was expected* . . .

Cheer up, folks, I'll think of something.

I could hear Luce's breath shivering.

When I die it will be of *noblesse oblige.*

"OK," I said. "Time to get it together. We are going to have to get into the control room, wherever that is, and smash everything."

"Is that all you want?" Luce was grinning like a pirate. "If we could get in there, shit, we could take this place over."

I said, "I get the feeling we don't want the same things."

"Never mind that," Luce said. "Tell me what you want and I'll do it." She turned those headlight eyes on me: Robin, hunkered down in the Batcave, preparing for an orgy of collusion, or was that Lois Lane, doing an Ophelia?

"We've got to figure out how to get there."

"Right on." Her big grin was lighting up the place. "I think I know the way."

She had a bunch of maps scribbled on napkins, from memory—her idea of places she had been on the job, how the undergound passages might be laid out. It was going to take some doing, but together we were going to make sense of them. She thought she knew where the central office was, what to do when we found it, every time I nodded or said OK she would get that crazy grin. We agreed we would lie low until the lights went down and wait for the graveyard shift; if what she said was halfway true most of the guards would be too drunk or stoned to go to work, and that would make it the best time. As we talked a supper tray slid out of the slot and we fell on it. By the time we had finished eating we had a fair idea of which way we would head once we took off and what we were going to do—up to a point. When we finished rehearsing it we rolled up in discarded negligees and pulled ourselves into corners to catch a little sleep.

I woke to hear soft movements, cursing, a slap. Kaa Naaji was squatting on his heels again, looking so mournful that even in the dimness it was easy to figure out what had happened. Luce was rolling over, huffy in a tangle of gaudy nightclothes, while Kaa Naaji nursed the red fingermarks on his cheek in a mixture of delight and woe.

I said, "Maybe you ought to let her be."

"But she smiled at me before."

"She isn't smiling now." Even her back looked angry.

"Ah, my friend, in time she may change."

"How long are you going to hang around like this, you know, being unrequited?"

"For as long as it takes." His eyes shone like Christmas bulbs. "It's one of the things I came here for."

"A rap in the mouth?"

"Something to follow."

"You know you're never going to get her. What's the point?"

He was smiling. "Boone, there is always the outside chance, and so I have that to live for."

"What if she gets fed up and knocks your head off?"

He couldn't stop smiling. "There are worse things than dying for love."

"Name one."

He was looking right through me. "Having nothing to live for."

"You're telling yourself stories. What happens if this one ends?"

"Then I will think of another." His eyes were clear. "Is that so bad?"

"Have it your way," I said, and rolled over. So I let it lay for the time being because there was no way for me to disabuse him. I was not even sure I wanted to. He was sitting there gleaming in the shadows, happy with his story at least for the time being. Maybe we all tell ourselves stories in order to be able to keep on going, and maybe he was lucky to have hit on his. I pulled my collection of filmy rags around me and turned to the wall but no matter which way I rolled or how I shifted I could not get comfortable. Damn fool, I thought, poor little damn fool with his poor little stories, and then I sat up fast because the thoughts were moving behind my eyes, picked out in lights: . . . because it is expected. *What's the difference between that and what you're doing?*

Back, damn you, back. Shut up.

I must have gone oof, the noise you make when you are hit in the stomach, because the old lady heard me and sat up. Kaa Naaji was waiting too, so I shook Luce because like it or not for the time being, at least, I was the leader.

"What?"

"It's time."

IV

Outtakes

"You have doubtless guessed why I called an emergency meeting in the dead of night like this. Our paying guests are quiescent for the moment, but they are all going to be out and around in just a few hours and before the business day starts I would like to take stock. We are going to marshal our resources and we may have to take some staff off their usual duties long enough to deal with this, but we are going to have to get this thing under control."

"Don't say I didn't warn you."

"Dante, please. As I was saying, I want to thank you all for your extra effort and the overtime hours you have devoted to keeping everything running smoothly in spite of the escape, I think once we can get this under control we are going to make a fortune."

("I thought we were going to . . . "

"Dante, hush.")

"I told you we had a good thing going."

"Let's not pat ourselves on the back yet, James. You've all done an excellent job of covering and exploiting but the Escape of the Fearsome Foursome seems to have gotten out of range, for the moment, to call a spade a spade I would have to say that we have lost them temporarily, and I cannot stress too heavily that we are in a state of emergency and urge you all to do your best until we recover them. Now, James?"

"Well fortunately this happened at an ebb viewing time, most of our paying guests are safely in the sack, and the late-nighters are all watching a prepared loop. I have in mind an escape story we can give out in measured installments so we can keep this thing going whether we get the Fearsome Foursome back or not, Corky is working on continuity and we have even prepared Casting and Costume to provide identical substitutes for any on-the-surface action we may want to film independent of the escape itself."

("That's all very well, but . . . ")

"Furthermore, I would have to say right now that I think Corky's story line is far better than the original and if you folks are willing to let it run we can really clean up. Furthermore our jobbers have filled rush orders on the comic books and the T-shirts and if those do well we're prepared to follow up with an entire Fearsome Foursome line . . . "

"Jimmy you don't have any idea what we're up against. We have to get them back."

"That's your department, Dante. Everything is fine in mine."

"You're the one who let them get out of control."

"And we're covering beautifully. Getting them back is your department."

"I cannot do it without help. Dearest, please let me speak."

"All right, Dante."

"I have tried to make it plain that my staff was spread too thin by the new phase in the operation and what with the new element we have had to hire, all the drunks and the desertions, it's effectively cut by half. In addition to which the escape has pushed us to the limit because A, we don't know where the Fearsome Foursome are, and B, we don't have enough staff to cover every place they

226

might turn up. I think the situation is desperate and Jimmy's tubthumping about audience and revenues is quite beside the point. Furthermore, as the rest of you may not know, I have already asked Dearest to have Pop let us terminate this before we lose control altogether, and I hate forcing your hand like this, Dearest, I mean in front of everybody, but I guess I want to know what Pa said."

"He said it was recommended."

"But you're letting a fortune go down the drain."

"Shut up, Jimmy, and let your brother talk. All right, Dante, now that we have Pa's permission to terminate, I'd like to know precisely how you intend to proceed."

"I've already told you, my staff can't even locate them, and furthermore . . . Oh. If we can't locate them we can't . . . "

"You see, Dante, we may both want it, Pa may want it, but it's not as easy as you might think."

* * *

"You mean we're trapped here."

"Yes, Dottie, if you want to call it that."

"Oh Fred."

"But I think there's another way of looking at it."

"What do you mean?"

"What I mean is, well, honey, let's look at it this way. We've never been closer than we are here right in front of the cameras."

"That's true."

"What's more we are making an important contribution here, you and I are giving the world an intimate look at the way a family works."

"Oh Fred, you sound like the promo they got out on us."

"Well what if I do? It's all true. We're reaching millions of viewers this way, our values are being communicated to them hour by hour as we live and work, the day-to-day nobility, the daily ups and downs, and if our values become their values, why think what we will have done to brighten up this poor old world."

"You mean we're having a real influence."

"My dear, we are role models for the world."

"You make it sound so—significant."

"It is significant, Dorothy, it's a noble sacrifice. We are going to go down in the history books."

"What about your business?"

"I've appointed Randall my deputy. I can make the major decisions from here."

"When the boys get older they're going to want to go away to school and what are we going to do about colleges? Where are they going to find wives?"

"Wait a minute, my dear, this isn't forever."

"It isn't?"

"Try not to be disappointed. This is show business, Dottie, and sooner or later the public is going to tire of us."

"How could they?"

"And when our ratings fall below a certain point they are going to have to drop us, and then we'll get to go home."

"But we'll make it good in the meantime."

"My dear, we are going to make it very good."

* * *

"Corky, when you burst in here, and late for the meeting at that, you said they were heading this way. Did you know what you were talking about?"

"Well I thought they were."

"Then where are they?"

"I wish I knew."

"Are you sure you're not lying to take our mind off the issues?"

228

"Look, Dearest, they are down here somewhere. On my way in I passed five guards who were out cold or dead, and I think they have stripped the wiring off the alarm."

"At least we have some idea where to concentrate our forces."

"Right, Dante, but we're going to have to move faster than I thought. Children, we are going to have to go along with Dante's suggestion, which is to pull staff out of all other sectors to get on with the chase and capture, I think that includes using all the core groupers Cort has assembled, do you think we can trust them, Cort?"

"Cort?"

"Hey, Dearest. He's not here."

"Where is he? He's supposed to be here."

"Well he isn't. What's more he isn't coming."

"How do you know that, Dante?"

"He can't get in. I just tried the door and it's locked."

"Then go and find him."

"Locked. We're trapped."

"We have to get out and find them. Children, we have to find them and terminate. Pa says if we don't . . . "

"If we don't, what?"

"I've been trying to avoid telling you this but what can I do, one woman alone? You know your father, this may be just talk, the truth is, if we don't find the Fearsome Foursome and terminate them, well, I don't know how to say this but . . . "

"Dearest, what's the matter?"

"He's threatened to terminate us."

Boone Castle

We were running again, moving in formation along labyrinthine corridors, Luce and me leading, the other two trotting behind; she was pounding along next to me and I tried not to hear her muttering, humming, crooning in my ear as we tore along.

"First we'll take the bastards, then we'll take the place, right Boone?"

Without missing a beat I said, "Right, Luce."

"And once we have the place the sky will be the limit, right?"

"If you say so, Luce."

"It's going to be the two of us together, Boone." She was plunging like somebody's prize trotter, throwing her knees high and setting her feet wide, going along on hope and adrenalin, I had to keep her moving but some flash of self-preservation made me add:

"Up to a point."

"Together we can . . . You and me are going to be together, Boone, right?" She broke stride and looked at me, her face was so naked it was embarrassing. "Boone?"

I didn't want to answer. "I don't know."

"Well we'll talk about it later," she said, and put on a burst of speed so she wouldn't have to hear me say we wouldn't.

She led us to the door marked CONFERENCE ROOM and sealed it with her weapon, melting the edges to fuse them and then grinning at me with pointed teeth. With any luck they're all in there and we're home free."

"I hope you're right."

"Sorry I'm late, I . . . " Somebody new rounded the corner at a dead run and barreled into Ev. He turned, doing a slow take. "What are you doing here?"

Kaa Naaji stepped right up to him. "What are you doing here? Hey, you're the Indian, the biochemist."

"'How do you know that?"

Luce was getting into position, kneeling behind him.

"Look, Mr. Mahadevan, we have a special place for you in the operation, a position in our core group that . . . "

"Not any more," Kaa Naaji said, and gave him a push,

so that he went head over silver heels. Luce bopped him.

I said, "Neat work."

"Damn right. Look at that sucker. See that suit on him? Silver. That can mean only one thing." Her voice was hoarse with significance. *"This is one of them."*

"How do you know?"

"Because I know." She was grinning: *praise me.*

Kaa Naaji said, "My friends, we must hurry." He was right. Our victim in the silver suit was stirring and by this time there were shouts and thumpings on the other side of the door marked CONFERENCE ROOM.

We took off. At the end of the corridor we took a turn that carried us down on an incline until we hit a corridor that was wider than any of the others. As we went along the walls around us fell away to leave us in an open place; the tunnel fluorescents gave way to a creepy sunlight glow and damn if we didn't find ourselves at the end of an old-time street, Little Old New York that I had seen in early movies without number. There were trees growing out of holes in the sidewalks and flowers sprouting in window-boxes; there were cars on the street like they used to have in the old days and there was even a hansom cab pulled up outside the drugstore, but the driver was missing and the horse looked stuffed. Unless I had the location confused with some other set from some other movie, the dear old chestnut vender would be coming around the corner in just another minute; the lovable cop would round the corner swinging his billy club just in time to see the happy gang of kids open the fire hydrant so they could play in the spray; the stars were going to turn up in another minute too—unless they were us.

Weird: New York without burnt-out blocks and rats and rape-murderers, with no muggers abroad and no sign that there would ever be any, because everything was too nice. A part of me wanted to move into one of those brownstones and wait for a nice lady to bring me my pipe and slippers, but the rest of me knew better. I did not break out of the Chateau d'If and escape the Chinese dragon and the flaming belltower just to be sucked into one of their simple-minded storylines; I was damned if I was going to star in any more of their corny adventures, so I put out my arm like a traffic guard, trying to get everybody to stop.

"My," Ev was saying, "It kind of takes you back."

I said, "We can't stay. It's another of their setups."

Luce said, "No."

"We'd better turn back while we still can."

"Wrong." Luce hit my arm. "It's not what you think. Listen, I know this place."

"Damn right you do. The whole world does. It's the street they used in *Cover Girl*, Gene Kelly and Rita Hayworth started dancing down it in 1944. It's a fucking movie set." I only half-heard what I was saying. It was *what? Why?* What was I . . . what were we? "Now, will you come on?"

"No. Listen, I was down here before." She pulled me aside so we could huddle. "I was down here with a crew, on cleanup and removal."

"Hauling out the stiffs."

"Will you shut up and let me . . . " She grabbed my shoulder just above the collarbone and dug in. "That's better. OK, what we were handling was not your ordinary leftover, this one was done up in one of the Reynolds Wrap numbers with the diamond dog-collar."

"You mean like the one we hit outside the conference room."

"Don't you get it?" Her fingers hurt and when I tried to pull away she only gripped harder. Her breathing was hoarse. "Don't you get it? *He was one of them.*"

"So you think these are staff quarters."

"No. More." She put her head close to mine. Kaa Naaji had joined the circle and he leaned so his head touched hers; his hand kept flying up to stroke her shoulder but he knew better. She said, "I think this is where it's at. What do you think?"

"I don't know."

"I think we should find them." She had cast me as leader and she was waiting for my OK.

Kaa Naaji said, "What do you think?"

Ev had caught up. "Honey, we might as well. Where else would we go?"

"How do we know this isn't another one of their . . . "

"Dammit to hell Boone, we're on to something."

"All right," I said because they all wanted it. "Let's go."

She took off and the others followed before I even had a chance to say hey wait, or let's search the buildings. Kaa Naaji kept up neatly but Ev had to run to make the pace. I saw her catch her side once more and then straighten, I thought: can't have that, but she put on a burst of speed so we went along together. I thought there would be more New York around the next corner, Central Park before they built on it, or skaters on a pond, but instead we were on an Andy Hardy street, little white homes with green shutters and big green lawns that I lusted after, thinking what it must have been like to live there and go to high school in a car with a rumbleseat. I thought I heard the evening paper thwapping against front doors as the paperboy swung past on his bicycle and I imagined the sounds of ice clinking in lemonade glasses and the creak of the old porch swing. A part of me wanted to go and live there forever but at the same time I was thinking: oh shit, not that old trick. How can they make me want what wasn't? We were in nostalgia country and I couldn't for the life of me figure out how they could strike chords of memory that I had never before heard sounded, or what they were trying to do and whether they had laid all this on for me or whether we were involved in something even more complicated. Luce said customers never got this far. Maybe all this was for *them*.

Around the corner the pavement gave way to a dirt two-track road and the trees got thicker; damn if we weren't going along through a woods and by that time my misgivings were so great that I couldn't stop for fear of what might be coming along behind me but I didn't really want to keep going either because I was even more troubled by the prospects, what might be massing ahead. It didn't much matter what I thought because Luce was forging ahead. She was going at a dead run with Kaa Naaji hard on her heels and Ev struggling to keep up, so that I had to go ahead anyway to catch up with Ev and help her keep going; I slipped my arm around her waist and we ran together, me lifting her when her feet couldn't work fast enough to get her over a rock or a gully. She was trying to tell me something complicated but I just shushed her, although I knew I was going to have to call a halt in another minute or we would fall so far behind that we would never be able to catch up.

As it turned out I didn't have to because the woods thinned out and there we were in a little clearing dotted with daisies. There was a cutesy gravel path lined with a tickety-boo little picket fence with charming roses twining along it, leading the way to the house.

It was Swiss style, a mixture of early Heidi and ski chalet. There were more roses twined around every available inch of porch railing and when I looked beyond it I could see goats grazing on a little hill, silhouetted against a cyclorama sky. I could hear a choir singing somewhere in the middle distance but when I looked around for the church in the glen I found instead a speaker lashed in the top of a magnolia tree. The tree was a fake, in magnificent full bloom.

"I think this is it." Before anybody could stop her, Luce headed up the steps.

"Please, my friend, be careful."

"No time for that." She opened the wooden door with the heart-shaped peephole and went on in.

Kaa Naaji said, "We can't let her go this alone."

"Wait."

Ev said, "Let me get my breath."

"Hey." Luce was back on the steps now, looking baffled. "Maybe this isn't it after all. There's nobody home."

I thought: Right, and after we've eaten their porridge we'll break the chair by accident and fall asleep on their clever little beds, and when they come back and find us . . . I hated it.

Luce said, "Come on. This could still be it."

Was it? A quick picture flashed through my mind—us grappling with bears, or trashing the place, running a bulldozer through the artificial flower borders, bringing down fire and destruction on the artificial everything; if we wrecked it, at least that would be something, and anything would be an improvement over this fairytale limbo we had wandered into. I went on in past her and the others followed.

It was not what I expected. The cute details, the arch arrangements ended at the door. There were no lederhosen hanging inside, no homespun smocks, no signs of a shepherd or a bear family who had gone out for a stroll. I didn't see any quaint old oaken furniture or rounds of goat cheese or any of the rest of it—not even the table with the bowls of porridge still steaming. Instead the room looked as sterile and bright as any laboratory: well lighted, scrubbed and empty except for the suitcase.

The what?

Any traveling salesman could have left it there, or any lady taking her pet on a trip. Maybe it only looked like a suitcase, planted on a lab table in the middle of the room, looking unassuming in the fluorescent lighting, even cheap. It was black leatherette with chrome snaps and lock and wire mesh over one end, and whatever it was, somebody had gone to great pains to make it look like a carrier for a middle-sized pet.

I said, "The purloined letter."

Luce said, "What?"

When I bent over to look in the end I could make out a

complex of tiny dots of light blinking behind the mesh.

"It's only a stupid suitcase."

"That's what they want us to think. They want us to think it's only . . . " I reached for the handle.

Before I could touch it the thing gave off sparks. *"Don't."*

Was it a speaker or what? I went around the other end, thinking the end without the mesh might be its blind side.

"I'm warning you."

Luce whispered, "Maybe this is it after all."

I reached for the handle and it zotted me—an electric shock to the elbow.

The voice was shrill. "Don't *touch*."

There was something about it: what? A flicker of panic? Whatever it was, it made me feel better about everything, as if for once we were doing something they couldn't manipulate, something not according to the books, and for the first time we had made somebody in this place apprehensive. I said, "What are you, anyway?"

"How did you get in here? This place is impenetrable." The lights in the mesh end of the suitcase were winking erratically. "Only my family is permitted here."

"Your *what*?"

It seemed to know Luce was making a feint for the handle and it zotted her. "Stand back."

"What did I tell you?" She nursed her hand, grinning. "This is it."

"I gave orders to have you terminated. All of you."

I said, "Well somebody slipped up."

"Well somebody is going to pay."

"Do you have a name?" I kept trying to decide which part of the thing to look at while we were talking: the handle? the screening on the end or the hinges or the lock?

"Will you hold still?" It crackled in my direction. "The children call me Pa."

"Then you're a person."

"Don't tax me, idiot. You can see what I am."

"You're a suitcase."

Without my touching it, the thing sent a shock across the back of my neck; maybe I had it coming. "As ought to be apparent, I am neither."

Luce growled. "I don't see why we have to stand around and listen to this thing . . . "

She jumped as it sent currents in her direction, talking smoothly even as it did so. "You see, for the time being at least, I am legally dead. I have some of the best minds in the world working on my particular problem, but it's going to take time."

"Ah," Kaa Naaji said, "I have learned not to pin my hopes on technology. It is a hard lesson, my friend."

I could have sworn I saw blue lightning crackling between the thing and Kaa Naaji, who jerked in pain. It said, "Keep your opinions to yourself." It hummed to itself for a minute and then went on. "The length of time depends on whether the brains I have acquired over the years are good at what they are doing, and if they aren't, we'll have to recruit more and better brains, but I am patient, to say the very least, and I have the means. I am devoting my entire fortune to this enterprise, and as long as there are customers for Happy Habitat, my children will bring in even more."

I said, "You're a person in there."

"In a manner of speaking. Although I am technically legally dead, all the important parts of me have been printed into circuits. The package is quite neat, really. From here I can conduct my business quite handsomely, and as you have probably guessed, the suitcase is only a disguise."

Did I detect a note of vanity?

It said, "I don't really look like this. If you saw what I really looked like you would be impressed, but the suitcase makes an excellent cover. When I want to I can go about without attracting attention, I can sit unobtrusively in the plaza or the paramotel and check on various aspects of my operation, I can . . . I can also kill you if you try to touch me." It sent a charge through Luce, who had been trying to sneak up on it.

She bunched herself to spring on it and I held her back. She said, low, "I don't believe it can really kill us." Then she backed off and began circling at a respectful distance, studying it.

The thing was saying, "I am unclear as to why you have not been terminated or how you got this far but you can think of your presence here as only a temporary inconvenience. My boys will be here any minute to finish you."

Luce said, "Don't be so sure."

I thought I saw it jump. "It's only a matter of time."

"Have it your way," Luce said, still circling.

"While we're waiting," it said, "I'd like to know what you think of this place."

I said, "I think you ought to be ashamed."

"*Watch it.*" It sent a charge across the back of my neck but I thought it was weaker than the last. Did the thing, after all, have limited power? "I have imagined a country of wit and magnitude and I have brought it into being. Who among you can claim as much?"

Nobody said anything.

"Amusement park, real-life exhibits, underground complex, all. They all sprang from my imagination. I designed it, my people brought it into being, you are at the center of fifty years of planning."

I said, "It's phony." I kept on in spite of its barrage of little shocks. "It's a freak show and it stinks."

"My friend it is only the beginning. You have had a chance to look around?"

I couldn't stop the slide-show in my head; the phony jungle, the real corpses in the Indian massacre, the monstrous cuteness of the parks were intercut with shots of us running, the relentless camera tracking, throwing our own images back at us. "More than I'd like."

238

"Then you have seen how harmonious I have made everything. Rather than re-create nature here, I have chosen to improve on it—the gardens, the functional objects, the avenues were all conceived to be more beautiful than anything in nature, more disciplined, and that is all part of the plan."

I said, "Not everybody wants that."

"What do I care? That is no concern of mine." It hummed for a minute, collecting its thoughts? "When I was first reduced to what you see here, something small and neat enough to fit into a suitcase, I was thrown in on my own thoughts as never before. I had managed to thwart death. I was designing a new setting for myself— why not a new world? And if I was going to make a new world, why not make it to my liking? As you can see, I have accomplished that. I think you would have to admit that what you see is beautiful."

"It's all fake."

"Beauty is a state of mind. If I can shape my own world to be beautiful then I can surround myself with people who will be beautiful. If you can prune a tree why can't you do the same to a man?"

"Because he won't like it, for one thing, and for another thing . . . "

It sent out a couple of zots. *Don't you recognize a rhetorical question when you hear one?* Any fool knows that man's greatest enemy is human nature, his own propensity for violence, his lust and his greed. Now I think we're on the verge of winning this battle with our own natures, I am going to celebrate the victory here. I have created the ideal setting, and I am going to surround myself with an ideal society. First come my family, and then the chosen few."

Luce was scowling significantly: shall we jump it? I shook my head. I said, "Nobody wants your candy forests."

"Millions of people have. Why do you think they come

to Happy Habitat? Even you have basked in my artificial sunlight and enjoyed the grass under my synthetic trees. Open yourself to it. You'll see."

"People are killing each other up there."

"Oh, that. That's only the surface operation. The means. The real end is down here. Think of a civilization in which nothing is ugly. Think what that will make of the people who live in it, how well they will behave." It paused for so long that for a minute I thought it had broken down. Luce looked at me: Now? I waved her back. After a long while it said, "We are still in the last stages of construction, and we have begun the gathering in. The core group, the best minds. Too bad about you, little Indian, you were to have been among them."

Kaa Naaji said, "I'd rather die."

"Perhaps you shall, we have gathered the best scientists, along with some of the greatest artists, well, one or two at least, just to lighten the atmosphere. When my group is complete and everything is ready we will simply cut ourselves off and destroy the rest. There will be no more evil in the world. We will have entered Phase Four."

"You couldn't possibly."

"Your woman friend saw the capsules out there at the perimeter. You, Lucia di Lammermoor Finley."

"You mean those big silver things?"

("Is that your real name?"

"Damn suitcase knows more than I thought.")

"They contain a nerve gas so powerful and so pervasive that it will all be over within minutes. We will be alone down here, and perfectly safe. Given time, intelligence and money enough, a man can do anything. Why not live forever in a world of one's own devising?"

"It's monstrous."

"Perhaps." It missed a beat while it considered. "But don't you think it's better than waiting around for death?"

240

"Boone, somebody's coming."

I thought I heard a distant drumming: running feet.

The suitcase chortled. "I told you. All I had to do was stall you long enough."

Luce said, "What are we going to do?"

"Idiots, there's no escape."

"My friends, I do not believe this to be the case." The drumming sound separated itself into the sounds of people running; I could hear shouts in the woods outside, people thudding down the gravel path, and there was Kaa Naaji, pushing aside a section of the wall to reveal a button and pushing it. An elevator door opened. "You trust me, don't you?"

"Yes, Kaa Naaji. Yes."

He beamed. "Then I think we can get out this way."

"What about that thing?" Luce was rattling next to me, her big hands turning.

"It depends on what you want next."

Her expression was so naked that I had to turn away. She said, "I want what you want."

"I want to stop it."

"Then we'd better bring it along. Hostage, right?"

It was crackling and zotting. "Don't you touch me."

"Why not?" Luce grabbed it anyway. "If you want to kill me go ahead." She hit me with a look like a thrown axe. "I'm only doing what he wants."

"Put me down."

"Let's go."

"Can you make it, Ev?"

"I'll be all right."

"Put me down. This is your last warning."

We were in the elevator and the doors shut just as the first of the goons in the silver suits came crashing into the woodsman's hut.

Once we were in the elevator we all looked at the suitcase, waiting. It had threatened to kill us, it kept sending little charges at us, but it wasn't doing much. I puzzled over it as the charges I felt got weaker and weaker. Its lights winked madly through the screen mesh, Luce grimaced again and again as it sent currents through her, but she held on grimly as the elevator took us up.

I said, "You aren't going to kill anybody. You can't."

"That's all you know."

Luce stopped wincing, so I assumed the little charges had stopped.

I said, "You were never even equipped for it."

"To tell the truth," it said, "I never thought it would be necessary."

"You thought you were safe—in this?" I nudged the case with my toe.

"Until you came along I was."

"That's pathetic."

Its voice was steely. "You have reckoned without the last resort."

"What?"

"Ooop," Luce said as the elevator doors opened. "We're up."

Evaline

God I'm tired.

First I was high as a kite on being free and I ran along as fast as anybody. I even had time to consider the young men, interesting since I am supposed to be beyond all that, a fact I acknowledged the day before yesterday when I let my face go and washed the color out of my hair. At first I ran along thinking I might have one of them when this is all over, maybe the Indian, who is so sad, and maybe Boone, but I could tell from their eyes nobody thinks of me that way. My face tells the world I am an old woman now. I had to do it to get out, I would rather be

242

hideous and free, but now I have to wonder whether I'm going to màke it.

I'm not running very well. It was that old-time city street that brought it all in on me. There we were in a New York that I remembered from real life, it was laid out like a page from an old lady's memory book. I looked at it and thought: I was alive then, I'm still alive; I am an old, old person, and I couldn't move another step because it was all too much. Boone had to help me and Luce, that is trembling with desire for him, Luce never gave us a second glance because I am so old and ugly I am no threat. By the time we reached the hut I was trembling with exhaustion and beginning to be frightened because I understood for the first time that I might not make it after all; wanting it was no guarantee. I popped my last upper then, I was in a sweat and my hand was shaking and after I took it I felt not much better.

Either it isn't working or I'm not.

I don't think I can go the whole distance. Worse yet: I am slowing them down. I keep looking at that suitcase, the old man, the man in the suitcase and I wonder: Is that better? Would I rather be a suitcase, in a suitcase, than have to be this tired?

I think I would rather let go. I think about sleep. But there is Val's screenplay, and I have to . . . I have been charged.

The elevator brought us up in the lobby of the green glass hotel, outside I could see a pink dawn breaking. There were tanned and healthy-looking people wandering into the lobby, the early morning risers coming down to breakfast and last night's revelers heading off to bed. They were glossy with youth and health and money and when they saw me they were offended. They shrank at the sight of my face, all those wrinkles. People don't like anybody to be old.

Well old people don't like it either.

I stopped Boone. "I'm making us conspicuous."

Kaa Naaji said, "I have an answer to that." He drew me into an alcove and tied a scarf across my face. "Now they will think you are only another Muslim woman. If anybody stops you, just tell them you are with the sheik."

"I'm slowing us down."

Boone said, "You're doing fine."

Luce put her foot on the suitcase and glared at me.

The suitcase said, "You know damn well you will never make it. Not with that pathetic body."

"How do you . . . " How did it find out about me? Can it see?

"I know when to get off a sinking ship," it said. "My next body is going to last forever."

I felt my own body pulling me down and at the same time I thought: *that might not be so bad, to lie down.* I said to it, "Why stick around after you're all used up?"

It just winked its lights at me and started broadcasting. "Help. Kidnap. Attendants. Help."

A couple of passers-by looked at us, but they could see nothing wrong. All they saw were four slightly untidy-looking people standing with their luggage.

"Guards, programmers, guards!"

Luce kicked it.

"Please, my circuits."

"Nobody knows who you are, suitcase, so I think you'd better shut up."

"I still have the means to kill you all."

She picked it up and shook it, staring into the end with the fine mesh, glaring at the winking lights. "Shut up or I'll open you."

With the veil in place I must have looked strange, but passable. We went by a mirrored wall and I took a quick glance, thinking, OK, right, maybe the body will get me through. At least it still looks good. At the same time exhaustion pulled at me, something even stronger was pulling too, something that said, Let it be over. We came out into the open and on the way across the plaza I turned my ankle and Boone had to come back and help until I could make it alone. So I am slowing them down, and if I want any of us to make it I am going to have to let them go. Before I can do that I have to make sure part of me goes on. I have to pass on the torch.

We are in a little park. So far as I know we are not being followed. We stop to get our breath.

I take Boone aside. "I want you to take something for me. I want you to take it out."

"What are you talking about?"

"In case I don't make it."

"You're going to make it, Ev." I can tell by his face he is saying it for my sake.

"I don't think so."

"Don't say that."

"Not even if it's true?"

"Don't even think it." He looks so distressed that I say, "All right." I undo the zipper to my jacket, saying, "Just promise me you'll take it, in case."

"If it'll make you feel better."

"Yes." I turn my back so he won't see when I unwind the scarf and lift Val's screenplay off my naked front. I had them lifted; in the days when I danced with Tiger anybody could have seen, they still had pretty tips then, that pointed up, but even in the days before I let my hair go grey they were giving up on me, I could look in the mirror and see the early signs. Even before I stopped looking in the mirror the muscle walls had begun to break, the silicone had slipped a little and, all right, I am an old lady, even I know it, recognize it, but I don't want Boone to have to see.

Even though I have decided to face the facts.

"What are you doing?"

I zip back up and turn to face him. Without the pressure of the screenplay my breasts are cold. I am cold. "This is a screenplay."

"A what?"

"I have. I had a lover." I turn so I won't have to see his look of incredulity. "It's all right, he was just as old as me."

"That's. Uh." He doesn't know what to say.

"You're too young to remember Valentine Stone."

He takes the packet from me. "I wrote a paper on him once."

Score one. "Then I don't have to explain."

"He was here?"

"He died here."

"That's terrible."

"This is his last screenplay. It's about this place."

He turns slowly. "Did you know I was—am a holomaker?"

"Then you're the right person." I touch his hand. "I want you to take this home."

He is temporarily confused. Faint changes of expression fleet across his face as he tries to decide what place he calls home.

"I mean out. Away from here."

"Of course." His face lightens.

"So the people will know."

"You'll be there to see it." He squeezes my hand and then slides the folder into the front of his shirt.

There is a vein pulsing in his temple; his shirt is open and for a second I want to kiss his throat but all my clocks have stopped rushing, even my pulse is slowing; a month ago I would have tried to seduce this boy and felt equal to it but now I see how young he is and understand at last all the differences between us. I touch his hand as I would touch the hand of a son I loved. "I think I can make it now."

He moves to help me. "You bet you can." He squeezes my shoulder like a son just home from college, home from the war, a loving son. "Come on, babe, let's go."

We have to leave the park. I move along with him, feet

246

plopping one in front of the other, moving right along because I know he expects it and although I wanted to get out of this place, to go somewhere and do something that would make a difference, I have passed on the torch and it is time to let down. Even if I did get out now I would let Boone take it, go ahead with it, because I am warm now, relaxed, courting lassitude; it began with the makeup and the hair and the clothes but they were only parts of it, the first signs, the outward signs of a relaxation of will. My flesh is going to fall away next and I am content to let it go; my feet are leaden and I will move ahead for my son's sake but when the time comes I will make him leave me behind because I am ready. How strange to be letting down at last, how voluptuous, almost like an escape . . .

Luce

All the thanks I get, I rescue the stupid bastard from his rotten dungeon and I hold off the guards while he and the Indian scramble up to the surface, I almost got my tail fried because I was the last up the ladder. I fight off the Chinese dragon and what thanks do I get? It was me that knew the way through the tunnels, I am the one who got them out of the woods and it was me that knew where it was at and delivered everybody in one piece and got them all out in one piece, stupid bastard wouldn't even be alive if it was not for me, and what do I get? I get to carry this fucking suitcase, that's what I get, I am carrying this fucking suitcase while Kaa Naa whoozit that gives me the creeps keeps plucking at my elbow and begging me to let him help while there is Boone that I would die for, going on ahead, so busy helping that old lady that he won't even look back to see how I am doing.

All right, he doesn't want to look at me, this face, even

Norman married me for security; I am used to it, my old man said it would shrink the testicles on a stone lion and my old lady said, You will have to make up for it by being extra sweet but shit, what did she know. I was going to make up for it by being important and I would have, too, except Boone. All right, I should have holed up back there in the Swiss cottage and sold out to the suitcase for a partnership, collared the rest and turned them in, and wouldn't that damn suitcase be grateful now. It would be slobbering all over me with promises of fringe benefits and extra paid vacations, plants in my office and a teakwood desk but no, I had to do what Boone wanted, I lost sight of the main chance because Boone.

I lost it all because of Boone and does he take a minute to thank me for it? Does he even look back: are you all right? Hell no. I steer them out of the tourist area and show him which way is the perimeter but does he take a minute to thank me? No. Does he even stop to ask if this thing is too heavy for me, or, Do you have any regrets, giving up your dreams of glory and throwing your career out the window just for me? Hell no, not him. He doesn't even notice. He doesn't even know, he just goes along helping that stupid old lady over twigs like she was the sexiest thing around, I might as well be a lamppost or a dumb tree for all he sees in me, well when I get out of here I am going to get a face job and then we'll see.

Maybe if he knew how I feel. When we get out I am going to take him aside and say something I never did before, not to anybody, I'll say, Daniel Boone Castle I'm in love with you that's the God's truth and he'll look right at me and he'll . . . No he won't. I am stuck inside a body that doesn't even signify and that is all he'll see, dumb bastard doesn't know, he doesn't even notice, I can't even get the sucker to look at me.

Worse yet, I can't get this suitcase to shut up.

It says, "I suppose you think you know what you're doing."

We're escaping. I say, "Damn right I do."

We're escaping, and so far it's so easy I have to wonder if they're letting us. I pretend to be a guard taking this group somewhere and nobody pays much attention. The staff I see could care less; they look sloppy in the uniform and they are going about their business with half a hand, laughing and fooling around in corners and letting things slip. You can already see the results. It is bad for the operation. The plaza is a disgrace, with shrubs dying and plastic glasses and crumpled food wrappers rolling around on the marble. I could see the service was bad at the restaurants, there were waiters yawning and scratching their asses while the customers got madder and finally went into the kitchens to get their own plates. In one place a guy was dumping his morning pancakes on the tablecloth but nobody made a move to clean it up and when he started dumping other people's dishes, nobody tried to get him to stop. I can tell you that kind of thing does not look good and frankly I think it is because they are hiring the wrong kind of types for this work, you need personnel who are going to carry on even when management is off on a wild goosechase, it is a matter of morale and discipline.

Where management is, is, they are all down there in the tunnels trying to locate us, they are down there with half of the custodials and all of Cleanup and Removal, and it is only a matter of time before they come funneling to the top. I move a little faster, coming up on Boone's heels. He and the old lady step up the pace. We are out of the resort area now, and passing through the environments. If I have it right the plaza is at the hub and we are moving out. Nobody notices us, nobody tries to follow, but I figure it is only a matter of time.

"They are going to catch you in another minute," the suitcase says.

"The hell you say."

"How do you know this isn't a trap?"

I say, "I just know." I don't.

"You'll see, this is a gigantic trap. You don't think you could get this far unless I let you, do you?"

"I don't know."

It says, "I suppose you know what will happen when they do catch you."

"Nobody is going to catch us."

"That's what you think. I'm a man of many resources."

"You are nothing but a suitcase."

"Have it your way." Damn suitcase makes it sound like: *It's your funeral.*

"I'll tell you what's going to happen if they do catch us. In case you wonder why I haven't already thrown you into the bushes. You personally are going to make them let us go." I give it a shake so it will know I mean business. "If you don't I am going to open you."

"Just try it," it says.

"Watch out or I will."

We are going along at a pretty good clip so I am quiet for a while, to conserve my breath. Boone is ahead, helping the old lady. Kaa Naaji is trotting at my right flank, two steps behind so I won't see him and get mad at him. Some of the plastic flowers are dropping off the jungle vines and the floor needs raking. The place doesn't look too good.

"Listen," the suitcase says, "I think we can make a deal."

"It's too late for deals."

"You don't know what I have to offer."

I let it bang against a low branch. "I warned you to shut up."

"You know he's never going to love you."

"What?"

"He doesn't even notice you."

Instead of saying, How do you know that, I just go along, shaking it and saying, "You don't know what you're talking about," even though I am afraid it does.

It says, "I've been around long enough to recognize a case of unrequited love."

"Yeah been around, all you can do is talk."

It says, "That's only lately. Now shut up and listen, and I'll tell you some of the things I can do for you."

I pretend not to be listening while it promises me a face job, a complete retread, a fabulous wardrobe. It promises I am going to be gorgeous, with this terrific body, I may even end up being happy. I am thinking that would not be bad, but I am also thinking, *This could be a trick.*

It says, "I can make you irresistible."

Why am I crying? "Go to hell."

It changes tack. "I can make you a vice president."

Why not? Then Boone would have to . . . "No you can't."

"I can do anything I want. I am the owner. Look at it this way," it says. "Everything would be different."

Yeah, right, I am thinking, there would be hell to pay. If I ran this operation, he would have to look at me.

The suitcase says, "Well?"

It would serve him right. "Shut up."

"What would you say to a piece of the action? Fifty–fifty."

Serve him right, then he would have to treat me . . . "Shut up."

Am I wavering?

Just then Boone looks over his shoulder at me: "Are you all right?"

The suitcase ups the ante. "Sixty-two."

"Fine." I smile at Boone. I can't stop smiling. "Just fine."

I can tell the suitcase is just about to raise it to sixty-five. I rattle its brains out. "I told you to shut up."

I guess I finally got to it. After a while it stopped moaning and shut up. We are going through the medieval courtyard, all the guards in the castle keep are so drunk they don't even look at us. There are ugly stains on the fronts of their tunics; they do not look sharp, I think. I think if this was my operation they would look sharp right enough. There are beer cans rolling in the courtyard, mingled with the half-gnawed joints and ruined wineskins and it doesn't look too authentic, nor does the golf cart parked by the tower look authentic, but when you let little things pass, like the stains on the tunics, pretty soon the whole thing begins to slip. I think I hear somebody screaming in one of the towers—some paying guest, maybe, accidentally trapped on the rack?

The suitcase says, "I can make him love you."

"Will you shut up about that?"

"It's what you want, isn't it?"

"You bloody can't and you bloody know it, so why don't you bloody shut up?"

Oh right, dammit, I am right and I know it, he would never love me even if I was soft and beautiful, and I could get all those other things, power, seventy-five per cent off the top and it wouldn't make any real difference because he doesn't, he won't; I know it, now I really know it, I am going along with the suitcase, swallowing bitterness and snuffling back the tears.

Shit, dammit, oh shit.

The suitcase says, "You know you are fighting a losing battle."

It is getting hard to see. "I warned you," I say, and throw the thing at Kaa Naaji.

Kaa Naaji

She had given me the suitcase, ah the handle is still warm from her hand; my friend Boone has accepted me because it is I who found the elevator and so aided our escape, and this time it is a real escape. I am useful now, I am important to them, what more can I want? I am trusted and now she whom I have loved beyond all loving has entrusted the strange speaking satchel to me so I run along, fueled by hope.

It is hope that makes me want to go on living. Perhaps none of us want that which we think we want, but only wish to be able to go on hoping. Did I not learn this when I attained my scientific goal and then languished, for the want of another.

Right now I want her.

I want to get out.

If I gain these, what else will I want?

It is enough that I want.

"Ah my friend," I say to the suitcase as we go along, "I think we have certain experiences in common. Although we both expected to make great gains through the miracle of technology, we have both found out that true happiness is in the realm of the spirit."

"Speak for yourself, Charlie."

"Please. My name is Kaa Naa Mahadevan."

"Well you can call me Pa."

"Very well, Pa. Is that really you in there?" I do not know what to expect: some parts of a real person or a clever microphone or only a set of humming silver works.

The voice is too distraught to be artificial. "You bet your ass it is."

"Are you truly a deceased human being?"

"Not deceased. Legally dead, and if you can't tell the difference maybe you don't belong in my core group after all."

"Yet you are confined to this satchel." I am pondering.

"Only temporarily. I've got a whole squad working on transplants, me into somebody, if we can all agree on the receptacle, and another bunch working on simulacra and somebody else assembling spare parts, so it's only a matter of . . ."

"Is it lonely inside the suitcase?"

"Only boring, but I can wait. Listen, Charlie . . ."

"Kaa Naa . . . "

" . . . and listen hard. I am prepared to make a deal."

I shake my head but of course the suitcase cannot see. "No deals."

It says, "You know I had you earmarked for the core group."

"You have already told me." I do not wish to listen to its blandishments.

"You were to be one of the surviving minds."

"At what cost? I think that would be lonely indeed."

"Well I'm prepared to up the ante. How would you like a spot in management?" It is waiting for my reply.

"While the rest of the world dies?"

"Who needs them?" it says. "P.S., there will be no survivors, so if you know what's good for you . . . "

"I think you are a monster."

"Don't be ridiculous. Can we talk frankly for a minute? Now listen, you are not traveling in very good company. That female is a personal and public disaster, and the guy is charming but ineffectual, and as for the old lady . . . "

"Please, you are speaking of my friends."

" . . . she's going to die anyway, but you . . . "

"Sir." I am very formal with it. I will not call it Pa again. "I do not wish to survive at the expense of my friends."

"Friendship is an illusion."

"You are the one who makes illusions. You." I set it down on a rock and stare hard at the wire mesh on the end. I berate it. "What do you know about want, or what truly satisfies? You are the charlatan, my friend. Look at the promises you made to get me here. Adventure, people who needed me . . . "

"Well didn't I deliver? And that was only a sample."

"Nothing worked." I remember the fraudulent jungle, the ersatz battle with the water buffalo; most bitterly I remember Boone's reproaches, how long it took me to regain his trust. "Nothing you have to offer is real."

"All right," the suitcase says, "what if it isn't? I've already told you, the surface operation is only the means to an end."

"Aha, and how do you know your end is going to be real?"

It snaps. "Don't ask questions."

I pursue my point. "You do not mind if it is not?"

"It doesn't matter, stupid. What matters is that I control it. That's good enough for me."

"Well," I say, getting up because I have won the argument, "I do not want your lies."

"What makes you think my lies are any worse than yours? They serve the purpose. We all tell ourselves things to keep going, who's to say your stories are any better than mine?"

"Aha." I have it now. "Mine are real."

"Have it your way." Can a suitcase snort? It changes its approach. "OK, let's look at it this way. There may be a few bugs in the operation but with a guy like you on my team, we can work it out, all we have to do is start pulling together. You give a little, I'll give a little. You'll have everything you want."

"I don't want that." Ahead, I see my friends moving out of sight and I snatch up the suitcase because I cannot bear to lose them.

"Carte blanche," it says. "What do you say?"

"No thank you." I start running. "I prefer to wait for something real."

"You wouldn't know it if you saw it."

I choose not to answer.

"Hey, you're jouncing me."

"I think you had better be quiet now."

We are passing into a landscape I do not like. The terrain and the buildings look as if they belong to some distant future; the ground is flat and featureless, with the look and texture of tempered steel. All the buildings are either round or tall and triangular, like the pieces of some chessboard of the future, brilliant, and the place seems deserted. We do not see the lounging guards, the sidewalk cafes, we do not even see any customers. Perhaps this is the uncompleted setting the capsule advertised when it came to me in the Red Fort at Agra, speaking of HOPE FOR THE FUTURE. If this is so, then this too is a fake.

Pa says: "You're not going to like what's about to happen."

"You know what will happen?"

"I might."

"I do not care."

"You're going to be sorry."

"Quiet."

"Don't say I didn't warn you. You don't think I'm going to let you get away with this."

"I don't believe you can control it."

"We'll just see if I can." It seems to vibrate. "You'll never escape."

"Then I'll die trying."

"That can be arranged."

"You can't frighten me." This is true. I am going along in relative contentment, moving in company with that splendid woman I desired for so long, following my friend Boone. I have a place to go: back to the world. I have a mission: to make good my escape. I think this may be real danger and I am really in it. If this is so, then what more can I ask?

"You'll be sorry," the suitcase says.

"Aha my friend, you forget, you are in danger too."

"That's what you think."

"You think we brought you along because we admire you? My friend, satchel or not, you are our hostage and we will use you any way we must."

"Think what you want," it says, "but remember the whole thing may blow up in your face."

"I wish you would be quiet."

"Fool, do you want to die?"

"At least that would be real."

"Don't be so sure."

"My. Oh my, oh my." We have rounded a corner and come into what seems to be the village square, if this is a village. Luce goes first, holding her weapon, and my heart cries out. We move up behind her, I with the suitcase, Boone holding our failing friend, Ms. Evaline, so that we form a wedge. Looming high over the square is an enormous television screen with four imposing figures growing larger as they approach the cameras. They are magnificent, flickering in silver. They are us. As I gasp and fall back I hear a rattle and a snap and the sound of many feet drumming, and I recognize our old nemesis coming around the corner, still ferocious although a little tattered and disorganized. It is the Chinese dragon, which we last saw in the tunnels. Who brought it to the surface? How has it gotten here? Did they, it, the suitcase already know where we would be? Above us a legend is moving across the screen, blazing pink:

SOME MEET ITS MATCH**SEE THE FEARSOME FOURSOME MEET ITS MATCH**SEE THE

I think I hear someone say, "This is going to make a terrific movie."

The suitcase leaps in my hand. "All right, smarty, what did I tell you?"

Boone Castle

There was that damn dragon again, I thought: What's the use, we might as well lie down and let it run over us, but Luce was already tearing into it with her weapon, charring the whiskers, burning one ear, at least I think that was an ear, and when that didn't slow it down we all took whatever was handy and got ready to make our stand, Kaa Naaji swinging the suitcase, which was screaming for him to stop, us to stop, it to stop, me raising my fists and Luce getting ready to bludgeon the dragon with her weapon, which had jammed and which was too small even to make a dent. Ev was quicker than any of us, throwing her whole body. Instead of waiting for it to reach us and overwhelm us she hurled herself into its teeth and before I could try to pull her out or batter the huge head or deflect it, the thing had pushed her down and was mauling her, by which time Luce had her weapon working again and raked it back and forth over the dragon flanks, scorching the cloth and burning the people underneath. We heard screams from inside the cloth and when she directed her beam at the soft spot behind the dragon's spangled ruff there was more screaming and the thing quit hurting Ev and tried to pull itself together, blowing smoke and shaking its head. It backed off and instead of charging again it regrouped and trotted straight past us and out of the square, with some of those booted feet still drumming and the rest of them dragging as the wounded hauled the dead along with them because the dragon had to keep moving no matter what.

"The show," I said, "we are back in the fucking show. What are you *doing*?"

The lights in the suitcase winked. "I am only protecting myself."

"You stupid old fool, nobody lives forever."

"Prove it."

"Nobody even wants to." I was not even sure about tomorrow and yet here was this *thing* that had gone to all this trouble just to keep on going, would do whatever it could to keep on going no matter what the cost while I . . .

It crackled. "It's better than waiting around to die."

So it had found its own reason.

What made it

Why didn't it give up?

"Boone."

Ev's voice was so faint I barely heard it. I ran to her. "Are you all right?"

"Not exactly." She looked bad.

"You have to be. Come on Ev, you have things to do, you can't just . . . "

There was a big gash in her temple and one of the teeth was still stuck in her belly, wiggling when she breathed. She said, "I'm all right."

"Let me help you."

"I can't get up."

"Ev, please."

"Honey, you'd better beat it."

"We can't leave you."

"You're going to have to." She was bleeding everywhere but her face was peaceful. "Go ahead, Boone. It's all right."

"No it isn't." I rapped my ribcage, rattling the script. "The screenplay. You."

"It's all yours."

"But you wanted to."

"You can take it the rest of the way."

I wanted her to get up and be all right but I was afraid to touch her. If I did she was going to come apart. "Ev, you've run so hard and come so far. Oh Ev."

"I'd rather go where I'm going," she said.

"Don't say that." She didn't know where she—

She looked so damn serene. "I mean it, there's somebody I have to—"

"Oh Ev, please hang on."

She shook her head. "I'm going to be with him."

"*Ev.*"

Her eyes closed, I knew she was gone but I couldn't make myself get up and get on with it. I didn't want to leave her.

I felt hands on my shoulders, Kaa Naaji on one side: "Boone, my friend," Luce on the other: "We'd better hurry, Boone." I could hear the suitcase. "Now are you ready to talk about a deal?"

By that time they had me on my feet and they were dragging me out of the square. "Come on, they'll be after us in another minute," Luce said.

I looked up at the screen. "What difference does it make?" There we were on a thirty-second delay, larger than the picture on any billboard: Ev on the ground, the others pulling me to my feet. "What's the point? We can't get away from it."

Kaa Naaji said, "My friend, we have to try."

The suitcase said, "He's right, you know. You'll never get away."

"The hell you say." Luce gave the suitcase a shake. "We still have this to bargain with."

We went on. We came out of the science fiction setting and into what looked like a wasteland: rocks and sand and very few things that grew, the Deadly Desert in spades.

Luce said, "We're getting close to the perimeter."

The suitcase said, "You'll never make it. You'll burn to ash on my electronic shield."

She said, "If we do, you burn with us."

"That's what you think," the suitcase said. "I still have my resources."

"Yeah, bull," she said. "I don't think you have anything."

A trap opened on a rise in front of us and several people surfaced on an elevator platform. They were mostly young and good-looking in the glitter suits, tanned and only a little frantic in their diamond dog collars. Together, they made quite a crowd.

"Look," the suitcase said. "My family."

"Those are the ones in charge," Luce whispered. "See the silver uniforms?"

The suitcase zotted Kaa Naaji. "Put me down."

260

Kaa Naaji put it down.

"Corky," it said. "It's Father. Dearest, Dante, Jimmy, Cort . . . "

They were lithe and beautiful, rubbing against each other like cats. There was even the one Luce had knocked out in the corridor outside the conference room standing there with a bandage around his head. He said, "Mahadevan, you can still take advantage of my amazing free offer. All you have to do is hand over Pa there."

There was only one who didn't look so lithe: a big lady with a big front and all her hair glittering on top of her head; she had the silver dress like the Thirties matron in the movies, maybe Margaret Dumont, and she twined her hands in the kneelength silvered pearls. Her wrinkles quivered and her voice shook.

"Hello, Pa."

"It took you long enough."

"There were problems."

"Why have you let this go on for so long?"

"To tell the truth we . . . "

Luce said, "Shut up."

The big lady moved forward, flanked by two of the young ones, who were snaking the muzzles of their weapons like cobra heads, ready to fire at her command.

"You had better move away from my husband."

Kaa Naaji and I exchanged looks. He was ready to stand firm, and so was Luce. I said, "What if we don't?"

"Then we'll have to waste you."

"What about it? I mean, him?"

The suitcase said, "Caution, my dear."

She was looking at me with her hand raised like the starter at a race. I could swear she hesitated for a minute.

The suitcase said, "Perhaps I should remind you, Dearest, just which energy sources are wired into my circuits, and why I had that done?"

She said, "Oh, Pa, you never trusted me."

"I had to be prepared for any eventuality."

One of the young men said, "Maybe before we rescue you, you had better fill us in on Phase Four."

"Corky, shhh."

"Unless you rescue me there will be no Phase Four. If I go, you go."

The big lady looked at her children, distraught. She looked at the suitcase as if to ascertain whether it was on the level and it zotted and crackled a little as if to prove it was. "All right, Corky." She pushed him up front. "Deal with them."

He said, "You folks want out?"

I said, "What do you think we want?"

Luce put her foot on the suitcase. "And the sooner the better."

"Then step away from him."

She poked the suitcase with the tip of her weapon. "You mean this thing?"

"That's it, lady, leave our father alone."

"Not on your ass," she said. "Not until we're home free."

I said, "We get free passage and transportation. Understood?"

"Get away from him or I'm going to have to . . . " Corky's face was working. He didn't seem to know how to finish his sentence.

I said, "I don't think there's anything you can do."

He looked at the one called Dearest: what shall I? She looked at him. I think I heard a genteel whisper. "Corky, he's . . . "

"Damn right he's right," Luce said. "Now you'd all better clear off or I am going to open this thing. Like the thing says, you'll be sorry."

Dearest said, "No."

Corky said, "Wait, you fool."

All the people on the elevator platform said, "No."

The suitcase said, "Wait a minute, wait."

"*Ten.*" Luce started counting. "*Nine. Eight. Seven . . .* "

By that time the big lady and her son were back on the platform, huddling with the others.

"*Six. Five.*"

"Dearest. Children. Wait."

Corky raised his fist. "We'll be back."

"Don't abandon me."

Dearest said, "Sorry, Pa. We have to plan."

"Wait you fools."

"*Three. Two.*"

"You can't leave me like this." The suitcase was screaming. "Wait, you idiots, wait."

They were gone.

Luce looked at me. "How did you like that?"

I said, "You were terrific."

"Am I really?"

I should have paid closer attention to the trap opening, her moist mouth, but I thought the end was close now and we were really going to make it out in one piece so I got expansive, all right, careless. I said, "Fabulous."

She was grinning, she was stepping close to me. "Then maybe you and I can . . . you and I."

So I saw it at last and I thought fast, trying to head her off. "We can do it, we can get out."

She said, "More. You, me. Us." I didn't want to have to look into her naked eyes. Part of me was backtracking, trying to figure out what I had done to lead her on and the other part was feeling guilty because I had used her: just one more phase in the escape. I didn't know what to say to her so I pretended not to see.

Instead I turned to Kaa Naaji, saying, "Well, what's next?"

I heard her voice, very quiet. "Boone."

I wouldn't look at her.

"The truth."

I didn't turn.

She went on anyway. "Boone, I know you don't right now." She swallowed hard, I guess she found it bitter. "But even if you don't, do you think you could ever, ah— love . . ."

She put her hand on my shoulder, forcing me to look at her after all. I tried to keep my expression neutral, friendly, because anything I showed was going to hurt her. I guess it didn't work.

After a minute she said, "Yeah. Right. Shit."

"What did I tell you?" the suitcase said. "He doesn't care about you."

I was almost glad to see the Chinese dragon, all that was left of it after the last attack. The head and a few feet of body were hauling themselves up over the last hill behind us and gathering speed as the thing began roaring down the hill. At the same time the suitcase went into a frenzy of winking lights and suddenly began to tick.

"You can scare off my family, but you can't frighten me."

Kaa Naaji was ready to pick it up and start running with it but Luce shouldered him aside. She had one hand raised. "Wait."

"This is your last chance," the suitcase said.

Luce said, "Good."

"I warned you about the last resort." It was rattling ominously. "Well this is the last resort."

"Do it." Luce was grinning. "Get it over with."

Kaa Naaji said, "Wait," but it was already too late.

"If I don't get away nobody does." The thing was ticking louder. It had begun to glow, the clasp and handle and screen wire were all red hot. "I'm going to take you with me."

I looked at Kaa Naaji. "Down," I said. "It's going to . . ."

"No." Luce's voice was huge. She turned on me, shouting her rage. "Oh you damn bastard, why won't you let anybody love you," and then, before I could stop her, she threw herself between us and the glowing suitcase, starfishing in the blaze of light as he blew up.

There were bits raining everywhere: bits of Luce, Pa, even pieces of the dragon, which had whiplashed into her at the last second, as the head saw the suitcase glowing and made its escape, but when I raised my head at last I saw that Kaa Naaji and I were still in one piece because that tough crazy lady had taken most of it. He and I lay face down for a long time, trembling, and even when I tried to get up I couldn't at first because I was shaken, not so much by the explosion as by the force of that brute lady, her raging love, that I had brought all that down on myself without ever wanting it. I might still be lying there trying to get over it, but next to me Kaa Naaji was sobbing.

"I loved her," he said. "I was in love with her."

So I had to find the right thing to say to help him get going again. "I'm sure she knew it," I said.

"Do you think so?"

"I'm sure it made a big difference to her."

He sat up.

From where she fell it was not far to the perimeter. We could see the insulators twinkling on the conductor towers. I thought I heard the humming of the shield. Behind· us the dragon head wobbled crazily: all that was left. For a minute I thought it was going to catch up with us and we would have to tangle with it, but as I turned to watch it sank to the ground, its one remaining pair of legs buckling so that the scorched and ruined painted face was turned to the sky like a hideous flower.

When I turned back, Kaa Naaji was preparing to launch himself at the shield.

"Perhaps I can neutralize it," he said, "and you will be free."

"Not me. Us. We've got to beat it together."

"Perhaps this is what I was meant for."

"Not on my account, Kaa Naaji, please."

He was trying it on. "Perhaps I have found my function."

If he had found his function, what was going to be mine? I said, "Kaa Naaji, don't. That's not the point."

Too late. He was already well into his last goodbye. "If you make it back to civilization, Boone, you will tell them that I shorted out the force field in the interest of our mission, and remember, I was brave."

"I'll tell them no such thing," I said, trying to grab him. I was more than a little alarmed by all the sacrifices people were making, they seemed to be dying left and right on my behalf and I was tired of saying goodbye.

"Remember me." He wrenched free and whirled with a little farewell wave. Then he threw himself into the shield and there was a flurry of sparks and his clothing started smoking as he hurled himself on his belly, waiting for the explosion.

I closed my eyes.

Nothing happened.

When I opened them he was still lying there.

I went over to him. If there had ever been a shield it was gone now, and if there had been one we were both outside it. Safe? "I guess you'd better get up."

"You mean I'm not dead?"

I shook my head. "Not nearly." We both stood looking back. I don't know whether it was Pa's self-destruction and whatever he took with him or the final shorting out of the field that had begun it but there was a series of flashes on the horizon, clouds puffing up from a distance, as if from a lot of little explosions. Happy Habitat was not destroying itself but parts of it were shorting out even as we stood there, and whatever was left when it had quit popping and snapping and all the lights stopped flickering, it was not going to be the same, and so I guess I had accomplished what I set out to accomplish. They were done watching me. It was a relief. I said, "Come on, Kaa Naaji, let's find our way home."

"No," he said.

"But it's over."

"Yes." He was smiling. "That means I have to find something else to do."

"You idiot. Let's get out while we can."

"You go," he said. "Go outside and tell them. Ev gave you something to take back."

"Yeah, right." *So I still have that to do.* "What about you?"

"I am going back inside." He didn't even stop to shake hands as he turned back to the interior. He did look over his shoulder at me as he made his farewell, and he was beaming. "This is going to be a new country."

"You don't know that. The rest of that terrible family are still . . . "

"I am not without scientific training, it may be of some value in setting things right."

"They're probably going to kill you."

"Ah, but if they don't." He looked perfectly happy. "If they don't I will be needed."

"Kaa Naaji, you're kidding yourself."

He said the quintessential Indian thing: "As you wish."

I thought: *At least I know the show is over.* I started walking the other way, away from Happy Habitat.

So I went the last several miles alone, over flat, rubbly terrain that was little better than a desert, stumbling along, hungry and thirsty, tired and so preoccupied that at first I did not notice the sound of the jet engine. Walking had gotten to be an end in itself, and I was forcing one foot to follow the other foot, concentrating so closely on the sand and rocks that I did not even see the plane until the parachute with the survival kit flamed orange overhead, brightening the sky, if that was sky, and blossoming down. I waved; the plane dipped its wings: wait here. It zoomed off.

I sat down and ripped the bundle open. There was food inside, along with a canteen, a kit filled with antibiotics, a puptent and an inflatable mattress. Rolled inside the mattress was a packet. I ate and drank first and when I finally had enough I opened the oilskin pouch and the documents. Documents? Letters. Letters? My fan mail.

"Dear Mr. Castle, I sure enjoyed you in the . . . "

"looking forward to seeing more . . . "

"Dear Mr. Castle, you may not know me, but . . . "

"especially liked the . . . "

"Mr. Castle, I . . . "

My God my fan mail; I read it not knowing whether I had come all this way and lost all those people and still not broken out of Pa's pretend playland or whether I had broken out after all, and come into the desert to find out that

There was a cold wind on my back.

"Boone, I am so proud of you. Love, Mother."

The wind rose and I was shaking. In the distance I could hear the sound of motors, a large land vehicle just about to roll over the horizon: rescuers or something worse? I was shaking, exhausted, I couldn't run any more and I didn't know

Thank you for all your cards and letters, friends, it's nice to know that

Is it that we do it for each other?

I don't know whether to run or turn and greet them or whether I am just going to lie here and give up

O God, if life's a show

Then I guess the show must go on

Precisely because you are watching.